Nobody's Man

by
E. Phillips Oppenheim

Nobody's Man
by E. Phillips Oppenheim

Copyright © 2024

All Rights reserved.

No part of this publication may be reproduced, stored in a retrieval system, or transmitted in any form or by any means, electronic, mechanical, photocopying or Otherwise, without the written permission of the publisher.
The author/editor asserts the moral right to be identified as the author/editor of this work.

ISBN: 978-93-64289-67-2

Published by
DOUBLE 9 BOOKS
2/13-B, Ansari Road
Daryaganj, New Delhi – 110002
info@double9books.com
www.double9books.com
Tel. 011-40042856

This book is under public domain

ABOUT THE AUTHOR

Edward Phillips Oppenheim was an English author who lived from October 22, 1866, to February 3, 1946. He wrote a lot of best-selling genre fiction with glamorous characters, international drama, and fast-paced action. They were popular forms of fun because they were easy to read. In 1927, he was on the cover of Time magazine. Edward Phillips Oppenheim was born in Tottenham, London, on October 22, 1866. His parents were Henrietta Susannah Temperley Budd and a leather merchant named Edward John Oppenheim. He went to Wyggeston Grammar School until the sixth form in 1883, but had to quit because his family couldn't afford it. For almost twenty years, he worked in his father's business. His father helped pay for the release of his first book, which did just enough to cover its costs. It was under the name "Anthony Partridge" that he released five of his books from 1908 to 1912. To help Oppenheim's writing career, Julien Stevens Ulman (1865–1920), a rich New York leather merchant who liked Oppenheim's books, bought the leather works around 1900 and made him a paid director. He quickly came up with a method that worked and made a name for himself. John Buchan, who was just starting out as a suspense writer, called Oppenheim "my master in fiction" and "the greatest Jewish writer since Isaiah" in 1913.

CONTENTS

CHAPTER I 7
CHAPTER II 16
CHAPTER III 21
CHAPTER IV 27
CHAPTER V 33
CHAPTER VI 39
CHAPTER VII 44
CHAPTER VIII 52
CHAPTER IX 57
CHAPTER X 66
CHAPTER XI 72
CHAPTER XII 79
CHAPTER XIII 84
CHAPTER XIV 90

BOOK TWO
CHAPTER I 94
CHAPTER II 101
CHAPTER III 106
CHAPTER IV 112
CHAPTER V 118

CHAPTER VI	124
CHAPTER VII	131
CHAPTER VIII	136
CHAPTER IX	141
CHAPTER X	146
CHAPTER XI	153
CHAPTER XII	158
CHAPTER XIII	165
CHAPTER XIV	170
CHAPTER XV	176
CHAPTER XVI	182
CHAPTER XVII	187
CHAPTER XVIII	195
CHAPTER XIX	203
CHAPTER XX	206
CHAPTER XXI	210
CHAPTER XXII	214

CHAPTER I

Andrew Tallente stepped out of the quaint little train on to the flower-bedecked platform of this Devonshire hamlet amongst the hills, to receive a surprise so immeasurable that for a moment he could do nothing but gaze silently at the tall, ungainly figure whose unpleasant smile betrayed the fact that this meeting was not altogether accidental so far as he was concerned.

"Miller!" he exclaimed, a little aimlessly.

"Why not?" was the almost challenging reply. "You are not the only great statesman who needs to step off the treadmill now and then."

There was a certain quiet contempt in Tallente's uplifted eyebrows. The contrast between the two men, momentarily isolated on the little platform, was striking and extreme. Tallente had the bearing, the voice and the manner which were his by heritage, education and natural culture. Miller, who was the son of a postman in a small Scotch town, an exhibitioner so far as regards his education, and a mimic where social gifts were concerned, had all the aggressive bumptiousness of the successful man who has wit enough to perceive his shortcomings. In his ill-chosen tourist clothes, untidy collar and badly arranged tie, he presented a contrast to his companion of which he seemed, in a way, bitterly conscious.

"You are staying near here?" Tallente enquired civilly.

"Over near Lynton. Dartrey has a cottage there. I came down yesterday."

"Surely you were in Hellesfield the day before yesterday?"

Miller smiled ill-naturedly.

"I was," he admitted, "and I flatter myself that I was able to make the speech which settled your chances in that direction."

Tallente permitted a slight note of scorn to creep into his tone.

"It was not your eloquence," he said, "or your arguments, which brought failure upon me. It was partly your lies and partly your tactics."

An unwholesome flush rose in the other's face.

"Lies?" he repeated, a little truculently.

Tallente looked him up and down. The station master was approaching now, the whistle had blown, their conversation was at an end.

"I said lies," Tallente observed, "most advisedly." The train was already on the move, and the departing passenger was compelled to step hurriedly into a carriage. Tallente, waited upon by the obsequious station master, strolled across the line to where his car was waiting. It was not until his arrival there that he realised that Miller had offered him no explanation as to his presence on the platform of this tiny wayside station.

"Did you notice the person with whom I was talking?" he asked the station master.

"A tall, thin gentleman in knickerbockers? Yes, sir," the man replied.

"Part of your description is correct," Tallente remarked drily. "Do you know what he was doing here?"

"Been down to your house, I believe, sir. He arrived by the early train this morning and asked the way to the Manor."

"To my house?" Tallente repeated incredulously.

"It was the Manor he asked for, sir," the station master assured his questioner. "Begging your pardon, sir, is it true that he was Miller, the Socialist M.P.?"

"True enough," was the brief reply. "What of it?"

The man coughed as he deposited the dispatch box which he had been carrying on the seat of the waiting car.

"They think a lot of him down in these parts, sir," he observed, a little apologetically.

Tallente made no answer to the station master's last speech and merely waved his hand a little mechanically as the car drove off. His mind was already busy with the problem suggested by Miller's appearance in these parts. For the first few minutes of his drive he was back again in the turmoil which he had left. Then with a little shrug of the shoulders he abandoned this new enigma. Its solution must be close at hand.

Arrived at the edge of the dusty, white strip of road along which he had travelled over the moors from the station, Tallente leaned forward and watched the unfolding panorama below with a little start of surprise. He had passed through acres of yellowing gorse, of purple heather and mossy turf, fragrant with the aromatic perfume of sun-baked herbiage. In the distance, the moorland reared itself into strange promontories, out-flung to the sea. On his right, a little farm, with its cluster of out-buildings, nestled in the bosom of the hills. On either side, the fields still stretched upward like patchwork to a clear sky, but below, down into the hollow, blotting out all that might lie beneath, was a curious sea of rolling white mist, soft and fleecy yet impenetrable. Tallente, who had seen very little of this newly chosen country home of his, had the feeling, as the car crept slowly downward, of one about to plunge into a new life, to penetrate into an unknown world. A man of extraordinarily sensitive perceptions, leading him often outside the political world in which he fought the battle of life, he was conscious of a curious and grim premonition as the car, crawling down the precipitous hillside, approached and was enveloped in the grey shroud. The world which a few moments before had seemed so wonderful, the sunlight, the distant view of the sea, the perfumes of flowers and shrubs, had all gone. The car was crawling along a rough and stony road, between hedges dripping with moisture and trees dimly seen like spectres. At last, about three-quarters of the way down to the sea, after an abrupt turn, they entered a winding avenue and emerged on to a terrace. The chauffeur, who had felt the strain of the drive, ran a little past the front door and pulled up in front of an uncurtained window. Tallente glanced in, dazzled a little at first by the unexpected lamplight. Then he understood the premonition which had sat shivering in his heart during the long descent.

The mist, which had hung like a spectral curtain over the little demesne of Martinhoe Manor, had almost entirely disappeared when, at a few minutes before eight, with all traces of his long journey obliterated, Andrew Tallente stepped out on to the stone-flagged terrace and looked out across the little bay below. The top of the red sandstone cliff opposite was still wreathed with mists, but the sunlight lay upon the tennis lawn, the flower gardens below, and the rocks almost covered by the full, swelling tide. Tall, and looking slimmer than ever in his plain dinner garb, there were some indications of an hour of strange and unexpected suffering in the tired face of the man who gazed out in somewhat dazed fashion at the little panorama which he had been looking forward so eagerly to seeing again. Throughout the long journey down from town, he had felt an unusual and almost boyish enthusiasm for his coming holiday. He had thought of his tennis racquet and fishing rods, wondered about his golf clubs and his guns. Even the unexpected encounter with Miller had done little more than leave an unpleasant taste in his mouth. And then, on his way down from "up over," as the natives called that little strip of moorland overhead, he had vanished into the mist and had come out into another world.

"Andrew! So you are out here? Why did you not come to my room? Surely your train was very punctual?"

Tallente remained for a moment tense and motionless. Then he turned around. The woman who stood upon the threshold of the house, framed with a little cascade of drooping roses, sought for his eyes almost hungrily. He realised how she must be feeling. A dormant vein of cynicism parted his lips as he held her fingers for a moment. His tone and his manner were quite natural.

"We were, I believe, unusually punctual," he admitted. "What an extraordinary mist! Up over there was no sign of it at all."

She shivered. Her eyes were still watching his face, seeking for an answer to her unasked question. Blue eyes they were, which had been beautiful in their day, a little hard and anxious now. She wore a white dress, simple with the simplicity of supreme and expensive art. A rope of pearls was her only ornament. Her hair was somewhat elaborately coiffured, there was a touch of rouge upon her cheeks, and the unscreened evening sunlight was scarcely kind to her rather wan features and carefully arranged complexion. She still had her claims to beauty, however. Tallente admitted that to himself as he stood there appraising her, with a strange and almost impersonal regard,— his wife of thirteen years. She was beautiful, notwithstanding the strained look of anxiety which at that moment disfigured her face, the lurking fear which made her voice sound artificial, the nervousness which every moment made fresh demands upon her self-restraint.

"It came up from the sea," she said. "One moment Tony and I were sitting out under the trees to keep away from the sun, and the next we were driven shivering indoors; It was just like running into a fog bank in the middle of the Atlantic on a hot summer's day."

"I found the difference in temperature amazing," he observed. "I, too, dropped from the sunshine into a strange chill."

She tried to get rid of the subject.

"So you lost your seat," she said. "I am very sorry. Tell me how it happened?"

He shrugged his shoulders.

"The Democratic Party made up their mind, for some reason or other, that I shouldn't sit. The Labour Party generally were not thinking of running a candidate. I was to have been returned unopposed, in acknowledgment of my work on the Nationalisation Bill. The Democrats, however, ratted. They put up a man at the last moment, and—well, you know the result—I lost."

"I don't understand English politics," she confessed, "but I thought you were almost a Labour man yourself."

"I am practically," he replied. "I don't know, even now, what made them oppose me."

"What about the future?"

"My plans are not wholly made."

For the first time, an old and passionate ambition prevailed against the thrall of the moment.

"One of the papers this morning," she said eagerly, "suggested that you might be offered a peerage."

"I saw it," he acknowledged. "It was in the Sun. I was once unfortunate enough to be on the committee of a club which blackballed the editor."

Her mouth hardened a little.

"But you haven't forgotten your promise?"

"'Bargain' shall we call it?" he replied. "No, I have not forgotten."

"Tony says you could have a peerage whenever you liked."

"Then I suppose it must be so. Just at present I am not prepared to write 'finis' to my political career."

The butler announced dinner. Tallente offered his arm and they passed through the homely little hall into the dining room beyond. Stella came to a sudden standstill as they crossed the threshold.

"Why is the table laid for two only?" she demanded. "Mr. Palliser is here."

"I was obliged to send Tony away—on important business," Tallente intervened. "He left about an hour ago."

Once more the terror was upon her. The fingers which gripped her napkin trembled. Her eyes, filled with fierce enquiry, were fixed upon her husband's as he took his place in leisurely fashion and glanced at the menu.

"Obliged to send Tony away?" she repeated. "I don't understand. He told me that he had several days' work here with you."

"Something intervened," he murmured.

"Why didn't you wire?" she faltered, almost under her breath. "He couldn't have had any time to get ready."

Andrew Tallente looked at his wife across the bowl of floating flowers.

"Ah!" he exclaimed. "I didn't think of that. But in any case I did not make up my mind until I arrived that it was necessary for him to go."

There was silence for a time, an unsatisfactory and in some respects an unnatural silence. Tallente trifled with his *hors d'oeuvres* and was inquisitive about the sauce with which his fish was flavoured. Stella sent away her plate untouched, but drank two glasses of champagne. The light came back to her eyes, she found courage again. After all, she was independent of this man, independent even of his name. She looked across the table at him appraisingly. He was still sufficiently good-looking, lithe of frame and muscular, with features well-cut although a little irregular in outline. Time, however, and anxious work were beginning to leave their marks. His hair was grey at the sides, there were deep lines in his face, he seemed to her fancy to have shrunken a little during the last few years. He had still the languid, high-bred voice which she had always admired so munch, the same coolness of manner and quiet dignity. He was a personable man, but after all he was a failure. His career, so far as she could judge it, was at an end. She was a fool to imagine, even for a moment, that her whole future lay in his keeping.

"Have you any plans?" she asked him presently. "Another constituency?"

He smiled a little wearily. For once he spoke quite naturally.

"The only plan I have formulated at present is to rest for a time," he admitted.

She drank another glass of champagne and felt almost confident. She told him the small events of the sparsely populated neighbourhood, spoke of the lack of water in the trout stream, the improvement in the golf links, the pheasants which a near-by landowner was turning down. They were comparative newcomers and had seen as yet little of their neighbours.

"I was told," she concluded, "that the great lady of the neighbourhood was to have called upon me this afternoon. I waited in but she didn't come."

"And who is that?" he enquired.

"Lady Jane Partington of Woolhanger—a daughter of the Duke of Barminster. Woolhanger was left to her by an old aunt, and they say that she never leaves the place."

"An elderly lady?" he asked, merely with an intent of prolonging a harmless subject of conversation.

"On the contrary, quite young," his wife replied. "She seems to be a sort of bachelor-spinster, who lives out in that lonely place without a chaperon and rules the neighborhood. You ought to make friends with her, Andrew. They say that she is half a Socialist.—By the by, how long are we going to stay down here?"

"We will discuss that presently," he answered.

The service of dinner came to its appointed end. Tallente drank one glass of port alone. Then he rose, left the room by the French windows, passed along the terrace and looked in at the drawing-room, where Stella was lingering over her coffee.

"Will you walk with me as far as the lookout?" he invited. "Your maid can bring you a cloak if you are likely to be cold."

She responded a little ungraciously, but appeared a few minutes later, a filmy shawl of lace covering her bare shoulders. She walked by his side to the end of the terrace, along the curving walk through the plantation, and by the sea wall to the flagged space where some seats and a table had been fixed. Four hundred feet below, the sea was beating against jagged rocks. The moon was late and it was almost dark. She leaned over and he stood by her side.

> "Stella," he said, "you asked me at dinner when we were leaving here.
> You are leaving to-morrow morning by the twelve-thirty train."

"What do you mean?" she demanded, with a sudden sinking of the heart.

"Please do not ask," he replied. "You know and I know. It is not my wish to make public the story of our—disagreement."

She was silent for several moments, looking over into the black gulf below, watching the swirl of the sea, listening to its dull booming against the distant rocks, the shriek of the backward-dragged pebbles. An owl flew out from some secret place in the cliffs and wheeled across the bay. She drew her shawl around her with a little shiver.

"So this is the end," she answered.

"No doubt, in my way," he reflected, "I have been as great a disappointment to you as you to me. You brought me your great wealth, believing that I could use it towards securing just what you desired in the way of social position. Perhaps that might have come but for the war. Now I have become rather a failure."

"There was no necessity for you ever to have gone soldiering," she reminded him a little hardly.

"As you say," he acquiesced. "Still, I went and I do not regret it. I might even remind you that I met with some success."

"Pooh!" she scoffed. "What is the use of a few military distinctions? What are an M.C. and a D.S.O. and a few French and Belgian orders going to do for me? You know I want other things. They told me when I married you," she went on, warming with her own sense of injury, "that you were certain to be Prime Minister. They told me that the Coalition Party couldn't do without you, that you were the only effective link between them and Labour. You had only to play your cards properly and you could have pushed out Horlock whenever you liked. And now see what a mess you have made of things! You have built up Horlock's party for him, he offers you an insignificant post in the Cabinet, and you can't even win your seat in Parliament."

"Your epitome of my later political career has its weak points, but I dare say, from your point of view, you have every reason for complaint," he observed. "Since I have failed to procure for you the position you desire, our parting will have a perfectly natural appearance. Your fortune is unimpaired—you cannot say that I have been extravagant—and I assure you that I shall not regret my return to poverty."

"But you won't be able to live," she said bluntly. "You haven't any income at all."

"Believe me," he answered quietly, "you exaggerate my poverty. In any case, it is not your concern."

"You wouldn't—"

She paused. She was a woman of not very keen perceptions, but she realised that if she were to proceed with the offer which was half framed in her mind, the man by her side, with his, to her outlook, distorted sense of honour, would become her enemy. She shrugged her shoulders, and turning towards him, held out her hand.

"It is the end, then," she said. "Well, Andrew, I did my best according to my lights, and I failed. Will you shake hands?"

He shook his head.

"I cannot, Stella. Let us agree to part here. We know all there is to be known of one another, and we shall be able to say good-by without regret."

She drifted slowly away from him. He watched her figure pass in and out among the trees. She was unashamed, perhaps relieved,—probably, he reflected, as he watched her enter the house, already making her plans for a more successful future. He turned away and looked downwards. The darkness seemed, if possible, to have become a little more intense, the moaning of the sea more insistent. Little showers of white spray enlaced the sombre rocks. The owl came back from his mysterious journey, hovered for a moment over the cliff and entered his secret home. Behind him, the lights in the house went out, one by one. Suddenly he felt a grip upon his shoulder, a hot breath upon his cheek. It was Stella, returned dishevelled, her lace scarf streaming behind, her eyes lit with horror. "Andrew!" she cried. "It came over me—just as I entered the house! What have you done with Anthony?"

CHAPTER II

Tallente's first impressions of Jane Partington were that an exceedingly attractive but somewhat imperious young woman had surprised him in a most undignified position. She had come cantering down the drive on a horse which, by comparison with the Exmoor ponies which every one rode in those parts, had seemed gigantic, and, finding a difficulty in making her presence known, had motioned to him with her whip. He climbed down from the steps where he had been busy fastening up some roses, removed a nail from his mouth and came towards her.

"How is it that I can make no one hear?" she asked. "Do you know if Mrs. Tallente is at home?"

Tallente was in no hurry to reply. He was busy taking in a variety of pleasant impressions. Notwithstanding the severely cut riding habit and the hard little hat, he decided that he had never looked into a more attractively feminine face. For some occult reason, unconnected, he was sure, with the use of any skin food or face cream, this young woman who had the reputation of living out of doors, winter and summer, had a complexion which, notwithstanding its faint shade of tan, would have passed muster for delicacy and clearness in any Mayfair drawing-room. Her eyes were soft and brown, her hair a darker shade of the same colour. Her mouth, for all its firmness, was soft and pleasantly curved. Her tone, though a trifle imperative, was kindly, gracious and full of musical quality. Her figure was moderately slim, but indistinguishable at that moment under her long coat. She possessed a curious air of physical well-being, the well-being of a woman who has found and is enjoying what she seeks in life.

"Won't you tell me why I can make no one hear?" she repeated, still good-naturedly but frowning slightly at his silence.

"Mrs. Tallente is in London," he announced. "She has taken most of the establishment with her."

The visitor fumbled in her side pocket and produced a diminutive ivory case. She withdrew a card and handed it to Tallente, with a glance at his gloved hands.

"Will you give this to the butler?" she begged. "Tell him to tell his mistress that I was sorry not to find her at home."

"The butler," Tallente explained, "has gone for the milk. He shall have the card immediately on his return."

She looked at him for a moment and then smiled.

"Do forgive me," she said. "I believe you are Mr. Tallente?"

He drew off his gloves and shook hands.

"How did you guess that?" he asked.

"From the illustrated papers, of course," she answered. "I have come to the conclusion that you must be a very vain man, I have seen so many pictures of you lately."

"A matter of snapshots," he replied, "for which, as a rule, the victim is not responsible. You should abjure such a journalistic vice as picture papers."

"Why?" she laughed. "They lead to such pleasant surprises. I had been led to believe, for instance, by studying the Daily Mirror, that you were quite an elderly person with a squint."

"I am becoming self-conscious," he confessed. "Won't you come in? There is a boy somewhere about the premises who can look after your horse, and I shall be able to give you some tea as soon as Robert gets back with the milk."

He cooeed to the boy, who came up from one of the lower shelves of garden, and she followed him into the hall. He looked around him for a moment in some perplexity.

> "I wonder whether you would mind coming into my study?" he suggested.
> "I am here quite alone for the present, and it is the only room I use."

She followed him down a long passage into a small apartment at the extreme end of the house.

"You are like me," she said. "I keep most of my rooms shut up and live in my den. A lonely person needs so much atmosphere."

"Rather a pigsty, isn't it?" he remarked, sweeping a heap of books from a chair. "I am without a secretary just now—in fact," he went on, with a little burst of confidence engendered by her friendly attitude, "we are in a mess altogether."

She laughed softly, leaning back amongst the cushions of the chair and looking around the room, her kindly eyes filled with interest.

"It is a most characteristic mess," she declared. "I am sure an interviewer would give anything for this glimpse into your tastes and habits. Golf clubs, all cleaned up and ready for action; trout rod, newly-waxed at the joints—you must try my stream, there is no water in yours; tennis racquets in a very excellent press—I wonder whether you're too good for a single with me some day? Typewriter—rather dusty. I don't believe that you can use it."

"I can't," he admitted. "I have been writing my letters by hand for the last two days."

She sighed.

"Men are helpless creatures! Fancy a great politician unable to write his own letters! What has become of your secretary?"

Tallente threw some books to the floor and seated himself in the vacant easy-chair.

"I shall begin to think," he said, a little querulously, "that you don't read the newspapers. My secretary, according to that portion of the Press which guarantees to provide full value for the smallest copper coin, has 'disappeared'."

"Really?" she exclaimed. "He or she?"

"He—the Honourable Anthony Palliser by name, son of Stobart Palliser, who was at Eton with me."

She nodded.

"I expect I know his mother. What exactly do you mean by 'disappeared'?"

Tallente was looking out of the window. A slight hardness had crept into his tone and manner. He had the air of one reciting a story.

"The young man and I differed last Tuesday night," he said. "In the language of the novelists, he walked out into the night and disappeared. Only an hour before dinner, too. Nothing has been heard of him since."

"What a fatuous thing to do!" she remarked. "Shall you have to get another secretary?"

"Presently," he assented. "Just for the moment I am rather enjoying doing nothing."

She leaned back amongst the cushions of her chair and looked across at him with interest, an interest which presently drifted into sympathy. Even the lightness of his tone could not mask the inwritten weariness of the man, the tired droop of the mouth, and the lacklustre eyes.

"Do you know," she said, "I have never been more intrigued than when I heard you were really coming down here. Last summer I was in Scotland—in fact I have been away every time the Manor has been open. I am so anxious to know whether you like this part of the world."

"I like it so much," he replied, "that I feel like settling here for the rest of my life."

She shook her head.

"You will never be able to do that," she said, "at least not for many years. The country will need so much of your time. But it is delightful to think that you may come here for your holidays."

"If you read the newspapers," he remarked, a little grimly, "you might not be so sure that the country is clamouring for my services."

She waved away his speech with a little gesture of contempt.

"Rubbish! Your defeat at Hellesfield was a matter of political jobbery. Any one could see through that. Horlock ought never to have sent you there. He ought to have found you a perfectly safe seat, and of course he will have to do it."

He shook his head.

"I am not so sure. Horlock resents my defeat almost as though it were a personal matter. Besides, it is an age of young men, Lady Jane."

"Young men!" she scoffed. "But you are young."

"Am I?" he answered, a little sadly. "I am not feeling it just now. Besides, there is something wrong about my enthusiasms. They are becoming altogether too pastoral. I am rather thinking of taking up the cultivation of roses and of making a terraced garden down to the sea. Do you know anything about gardening, Lady Jane?"

"Of course I do," she answered, a little impatiently. "A very excellent hobby it is for women and dreamers and elderly men. There is plenty of time for you to take up such a pursuit when you have finished your work."

"Fifteen thousand intelligent voters have just done their best to tell me that it is already finished," he sighed.

She made a little grimace.

"Am I going to be disappointed in you, I wonder?" she asked. "I don't think so. You surely wouldn't let a little affair like one election drive you out of public life? It was so obvious that you were made the victim for Horlock's growing unpopularity in the country. Haven't you realised that yourself— or perhaps you don't care to talk about these things to an ignoramus such as I am?"

"Please don't believe that," he begged hastily. "I think yours is really the common-sense view of the matter. Only," he went on, "I have always represented, amongst the coalitionists, the moderate Socialist, the views of those men who recognise the power and force of the coming democracy, and desire to have legislation attuned to it. Yet it was the Democratic vote which upset me at Hellesfield."

"That was entirely a matter of faction," she persisted. "That horrible person Miller was sent down there, for some reason or other, to make trouble. I believe if the election had been delayed another week, and you had been able to make two more speeches like you did at the Corn Exchange, you would have got in."

He looked at her in some surprise.

"That is exactly what I thought myself," he agreed. "How on earth do you come to know all these things?"

"I take an interest in your career," she said, smiling at him, "and I hate to see you so dejected without cause."

He felt a little thrill at her words. A queer new sense of companionship stirred in his pulses. The bitterness of his suppressed disappointment was suddenly soothed. There was something of the excitement of the discoverer, too, in these new sensations. It seemed to him that he was finding something which had been choked out of his life and which was yet a real and natural part of it.

"You will make an awful nuisance of me if you don't mind," he warned her. "If you encourage me like this, you will develop the most juvenile of all failings—you will make me want to talk about myself. I am beginning to feel terribly egotistical already."

She leaned a little towards him. Her mouth was soft with sweet and feminine tenderness, her eyes warm with kindness.

"That is just what I hoped I might succeed in doing," she declared. "I have been interested in your career ever since I had the faintest idea of what politics meant. You could not give me a greater happiness than to talk to me—about yourself."

CHAPTER III

Very soon tea was brought in. The homely service of the meal, and Robert's plain clothes, seemed to demand some sort of explanation. It was she who provided the opening.

"Will your wife be long away?" she enquired.

Tallente looked at his guest thoughtfully. She was pouring out tea from an ordinary brown earthenware pot with an air of complete absorption in her task. The friendliness of her seemed somehow to warm the atmosphere of the room, even as her sympathy had stolen into the frozen places of his life. For the moment he ignored her question. His eyes appraised her critically, reminiscently. There was something vaguely familiar in the frank sweetness of her tone and manner.

"I am going to make the most idiotically commonplace remark," he said. "I cannot believe that this is the first time we have met."

"It isn't," she replied, helping herself to strawberry

"Are you in earnest?" he asked, puzzled.

"Do you mean that I have spoken to you?"

"Absolutely!"

"Not only that but you have made me a present."

He searched the recesses of his memory in vain. She smiled at his perplexity and began to count on her fingers.

"Let me see," she said, "exactly fourteen years ago you arrived in Paris from London on a confidential mission to a certain person."

"To Lord Peters!" he exclaimed.

She nodded.

"You had half an hour to spare after you had finished your business, and you begged to see the young people. Maggie Peters was always a friend of yours. You came into the morning-room and I was there."

"You?"

"Yes! I was at school in Paris, and I was spending my half-holiday with Maggie."

"The little brown girl!" he murmured. "I never heard your name, and when I sent the chocolates I had to send them to 'the young lady in brown.' Of course I remember! But your hair was down your back, you had freckles, and you were as silent as a mouse."

"You see how much better my memory is than yours," she laughed.

"I am not so sure," he objected. "You took me for the gardener just now."

"Not when you came down the steps," she protested, "and besides, it is your own fault for wearing such atrociously old clothes."

"They shall be given away to-morrow," he promised.

"I should think so," she replied. "And you might part with the battered straw hat you were wearing, at the same time."

"It shall be done," he promised meekly.

She became reminiscent.

"We were all so interested in you in those days. Lord Peters told us, after you were gone, that some day you would be Prime Minister."

"I am afraid," he sighed, "that I have disappointed most of my friends."

"You have disappointed no one," she assured him firmly. "You will disappoint no one. You are the one person in politics who has kept a steadfast course, and if you have lost ground a little in the country, and slipped out of people's political appreciation during the last decade, don't we all know why? Every one of your friends—and your wife, of course," she put in hastily, "must be proud that you have lost ground. There isn't another man in the country who gave up a great political career to learn his drill in a cadet corps, who actually served in the trenches through the most terrible battles of the war, and came out of it a Brigadier-General with all your distinctions."

He felt his heart suddenly swell. No one had ever spoken to him like this. The newspapers had been complimentary for a day and had accepted the verdict of circumstances the next. His wife had simply been the reflex of other people's opinion and the trend of events.

"You make me feel," he told her earnestly, "almost for the first time, that after all it was worth while."

The slight unsteadiness of his tone at first surprised, then brought her almost to the point of confusion. Their eyes met—a startled glance on her part, merely to assure herself that he was in earnest—and afterwards there was a moment's embarrassment. She accepted a cigarette and went back to her easy-chair.

"You did not answer the question I asked you a few minutes ago," she reminded him. "When is your wife returning?"

The shadow was back on his face.

"Lady Jane," he said, "if it were not that we are old friends, dating from that box of chocolates, remember, I might have felt that I must make you some sort of a formal reply. But as it is, I shall tell you the truth. My wife is not coming hack."

"Not at all?" she exclaimed.

"To me, never," he answered. "We have separated."

"I am so very sorry," she said, after a moment's startled silence. "I am afraid that I asked a tactless question, but how could I know?"

"There was nothing tactless about it," he assured her. "It makes it much easier for me to tell you. I married my wife thirteen years ago because I believed that her wealth would help me in my career. She married me because she was an American with ambitions, anxious to find a definite place in English society. She has been disappointed in me. Other circumstances have now presented themselves. I have discovered that my wife's affections are bestowed elsewhere. To be perfectly honest, the discovery was a relief to me."

"So that is why you are living down here like this?" she murmured.

"Precisely! The one thing for which I am grateful," he went on, "is that I always refused to let my wife take a big country house. I insisted upon an unpretentious place for the times when I could rest. I think that I shall settle down here altogether. I can just afford to live here if I shoot plenty of rabbits, and if Robert's rheumatism is not too bad for him to look after the vegetable garden."

"Of course you are talking nonsense," she pronounced, a little curtly.

"Why nonsense?"

"You must go back to your work," she insisted.

"Keep this place for your holiday moments, certainly, but for the rest, to talk of settling down here is simply wicked."

"What is my work?" he asked. "I tell you frankly that I do not know where I belong. A very intelligent constituency, stuffed up to the throat with schoolboard education, has determined that it would prefer a representative who has changed his politics already four times. I seem to be nobody's man. Horlock at heart is frightened of me, because he is convinced that I am not sound, and he has only tried to make use of me as a sop to democracy. The Whigs hate me like poison, hate me even worse than Horlock. If I were in Parliament, I should not know which Party to support. I think I shall devote my time to roses."

"And between September and May?"

"I shall hibernate and think about them."

"Of course," she said, with the air of one humoring a child, "you are not in earnest. You have just been through a very painful experience and you are suffering from it. As for the rest, you are talking nonsense."

"Explain, please," he begged.

"You said just now that you did not know where your place was," she continued. "You called yourself nobody's man. Why, the most ignorant person who thinks about things could tell you where you belong. Even I could tell you."

"Please do," he invited.

She rose to her feet.

"Walk round the garden with me," she begged, brushing the cigarette ash from her skirt. "You know what a terrible out-of-door person I am. This room seems to me close. I want to smell the sea from one of those wonderful lookouts of yours."

He walked with her along one of the lower paths, deliberately avoiding the upper lookouts. They came presently to a grass-grown pier. She stood at the end, her firm, capable fingers clenching the stone wall, her eyes looking seaward.

"I will tell you where you belong," she said. "In your heart you must know it, but you are suffering from that reaction which comes from failure to those people who are not used to failure. You belong to the head of things. You should hold up your right, hand, and the party you should lead should form itself about you. No, don't interrupt me," she went on. "You and all of us know that the country is in a bad way. She is feeling all the evils of a too-great prosperity, thrust upon her after a period of suffering. You can see the dangers ahead—I learnt them first from you in the pages of the reviews, when after the war you foretold the exact position in which we find ourselves to-day. Industrial wealth means the building up of a new democracy. The democracy already exists but it is unrepresented, because those people who should form its bulwark and its strength are attached to various factions of what is called the Labour Party. They don't know themselves yet. No Rienzi has arisen to hold up the looking-glass. If some one does not teach them to find themselves, there will be trouble. Mind, I am only repeating what you have told others."

"It is all true," he agreed.

"Then can't you see," she continued eagerly, "what party it is to which you ought to attach yourself—the party which has broken up now into half a dozen factions? They are all misnamed but that is no matter. You should stand for Parliament as a Labour or a Socialist candidate, because you understand what the people want and what they ought to have. You should draw up a new and final programme."

"You are a wonderful person," he said with conviction, "but like all people who are clear-sighted and who have imagination, you are also a theorist. I believe your idea is the true one, but to stand for Parliament as a Labour member you have to belong to one of the acknowledged factions to be sure of any support at all. An independent member can count his votes by the capful."

"That is the old system," she pointed out firmly. "It is for you to introduce a new one. If necessary, you must stoop to political cunning. You should make use of those very factions until you are strong enough to stand by yourself. Through their enmity amongst themselves, one of them would come to your side, anyway. But I should like to see you discard all old parliamentary methods. I should like to see you speak to the heart of the man who is going to record his vote."

"It is a slow matter to win votes in units," he reminded her.

"But it is the real way," she insisted. "Voting by party and government by party will soon come to an end. It must. All that it needs is a strong man with a definite programme of his own, to attack the whole principle."

He looked away from the sea towards the woman by his side. The wind was blowing in her face, blowing back little strands of her tightly coiled hair, blowing back her coat and skirt, outlining her figure with soft and graceful distinction. She was young, healthy and splendid, full of all the enthusiasm of her age. He sighed a little bitterly.

"All that you say," he reminded her, "should have been said to me by the little brown girl in Paris, years ago. I am too old now for great tasks."

She turned towards him with the pitying yet pleasant air of one who would correct a child.

"You are forty-nine years old and three months," she said.

"How on earth did you know that?" he demanded.

She smiled.

"A valuable little red book called 'Who's Who.' You see, it is no use your trying to pose as a Methuselah. For a politician you are a young man. You have time and strength for the greatest of all tasks. Find some other excuse, sir, if you talk of laying down the sword and picking up the shuttle."

He looked back seawards. His eyes were following the flight of a seagull, wheeling in the sunlight.

"I suppose you are right," he acknowledged. "No man is too old for work."

"I beg your pardon, sir."

They turned abruptly around. They had been so engrossed that they had not noticed the sound of footsteps. Robert, a little out of breath, was standing at attention. There was a disturbed look in his face, a tremor in his voice.

"I beg your pardon, sir," he repeated, "there is—some one here to see you."

"Some one?" Tallente repeated impatiently.

Robert leaned a little forward. The effort at lowering his voice only made his hoarse whisper sound more agitated.

"A police inspector, sir, from Barnstaple, is waiting in the study."

CHAPTER IV

Mr Inspector Gillian of Barnstaple had no idea of denying his profession. He had travelled over in a specially hired motor-car, and he was wearing his best uniform. He rose to his feet at Tallente's entrance and saluted a little ponderously.

"Mr. Andrew Tallente, sir?" he enquired.

Tallente silently admitted his identity, waved the inspector back to his seat—the one high-backed and uncomfortable chair in the room—and took an easy-chair himself.

"I have come over, sir," the man continued, "according to instructions received by telephone from Scotland Yard. My business is to ask you a few questions concerning the disappearance of the Honourable Anthony Palliser, who was, I am given to understand, your secretary."

"Dear me!" Tallente exclaimed. "I had no idea that the young man's temporary absence from polite society would be turned into a melodramatic disappearance."

The inspector took mental note of the levity in Tallente's tone, and disapproved.

"The Honourable Anthony Palliser disappeared from here, sir, on Tuesday night last, the night of your return from London," he said. "I have come to ask you certain questions with reference to that disappearance."

"Go ahead," Tallente begged. "Care to smoke a cigar?"

"Not whilst on duty, thank you, sir," was the dignified reply.

"You will forgive my cigarette," Tallente observed, lighting one. "Now you can go ahead as fast as you like."

"Question number one is this, sir. I wish to know whether Mr. Palliser's abrupt departure from the Manor was due to any disagreement with you?"

"In a sense I suppose it was," the other acknowledged. "I turned him out of the house."

The inspector did not attempt to conceal his gratification. He made a voluminous note in his pocketbook.

"Am I to conclude, then, that there was a quarrel?" he enquired.

"I do not quarrel with people to whom I pay a salary," Tallente replied.

"When you say that you turned him out of the house, that rather implies a quarrel, doesn't it? It might even imply—blows."

"You can put your own construction upon it," was the cool reply.

"Had you any idea where the honourable Anthony Palliser was going to?"

"I suggested the devil," Tallente confided blandly. "I expect he will get there some time. I put up with him because I knew his father, but he is not a young man to make a fuss about."

The inspector was a little staggered.

"I am to conclude, then," he said, "that you were dissatisfied with his work as your secretary?"

"Absolutely," was the firm reply. "You have no idea what a mess he was liable to make of things if he was left alone."

The inspector coughed.

"Mr. Tallente, sir," he said, "my instructions are to ask you to disclose the nature of your displeasure, if any, with the Honourable Mr. Anthony Palliser. In plain words, Scotland Yard desires to know why he was turned away from his place at a moment's notice."

"I suppose it is the duty of Scotland Yard to be inquisitive in cases of this sort," Tallente observed. "You can report to them the whole of the valuable information with which I have already furnished you, and you can add that I absolutely refuse to give any information respecting the—er—difference of opinion between the young man and myself."

The inspector did not conceal his dissatisfaction.

"I shall ask, you, sir," he said with dignity, "to reconsider that decision. Remember that it is the police who ask, and in cases of this sort they have special privileges."

"As soon as any criminal case arises from Anthony Palliser's disappearance," Tallente pointed out, "you will be in a position to ask me questions from a different standpoint. For the present I have given you just as much information as I feel inclined to. Shall we leave it at that?"

The inspector appeared to have become hard of hearing. He did not attempt to rise from his chair.

"Being your private secretary, sir," he said, "the Honourable Anthony Palliser would no doubt have access to your private papers?"

"Naturally," Tallente conceded.

"There might be amongst them papers of importance, papers whose possession by parties in the other camp of politics—"

"Stop!" Tallente interrupted. "Inspector Gillan, you are an astute man. Excuse me."

He crossed the room and, with a key which he took from a chain attached to his trouser button, opened a small but powerful safe fitted into the wall. He opened it confidently enough, gazed inside and remained for a moment transfixed. Then he took up a few little packets of papers, glanced them through and replaced them. He still stood there, dangling the key in his hard. The inspector watched him curiously.

"Anything missing, sir?" he asked.

Tallente swung the door to and came back to his chair.

"Yes!" he admitted.

"Can I make a note of the nature of the loss, sir?" the man asked, moistening his pencil.

"A political paper of some personal consequence," Tallente replied. "Its absence disquiets me. It also confirms my belief that Palliser is lying doggo for a time."

"A hint as to the contents of the missing paper would be very acceptable, sir," Inspector Gillian begged.

Tallente shook his head.

"For the present," he decided, "I can only repeat what I said a few moments ago—I have given you just as much information as I feel inclined to."

The inspector rose to his feet.

"My report will not be wholly satisfactory to Scotland Yard, sir," he declared.

"My experience of the estimable body is that they take a lot of satisfying," Tallente replied. "Will you take anything before you go, Inspector?"

"Nothing whatever, thank you, sir. At the risk of annoying you, I am bound to ask this question. Will you tell me whether anything in the nature of blows passed between you and the Honourable Anthony Palliser, previous to his leaving your house?"

"I will not even satisfy your curiosity to that extent," Tallente answered.

"It will be my duty, sir," the inspector said ponderously, "to examine some of your servants."

"Scotland Yard can do that for themselves," Tallente observed. "My wife and the greater part of the domestic staff left here for London a week ago."

The representative of the law saluted solemnly.

"I am sorry that you have not felt inclined to treat me with more confidence in this matter, Mr. Tallente," he said.

He took his leave then. Tallente heard him conversing for some time with Robert and saw him in the garden, interviewing the small boy. Afterwards, he climbed into his car and drove away. Tallente opened his safe and once more let the little array of folded papers slip through his hands. Then he rang the bell for Robert, who presently appeared.

"The inspector has quite finished with you?" his master asked.

Robert was a portly man, a little unhealthy in colour and a little short of breath. He had been gassed in the war and his nerves were not what they had been. It was obvious, as he stood on the other side of the table, that he was trembling.

"Quite, sir. He was enquiring about Mr. Palliser."

His master nodded.

"I am afraid he will find it a little difficult to obtain any information round here," he remarked. "There are certain things connected with that young man which may throw a new light upon his disappearance."

"Indeed, sir?" Robert murmured.

Tallente glanced towards the safe.

"Robert," he confided, "I have been robbed."

The man started a little.

"Indeed, sir?" he replied. "Nothing very valuable, I hope?"

"I have been robbed of papers," Tallente said quietly, "which in the wrong hands might ruin me. Mr. Palliser had a key to that safe. Have you ever seen it open?"

"Never, sir."

"When did Mr. Palliser arrive here?"

"On the evening train of the Monday, sir, that you arrived by on the Tuesday."

"Tell me, did he receive any visitors at all on the Tuesday?"

"There was a man came over from a house near Lynton, sir, said his name was Miller."

"Have you any idea what he wanted?"

"No certain idea, sir," Robert replied doubtfully. "Now I come to think of it, though, it seemed as though he had come to make Mr. Palliser some sort of an offer. After I had let him out, he came back and said something to Mr. Palliser about three thousand pounds, and Mr. Palliser said he would let him know. I got the idea, somehow or other, that the transaction, whatever it might have been, was to be concluded on Tuesday night."

"Why didn't you tell me this before, Robert?" his master enquired.

"Other things drove it out of my mind, sir," the man confessed. "I didn't look upon it as of much consequence. I thought it was something to do with Mr. Palliser's private affairs."

Tallente glanced at the safe.

"I saw this man Miller at the station," he said, "when I arrived."

"That would be on his way back from here, sir," Robert acquiesced. "I gathered that he was coming back again after dinner in a car."

"Did you hear a car at all that night?"

"I rather fancied I did," the man asserted. "I didn't take particular notice, though."

Tallente frowned.

"I am very much afraid, Robert," he said, "that wherever Mr. Palliser is, those papers are."

Robert shivered.

"Very good, sir," he said, in a low tone.

"Any speculations as to that young man's whereabouts," Tallente continued thoughtfully, "must necessarily be a matter of pure guesswork, but supposing, Robert, he should have wandered in that mist the wrong way—turned to the left, for instance, outside this window, instead of to the right—he might very easily have fallen over the cliff."

"The walk is very unsafe in the dark, sir," Robert acquiesced, looking down at the carpet.

"It was not my intention," Tallente remarked thoughtfully, "to kill the young man. A brawl in front of the windows was impossible, so I took him with me to the lookout. I suppose he was tactless and I lost my temper. I struck him on the chin and he went backwards, through that piece of rotten paling, you know, Robert—"

"I know, sir," the man interrupted, with a little moan. "Please don't!"

Tallente shrugged his shoulders.

"I took him at no disadvantage," he said coolly. "He knew how to use the gloves and he was twenty years younger than I. However, there it is. Backwards he went, all legs and arms and shrieks. And with him went the papers he had stolen.—At twelve o'clock to-night, Robert, I must go down after him."

"It's impossible, sir! It's a sheer precipice for four hundred feet!"

"Nothing of the sort," was the cool reply. "There are heaps of ledges and little clumps of pines and yews. All that you will have to do is to pull up the rope when I am ready. You can fasten it to a tree when I go down."

"It's not worth it, sir," the man protested anxiously. "No one will ever find the body down there."

"Send the boy home to stay with his parents to-night," Tallente continued. "Your wife, I suppose, can be trusted?"

"She is living up at the garage, sir," Robert answered. "Besides, she is deaf. I'll tell her that I am sleeping in the house to-night as you are not very well. And forgive me, sir—her ladyship left a message. She hoped you would lunch with her to-morrow."

Tallente strolled out again in a few minutes, curiously impatient of the restraint of walls, and clambered up the precipitous field at the back of the Manor. Far up the winding road which led back into the world, a motor-car was crawling on its way up over. He watched it through a pair of field glasses. Leaning back in the tonneau with folded arms, as though solemnly digesting a problem, was Inspector Gillian. Tallente closed the glasses with a little snap and smiled.

"The Bucket type," he murmured to himself, "very much the Bucket type."

CHAPTER V

The moon that night seemed to be indulging in strange vagaries, now dimly visible behind a mist of thin grey vapour, now wholly obscured behind jagged masses of black cloud, and occasionally shining brilliantly from a little patch of clear sky. Tallente waited for one of the latter moments before he finally tested the rope which was wound around the strongest of the young pine trees and stepped over the rustic wooden paling at the edge of the lookout He stood there balanced between earth and sky, until Robert, who watched him, shivered. "There is nothing to fear," his master said coolly. "Remember, I am an old hand at mountain climbing, Robert. All the same, if anything should happen, you'd better say that we fancied we heard a cry from down below and I went to see what it was. You understand?"

"Yes, sir!"

Tallente took a step into what seemed to be Eternity. The rope cut into his hands for the first three or four yards, as the red sand crumbled away beneath his feet, and he was obliged to grip for his life. Presently he gained a little ledge, from which a single yew tree was growing, and paused for breath.

"Are you all right, sir?" Robert called out from above.

"Quite," was the confident answer. "I shall be off again in a minute."

Tallente's head had been the wonder even of members of the Alpine Club, years ago in Switzerland. He found himself now in this strangest of all positions, absolutely steady and unmoved. Sheer below him, dark, rushing waves broke upon the rocks, sending showers of glittering spray upwards. Above, the little lookout with its rustic paling seemed almost more than directly overhead. The few stars and the fugitive moon seemed somehow set in a different sky. He felt a new kinship with a great gull who came floating by. He had become himself a creature of the wild places. Presently he began once more to let himself down, hand over hand, to where the next little clump of trees showed a chance of a precarious foothold. The rope chafed his fingers but he remained absolutely steady. Once he trusted for a moment to a yew tree, growing out of a fissure in the rock, which came out by the roots and went hurtling down into space. From overhead he heard Robert's terrified cry. The rope stood the strain of his sudden clutch, however, and all was well. A little lower down, holding on with one hand, he took his torch from his pocket and examined the surface of the cliff. Nothing apparently had been disturbed, nor was there any sign of any heavy body having been dashed through the undergrowth. Soon he went on again, and, working a little to the left, stood for a moment upon a green, turf-covered crag, a tiny plateau covered with the refuse of seagulls and a few stunted trees, from amongst which a startled hawk rose with a wild cry. He waited here until the moon shone once more and he could see the little strip of shingle below. Nowhere could he find any trace of the thing he sought.

At the end of half an hour's climbing, he reached the end of the rope. The little cove, filled with tumbled rocks and a narrow strip of beach, was still about eighty feet below. The slope here was far less precipitous and there was a foothold in many places amongst the thinly growing firs and dwarfed oaks. Calmly he let go the rope and commenced to scramble. More than once his foot slipped, but he was always in a position to save himself. The time came at last when he stood upon the pebbly beach, surprised to find that his knees were shaking and his breath coming fast. The little place was so enclosed that when he looked upwards it seemed as though he were at the bottom of a pit, as though the stars and the doubtful moon had receded and he was somehow in the bowels of the earth instead of being on the sea level. There were only a few feet of the shingle dry, and a great wave, breaking amongst the huge rocks, drenched him with spray. He proceeded with his task, however, searching methodically amongst the rocks, scanning the pebbly beach with his torch, always amazed that nowhere could he find the slightest trace of what he sought. Finally, drenched to the skin and utterly exhausted, he commenced once more the upward climb. He was an hour reaching the end of the rope. Then he blew the whistle and the rest was easy. Nevertheless, when the paling came into sight and he felt Robert's arms under his shoulders, he reeled over towards the seat and lay there, his clothes caked in red mud, the knees of his knickerbockers cut, blood on his hands and forehead, breathless. Robert forced brandy down his throat, however, and in a moment or two he was himself again.

"A miracle!" he gasped. "There is nothing there."

"There was something dark, I fancied, upon the strip of beach, sir,"
Robert ventured.

"I thought so too. It was a tarred plank of timber."

"Then the tide must have reached him."

Tallente rose to his feet and looked over.

"The sea alone knows," he said. "For the first time, though, Robert, I feel inclined to agree with the newspapers, who speak of the strange disappearance of the Honourable Antimony Palliser. Could any man go backwards over that palisading, do you think, and save his life?"

Robert shook his head.

"Miracles can't happen, sir," he muttered.

"Nevertheless," Tallente said, a little gloomily, "the sea never keeps what the land gives it. My fate will rest with the tides."

Robert suddenly gripped his master's arm. The moon had disappeared underneath a fragment of cloud and they stood in complete darkness. Both men listened. From one of the paths which led through the grounds from the beach, came the sound of muffled footsteps. A startled owl flew out and wheeled over their heads with a queer little cry.

"Who's that in the grounds, Robert?" Tallente demanded.

"I've no idea, sir," the latter replied, his voice shaking. "The cottage is empty. The boy went home—I saw him start off. There is no one else about the place."

Nevertheless, the footsteps came nearer. By and by, through the trees, came the occasional flash of an electric torch. Robert turned towards the house but Tallente gripped him by the arm.

"Stop here," he muttered. "We couldn't get away. Any one would hear our footsteps along this flinty path. Besides, there is the rope."

"It's someone else searching!" Robert whispered hoarsely.

The light grew nearer and nearer. A little way below, the path branched to the right and the left. To the left it encircled the tennis lawn and led to the Manor or back to the road. The path to the right led to the little lookout upon which the two men were standing. The footsteps for a moment hesitated. Then the light flashed out and approached. Whoever the intruder might be, he was making his way directly towards them. Tallente shrugged his shoulders.

"We must see this through, Robert," he said. "We were in a tighter corner at Ypres, remember. Keep as quiet as you can. Now, then."

Tallente flashed on his own torch.

"Who's there?" he asked sternly.

There was no answer. The torch for a moment remained stationary, then it began again to advance.

"What are you doing in my grounds?" Tallente demanded. "Who are you?"

A shape loomed into distinctness. A bulky man in dark clothes came into sight.

"I am Gillian—Inspector Gillian. What are you doing out here, Mr. Tallente?"

Tallente laughed a little scornfully.

"It seems to me that the boot is on the other leg," he said. "I should like to know what the mischief you mean by wandering around my grounds at this hour of the night without my permission?"

The inspector completed his climb and stood in the little circle of light. He took note of the rope and of Tallente's condition.

"My presence here, sir," the inspector announced, "is connected with the disappearance of the Honourable Anthony Palliser."

"Confidence for confidence," Tallente replied. "So is mine."

The inspector moved to the palisading. The top rail had been broken, as though it had given under the weight of some heavy body. He held up the loose fragment, glanced downwards into the dark gulf and back again to Tallente. "You've been over there," he said. "I have," Tallente admitted. "I've made a search that I don't fancy you'd have tackled yourself. I've been down the cliff to the beach."

"What reason had you for supposing that you might discover Mr. Palliser's body there?" the other asked bluntly.

Tallente sat on the stone seat and lit a cigarette.

"I will take you into my confidence, Mr. Inspector," he said. "This afternoon I strolled round here with a lady caller, just before you came, and I fancied that I heard a faint cry. I took no notice of it at the time, but to-night, after dinner, I wandered out here again, and again I fancied I heard it. It got on my nerves to such an extent that I fetched Robert here, a coil of rope, put on some shoes with spikes and tried to remember that I was an Alpine climber."

"You've been down to the beach and back, sir?" the inspector asked, looking over a little wonderingly.

"Every inch of the way. The last eighty feet or so I had to scramble."

"Did you discover anything, sir?"

"Not a thing. I couldn't even find a broken twig in any of the little clumps of outgrowing trees. There wasn't a sign of the sand having been disturbed anywhere down the face of the cliff, and I shouldn't think a human being had been on that beach during our lifetimes. I have had my night's work for nothing."

"It was just the cry you fancied you heard which made you undertake this expedition?"

"Precisely!"

The inspector held up the broken rail.

"When was this smashed?" he enquired.

"I have no idea," Tallente answered. "All the woodwork about the place is rotten."

"Doesn't it occur to you, sir, as being an extraordinarily dangerous thing to put it back in exactly the same position as though it were sound?"

"Iniquitous," Tallente agreed.

The inspector made a mental note. Tallente threw the remains of his cigarette into the sea. "I am going to bed now." he said. "Can I offer you any refreshment, Mr. Inspector, or are your investigations not yet complete?"

"I thank you, sir, but I require nothing. I have some men up in the wood there and I shall join them presently. I am staying in the neighborhood."

Tallente pointed to the rope.

"If you would care to search for yourself, Mr. Inspector, we'll help you down."

The man shook his head.

"Scarcely a job for a man of my build, sir. I have a professional climber coming to-morrow. I wish you had informed me of your intention to go down to-night."

"If you had informed me of your intention to remain in the neighborhood, that might have been possible," was the cool reply. The man took the loose wooden rail from its place and held it under his arm. "Walking off with a portion of my fence, eh?" Tallente asked.

The inspector made no direct reply. He turned his torch on to the broken end.

"A clue?" Tallente asked him lightly. The other turned away. "It is not my place, sir," he announced, "to share any discovery I might make with a person who has deliberately refused to assist the law."

"No one has convinced me yet," Tallente replied, "that Palliser's disappearance is a matter in which the law need concern itself." The inspector coughed. "I wish you good night, sir." He disappeared along the narrow path. They listened to his retreating footsteps. Tallente picked up his end of the rope. "I was right," he said, as he led the way back to the house. "Quite the Inspector Bucket type."

CHAPTER VI

At noon the next day, Tallente, nervously as well as physically exhausted with the long climb from the Manor, turned aside from the straight, dusty road and seated himself upon a lichen-covered boulder. He threw his cap on the ground, filled and lighted an old briar pipe, and gazed with a queer mixture of feelings across the moorland to where Woolhanger spread itself, a queer medley of dwelling house and farm buildings, strangely situated at the far end of the table-land he was crossing, where the moor leaned down to a great hollow in the hills. The open stretch of common which lay between him and his destination had none of the charm of the surrounding country. It was like a dark spot set in the midst of the rolling splendours of the moorland proper. There were boulders of rock of unknown age, dark patches of peat land, where even in midsummer the mud oozed up at the lightest footfall, pools and sedgy places, the home and sometimes the breeding place of the melancholy snipe. Of colour there was singularly little. The heather bushes were stunted, their roots blackened as though with fire, and even the yellow of the gorse shone with a dimmer lustre. But in the distance, a flaming carpet of orange and purple stretched almost to the summit of the brown hills of kindlier soil, and farther round, westwards, richly cultivated fields, from which the labourers seemed to hang like insects in the air, rolled away almost to the clouds.

Tallente looked at them a little wearily, impressed with the allegorical significance of his position. It seemed to him that he was in the land to which he belonged, the barren land of desolation and failure. The triumphs of the past failed for a moment to thrill his pulses. The memory of his well-lived and successful life brought him not an atom of consolation. The present was all that mattered, and the present had brought him to the gates of failure.—After all, what did a man work for, he wondered? What was the end and aim of it all? Life at Martinhoe Manor, with a faithful but terrified manservant, bookshelves ready to afford him the phantasmal satisfaction of another man's thoughts, sea and winds, beauties of landscape and colour, to bring him to the threshold of an epicurean pleasure which needed yet that one pulsating link with humanity to yield the full meed of joy and content. It all came back to the old story of man's weakness, he thought, as he rose to his feet, his teeth almost savagely clenching his pipe. He had become a conqueror of circumstances only to become a victim of the primitive needs of life.

At about a quarter of a mile from the house, the road branched away to the left to disappear suddenly over the edge of a drop of many hundreds of feet. Tallente passed through a plain white gate, down an avenue of dwarfed oaks, to emerge into an unexpectedly green meadow, cloven through the middle with a straight white avenue. Through another gate he passed into a drive which led through flaming banks of rhododendrons, now a little past their full glory, to the front of the house, a long and amplified building which, by reason of many additions, had become an abode of some pretensions. A manservant answered his ring at once and led him into a cool, white stone hall, the walls of which were hung from floor to ceiling with hunting and sporting trophies.

"Her ladyship is still at the farm, sir," the man announced. "She said if you came before she returned would you care to step round?"

Tallente signified his assent and was led through the house, across a more extensive garden, from which a marvellous view of the valley and the climbing slopes behind held him spellbound, by the side of a small, quaintly shaped church, to a circular group of buildings of considerable extent. The man conducted him to the front of a white-plastered cottage covered with roses, and knocked at the door.

"This is her ladyship's office, sir," he announced.

Lady Jane's invitation to enter was clear and friendly. Tallente found her seated behind a desk, talking to a tall man in riding clothes, who swung around to eye the newcomer with a curiosity which seemed somehow not altogether friendly. Lady Jane held out her hand and smiled delightfully.

"Do come in, Mr. Tallente," she begged. "I can't tell you how glad I am to see you. Now you will believe, won't you, that I am not altogether an idler in life? This is my agent, Mr. Segerson—Mr. Tallente."

Lionel Segerson held out his hand. He was a tall, well-built young Devonian, sunburnt, with fair curly hair, a somewhat obstinate type of countenance, and dressed in the dandified fashion of the sporting farmer.

"Glad to know you, Mr. Tallente," he said, in a tone which lacked enthusiasm. "I hope you're going to stay down in these parts for a time?"

Tallente made only a monosyllabic reply, and Lady Jane, with a little gesture of apology, continued her conversation with Segerson.

"I should like you," she directed, "to see James Crockford for yourself. Try and explain my views to him—you know them quite well. I want him to own his land. You can tell him that within the last two years I have sold eleven farms to their tenants, and no one could say that I have not done so on easy terms. But I need further convincing that Crocker is in earnest about the matter, and that he will really work to make his farm a success. In five good years he has only saved a matter of four hundred pounds, although his rental has been almost insignificant. That is the worst showing of any of the tenants on the estate, and though if I had more confidence in him I would sell on a mortgage, I don't feel inclined to until he has shown that he can do better. Tell him that he can have the farm for two thousand pounds, but he must bring me eight hundred in cash and it must not be borrowed money. That ought to satisfy him. He must know quite well that I could get three thousand pounds for it in the open market."

"These fellows never take any notice of that," Segerson remarked.

"Ungrateful beggars, all of them. I'll tell him what you say, Lady

Jane."

"Thank you."

"Anything else?" the young man asked, showing a disposition to linger.

"Nothing, thanks, until to-morrow morning." There was even then a slight unwillingness in his departure, which provoked a smile from Lady Jane as the door closed.

"The young men of to-day are terribly spoilt," she said. "He expected to be asked to lunch."

"I am glad he wasn't," Tallente observed.

She laughed.

"Why not? He is quite a nice young man."

"No doubt," Tallente agreed, without conviction. "However, I hate young men and I want to talk to you."

"Young men are tiresome sometimes," she agreed, rising from her chair.

"And older ones too, I am afraid!"

She closed her desk and he stood watching her. She was wearing an extraordinarily masculine garb—a covert-coating riding costume, with breeches and riding boots concealed under a long coat—but she contrived, somehow, to remain altogether feminine. She stood for a moment looking about her, as though wondering whether there were anything else to be done, a capable figure, attractive because of her earnest self-possession.

"Sarah," she called out.

The sound of a typewriter in an inner room ceased. The door was opened and a girl appeared on the threshold.

"You won't see me again to-day unless you send up for me," her mistress announced. "Let me have the letters to sign before five. Try and get away early, if you can. The car is going in to Lynton. Perhaps you would like the ride?"

"I should enjoy it very much, your ladyship," the girl replied gratefully. "There is really very little to do this afternoon."

"You can bring the letters whenever you like, then," Lady Jane told her, "and let Martin know that you are going in with him."

"You study your people, I see," Tallente remarked, as they strolled together back to the house.

"I try," she assented. "I try to do what I can in my little community here, very much as you, in a far greater way, try to study the people in your political programme. Of course," she went on, "it is far easier for me. The one thing I try to develop amongst them is a genuine, not a false spirit of independence. I want them to lean upon no one. I have no charities in connection with the estate, no soup kitchens or coal at Christmas, or anything of that sort. My theory is that every person is the better for being able to look after himself, and my idea of charity is placing him in a position to be able to do it. I don't want to be their Lady of the Manor and accept their rents and give them a dinner. I try to encourage them to save money and to buy their own farms. The man here who owns his own farm and makes it pay is in a position to lead a thoroughly self-respecting and honourable life. He ought to get what there is to be got out of life, and his children should be yeomen citizens of the best possible type. Of course, all this sort of thing is so much easier in the country. Very often, in the winter nights here, I waste my time trying to think out your greater problems."

"Problems," he observed, "which the good people of Hellesfield have just decided that I am not the man to solve."

"An election counts for nothing," she declared. "The merest whim will lead thousands of voters into the wrong polling booth. Besides, nearly all the papers admit that your defeat was owing to a political intrigue. The very men who should have supported you—who had promised to support you, in fact—went against you at the last moment. That was entirely due to Miller, wasn't it?"

"Miller has been my political bête noir for years," he confessed. "To me he represents the ignominious pacifist, whereas to him I represent the sabre-rattling jingo. I got the best of it while the war was on. To-day it seems to me that he has an undue share of influence in the country."

"Who are the men who really represent what you and I would understand as Labour?" she asked.

"That is too difficult a question to answer offhand," he replied. "Personally, I have come to the conclusion that Labour is unrepresentable—Labour as a cause. There are too many of the people yet who haven't vision."

They passed into the cool, geranium-scented hall. She pointed to an easy-chair by the side of which was set, on a small mahogany table, a silver cocktail shaker and two glasses.

"Please be as comfortable as you can," she begged, "for a quarter of an hour. If you like to wash, a touch of the bell there will bring Morton. I must change my clothes. I had to ride out to one of the outlying farms this morning, and we came back rather quickly."

She moved about the hall as she spoke, putting little things to rights. Then she passed up the circular staircase. At the bend she looked back and caught him watching her. She waved her hand with a little less than her usual frankness. Tallente had forgotten for a moment his whereabouts, his fatigue, his general weariness. He had turned around in his chair and was watching her. She found something in the very intensity of his gaze disturbing, vaguely analogous to certain half-formed thoughts of her own. She called out some light remark, scoffed at herself, and ran lightly out of sight, calling to her maid as she went.

CHAPTER VII

Luncheon was served in a small room at the back of the house. Through the wide-flung French windows was a vista of terraced walks, the two sunken tennis lawns, a walled garden leading into an orchard, and beyond, the great wood-hung cleft in the hills, on either side of which the pastoral fields, like little squares, stretched away upwards. From here there was no trace of the more barren, unkinder side of the moorland. The succession of rich colours merged at last into the dim, pearly hue where sky and cloud met, in the golden haze of the August heat, a haze more like a sort of transparent filminess than anything which really obscured.

Lady Jane, whose gift of femininity had triumphed even over her farm clothes, seemed to Tallente to convey a curiously mingled impression of restfulness and delicate charm in her cool, white muslin dress, low at the neck, the Paquin-made garment of an Aphrodite. She talked to him with all the charm of an accomplished hostess, and yet with the occasional fascinating reserve of the woman who finds her companion something more than ordinarily sympathetic. The butler served them unattended from the sideboard, but before luncheon was half way through they dispensed with his services.

"I suppose it has occurred to you by this time, Mr. Tallente," she said, as she watched the coffee in a glass machine by her side, "that I am a very unconventional person."

"Whatever you are," he replied, "I am grateful for."

"Cryptic, but with quite a nice sort of sound about it," she observed, smiling. "Tell me honestly, though, aren't you surprised to find me living here quite alone?"

"It seems to me perfectly natural," he answered.

"I live without a chaperon," she went on, "because a chaperon called by that name would bore me terribly. As a matter of fact, though, there is generally some one staying here. I find it easy enough to persuade my friends and some of my relatives that a corner of Exmoor is not half a bad place in the spring and summer. It is through the winter that I am generally avoided."

"I have always had a fancy to spend a winter on Exmoor," he confided.

"It has its compensations," she agreed, "apart, of course, from the hunting."

He felt the desire to speak of more vital things. What did hunting or chaperons more or less matter to the Lady Janes of the world! Already he knew enough of her to be sure that she would have her way in any crisis that might arise. "How much of the year," he asked, "do you actually spend here?"

"As much as I can."

"You are content to be here alone, even in the winter?"

> "More contented than I should be anywhere else," she assured him.
> "There is always plenty to do, useful work, too—things that count."

"London?"

"Bores me terribly," she confessed.

"Foreign travel?"

She nodded more tolerantly.

"I have done a little of it," she said. "I should love to do more, but travel as travel is such an unsatisfying thing. If a place attracts you, you want to imbibe it. Travel leaves you no time to do anything but sniff. Life is so short. One must concentrate or one achieves nothing. I know what the general idea of a stay-at-home is," she went on. "Many of my friends consider me narrow. Perhaps I am. Anyhow, I prefer to lead a complete and, I believe, useful life here, to looking back in later years upon that hotchpotch of lurid sensations, tangled impressions and restless moments that most of them call life."

"You display an amazing amount of philosophy for your years," he ventured, after a little hesitation. "There is one instinct, however, which you seem to ignore."

"What is it, please?"

"Shall I call it the gregarious one, the desire for companionship of young people of your own age?"

She shrugged her shoulders. She had the air of one faintly amused by his diffidence.

"You mean that I ought to be husband hunting," she said. "I quite admit that a husband would be a very wonderful addition to life. I have none of the sentiments of the old maid. On the other hand, I am rather a fatalist. If any man is likely to come my way whom I should care to marry, he is just as likely to find me here as though I tramped the thoroughfares of the world, searching for him. At last!" she went on, in a changed tone, as she poured out his coffee. "I do hope you will find it good. The cigarettes are at your elbow. This is quite one of the moments of life, isn't it?"

He agreed with her emphatically.

"A counsel of perfection," he murmured, as he sniffed the delicate Turkish tobacco. "Tell me some more about yourself?"

She shook her head.

"I am much too selfish a person," she declared, "and nothing that I do or say or am amounts to very much. I want you to let me a little way into your life. Talk either about your soldiering or your politics. You have been a Cabinet Minister and you will be again. Tell me what it feels like to be one of the world's governors?"

"Let us finish talking about you first," he begged. "You spoke quite frankly of a husband. Tell me, have you made up your mind what manner of man he must be?"

"Not in the least. I am content to leave that entirely to fate."

"Bucolic? Intellectual? An artist? A man of affairs?"

She made a little grimace.

"How can I tell? I cannot conceive caring for an ordinary person, but then every woman feels like that. And, you see, if I did care, he wouldn't be ordinary—to me. And so far as I am concerned," she insisted, with a shade of restlessness in her manner, "that finishes the subject. You must please devote yourself to telling me at least some of the things I want to know. What is the use of having one of the world's successful men tête-a-tête, a prisoner to my hospitality, unless I can make him gratify my curiosity?"

The thought created by her words burned through his mind like a flash of destroying lightning.

"One of the world's successful men," he repeated. "Is that how I seem to you?"

"And to the world," she asserted.

He shook his head sadly.

"I have worked very hard," he said. "I have been very ambitious. A few of my ambitions have been gratified, but the glory of them has passed with attainment. Now I enter upon the last lap and I possess none of the things I started out in life to achieve."

"But how absurd!" she exclaimed. "You are one of our great politicians. You would have to be reckoned with in any regrouping of parties."

"Without even a seat in the House of Commons," he reminded her bitterly. "And again, how can a man be a great politician when there are no politics? The confusion amongst the parties has become chaos, and I for one have not been clear-sighted enough to see my way through."

"Of course, I know vaguely what you mean," she said, "but remember that I am only a newspaper-educated politician. Can't you be a little more explicit?"

He lit another cigarette and smoked restlessly for a moment.

"I'll try and explain, if I can," he went on. "To be a successful politician, from the standard which you or I would aim at, a man needs not only political insight, but he needs to be able to adopt his views to the practical programme of one of the existing parties, or else to be strong enough to form a party of his own. That is where I have come to the cul-de-sac in my career. It was my ambition to guide the working classes of the country into their rightful place in our social scheme, but I have also always been an intensely keen Imperialist, and therefore at daggers drawn with many of the so-called Labour leaders. The consequence has been that for ten years I have been hanging on to the thin edge of nothing, a member of the Coalition Government, a member by sufferance of a hotchpotch party which was created by the combination of the Radicals and the Unionists with the sole idea of seeing the country through its great crisis. All legislation, in the wider sense of the term, had to be shelved while the country was in danger and while it was recovering itself. That time I spent striving to educate the people I wanted to represent, striving to make them see reason, to combat the two elements in their outlook which have been their eternal drawback, the elements of blatant selfishness and greedy ignorance. Well, I failed. That is all there is about it—I failed. No party claims me. I haven't even a seat in the House of Commons. I am nearly fifty years old and I am tired."

"Nearly fifty years old!" she repeated. "But what is that? You have—health, you are strong and well, there is nothing a younger man can do that you cannot. Why do you worry about your age?"

"Perhaps," he admitted, with a faint smile, and an innate compulsion to tell her of the thought which had lurked behind, "because you are so marvelously young."

"Absurd!" she scoffed. "I am twenty-nine years old—practically thirty. That is to say, with the usual twenty years' allowance, you and I are of the same age."

He looked across at her, across the lace-draped table with its bowls of fruit, its richly-cut decanter of wine, its low bowl of roses, its haze of cigarette smoke. She was leaning back in her chair, her head resting upon the fingers of one hand. Her face seemed alive with so many emotions. She was so anxious to console, so interested in her companion, herself, and the moment. He felt something unexpected and irresistible.

"I would to God I could look at it like that!" he exclaimed suddenly.

The words had left his lips before he was conscious that the thought which had lain at the back of them had found expression in his tone and glance. Just at first they produced no other effect in her save that evidenced by the gently upraised eyebrows, the sweetly tolerant smile. And then a sudden cloud, scarcely of discomfiture, certainly not of displeasure, more of unrest, swept across her face. Her eyes no longer met his so clearly and frankly. There was a little mist there and a silence. She was looking away through the windows to the dim, pearly line of blue, the actual horizon of things present. Her pulses were scarcely steady. She was possessed to a full extent of the her qualities of courage, physical and spiritual, yet at that moment she felt a wave of curious fear, the fear of the idealist that she may not be true to herself.

The moment passed and she looked at him with a smile. An innate gift of concealment, the heritage of her sex, came to her rescue, but she felt, somehow or other, as though she had passed through one of the crises of her life—that she could never be quite the same again. She had ceased for those few seconds to be natural.

"What does that wish mean?" she asked. "Do you mean that you would like to agree with me, or would you like to be twenty-nine?"

He too turned his back upon that little pool of emotion, did his best to be natural and easy, to shut out the memory of that flaming moment.

"At twenty-nine," he told her, "I was First Secretary at St. Petersburg. I am afraid that I was rather a dull dog, too. All Russia, even then, was seething, and I was trying to understand. I never did. No one ever understood Russia. The explanation of all that has happened there is simply the eternal duplication of history—a huge class of people, physically omnipotent, conscious of wrongs, unintelligent, and led by false prophets. All revolutions are the same. The purging is too severe, so the good remains undone."

There followed a silence, purposeful on her part, scarcely realised by him. She sought for means of escape, to bring their conversation down to the level where alone safety lay. She moved her chair a little farther back into the scented chamber, as though she found the sunlight too dazzling.

"You are like so many of the men who work for us," she said. "You are just a little tired, aren't you? You come down here to rest, and I dig up all the old problems and ask you to vex yourself with them. We must talk about slighter things. You are going to shoot here this season—perhaps hunt, later on?"

"I do not think so," he answered. "I have forgotten what sports mean. I may take a gun out sometimes. There is a little shooting that goes with the Manor, but very few birds, I believe. The last ten years seem to have driven all those things out of one's mind."

"Don't you think that you are inclined to take life a little too earnestly?" she asked. "One should have amusements."

"I may feel the necessity," he replied, "but it is not easy to take up one's earlier pleasures at my time of life."

"Don't think me inquisitive," she went on, "but, as I told you, I have looked you up in one of those wonderful books which tell us everything about everybody. You were a Double Blue at Oxford."

"Racquets and cricket," he assented. "Neither of them much use to me now."

"Racquets would help you with lawn tennis," she said, "but beyond that I find that not a dozen years ago you were a scratch golfer, and you certainly won the amateur championship of Italy."

"It is eleven years since I touched a club," he told her.

"Then you ought to be ashamed of yourself," she declared. "Games are part of an Englishman's life, and when he neglects them altogether there is something wrong. I shall insist upon your taking up lawn tennis again. I have two beautiful courts there, and very seldom any one to play with who has the least idea of the game."

His eyes rested for a moment upon the smoothly shaven lawns.

"So you think that regeneration may come to me through lawn tennis?" he murmured.

"And why not? You are taking yourself far too seriously, you know. How do you expect regeneration to come?"

"Shall I tell you what it is I lack?" he answered suddenly. "Incentive. I think my will has suddenly grown flabby, the ego in me unresponsive. You know the moods in which one asks oneself whether it is worth while, whether anything is worth while. Well, I am there at the crossroads. I think I feel more inclined to look for a seat than to go on."

"The strongest of us need to rest sometimes," she agreed quietly.

He relapsed into a silence so apparently deliberate that she accepted it as a respite for herself also. From the greater seclusion of her shadowy seat, she found herself presently able to watch him unnoticed,—the brooding melancholy of his face, the nervous, unsatisfied mouth, the discontent of his sombre brows. Then, even as she watched, the change in his expression startled her. His eyes were fixed upon the narrow ribbon of road which twisted around the other side of the house and led over the bleaker moors, seawards. The look puzzled her, gave her an uncomfortable feeling. Its note of appreciation seemed to her inexplicable. With a quaint, electrical sympathy, he caught the unspoken question in her eyes and translated it.

"You are beginning to doubt me," he said. "You are wondering if the shadow I carry with me is not something more than the mere depression of a man who has failed."

"You have not failed," she declared, "and I never doubt you, but there was something in your face just then which was strange, something alien to our talk. It was as though you saw something ominous in the distance."

"It is true," he admitted. "In the distance I can see the car I ordered to come and fetch me. There is a passenger—a man in the tonneau. I am wondering who he is."

"Some one to whom your man has given a lift, perhaps," she suggested.

He shook his head.

"I have another feeling—perhaps I should say an apprehension. It is some one who brings news."

"Political or—domestic?"

"Neither," he answered. "I thought that Fate had dealt me out most of her evil tricks when I came down here, a political outcast. She had another one up her sleeve, however. Do you read your morning papers?"

"Every day," she confessed. "Is it a weakness?"

"Not at all."

"You read of the disappearance of the Honourable Anthony Palliser?"

"Of course," she answered. "Besides, you told me about it, did you not, yesterday afternoon? I know one of his sisters quite well, and I was looking forward to seeing something of him down here."

"I was obliged to dismiss him at a moment's notice," Tallente went on. "He betrayed his trust and he has disappeared. That very imposing police inspector who broke up our tête-a-tête yesterday afternoon and I fear shortened your visit came on his account. He was the spokesman for a superior authority in London. They have come to the conclusion that I could, if I chose, throw some light upon his disappearance."

"And could you?"

He rose to his feet.

"You are the one person in the world," he said, "to whom I could tell nothing but the truth. I could."

They both heard the sound of footsteps in the hall. Lady Jane, disturbed by the ominous note in Tallente's voice, rose also to her feet, glancing from him towards the door, filled with some vague, inexplicable apprehension. Tallente showed no fear, but it was plain that he had nerved himself to face evil things. There was something almost ludicrous in this denouement to a situation which to both had seemed filled with almost dramatic possibilities. The door was opened by Parkins, the stout, discreet man servant, ushering in the unkempt, ill-tailored, ungainly figure of James Miller.

"This gentleman," Parkins announced, "wishes to see Mr. Tallente on urgent business."

CHAPTER VIII

The newcomer had distinctly the best of the situation. Tallente, who had expected a very different visitor, was for the moment bereft of words. Lady Jane, who, among her minor faults, was inclined to be a supercilious person, with too great a regard for externals, gazed upon this strange figure which had found its way into her sanctum with an astonishment which kept her also silent.

"Sorry to intrude," Mr. Miller began, with an affability which he meant to be reassuring. "Mr. Tallente, will you introduce me to the lady?"

Tallente acquiesced unwillingly.

"Lady Jane," he said, "this is Mr. James Miller—Lady Jane Partington."

Mr. Miller was impressed, held out his hand and withdrew it.

"I must apologize for this intrusion, Lady Jane, and to you, Tallente, of course. Mr. Tallente is naturally surprised to see me. He and I are political opponents," he confided, turning to Jane.

Her surprise increased, if possible.

"Are you Mr. Miller, the Democrat M.P.?" she asked,—"the Mr. Miller who was making those speeches at Hellesfield last week?"

"At your ladyship's service," he replied, with a low bow. "I am afraid if you are a friend of Mr. Tallente's you must look upon me as a very disagreeable person."

"If the newspapers are to be believed, your strategies up at Hellesfield scarcely give one an exalted idea of your tactics," she replied coldly. "They all seem to agree that Mr. Tallente was cheated out of his seat."

The intruder smiled tolerantly. He glanced around the room as though expecting to be asked to seat himself. No invitation of the sort, however, was accorded him. "All's fair in love and politics, Lady Jane," he declared. "We Democrats have our programme, and our motto is that those who are not with us are against us. Mr. Tallente here knew pretty well what he was up against."

"On the contrary," Tallente interrupted, "one never knows what one is up against when you are in the opposite camp, Miller. Would you mind explaining why you have sought me out in this singular fashion?"

"Certainly," was the gracious reply. "You have a very distinguished visitor over at the Manor, waiting there to see you. I came over with him and found your car on the point of starting. I took the liberty of hunting you up so that there should be no delay in your return."

"And who may this distinguished visitor he?" Tallente enquired, with unconscious sarcasm. "Stephen Dartrey," Miller answered. "He and Miss Miall and I are staying not far from you."

"Stephen Dartrey?" Lady Jane murmured. "Dartrey?" Tallente echoed. "Do you mean to say that he is over at the Manor now?"

"Waiting to see you," Miller announced, and for a moment there was a little gleam of displeasure in his eyes. Lady Jane sighed. "Now, if only you'd brought him over with you, Mr. Miller," she said, a shade more amiably, "you would have given me real pleasure. There is no man whom I am more anxious to meet." Miller smiled tolerantly. "Dartrey is a very difficult person," he declared. "Although he is the leader of our party, and before very long will be the leader of the whole Labour Party, although he could be Prime Minister to-morrow if he cared about it; he is one of the most retiring men whom I ever knew. At the present moment I believe that he would have preferred to have remained living his hermit's life, a writer and a dilettante, if circumstances had not dragged him into politics. He lives in the simplest way and hates all society save the company of a few old cronies."

"What does Dartrey want with me?" Tallente interrupted, a little brusquely. "It is no part of my mission to explain," Miller replied. "I undertook to come here and beg you to return at once." Tallente turned to Lady Jane. "You will forgive me?" he begged. "In any case, I must have been going in a few minutes."

"I should forgive you even if you went without saying good-by," she replied, "and I can assure you that I shall envy you. I do not want to turn your head," she went on pleasantly, as she walked by his side towards the door and across the hall, rather ignoring Miller, who followed behind, "but for the last two or three years the only political figures who have interested me at all have been Dartrey and yourself—you as the man of action, and Dartrey as the most wonderful exponent of the real, higher Socialism. I had a shelf made for his three books alone. They hang in my bedroom and I look upon them as my textbooks."

"I must tell Dartrey this," Miller remarked from behind. "I am sure he'll be flattered."

"What can he want with you?" Lady Jane asked, dropping her voice a little.

"I can't tell," Tallente confessed. "His visit puzzles me. He is the hermit of politics. He seldom makes advances and has few friends. He is, I believe, a man with the highest sense of honour. Perhaps he has come to explain to me why they threw me out at Hellesfield."

"In any case," she said, as they stood for a moment on the step, "I feel that something exciting is going to happen."

Miller, carrying his tweed cap in his hand, insisted upon a farewell.

"Sorry to have taken your guest away, Lady Jane," he said. "It's an important occasion, however. Would you like me to bring Dartrey over, if we are out this way before we go back?"

She shook her head.

"No, I don't think so," she answered quietly. "I might have an illusion dispelled. Thank you very much, all the same."

Mr. Miller stepped into the car, a little discomfited. Tallente lingered on the step.

"You will let me know?" she begged.

> "I will," he promised. "It is probably just a visit of courtesy. Dartrey must feel that he has something to explain about Hellesfield."

There was a moment's curious lingering. Each seemed to seek in vain for a last word. They parted with a silent handshake. Tallente looked around at the corner of the avenue. She was still standing there, gazing after the car, slim, cool and stately. Miller waved his cap and she disappeared.

The car sped over the moorland. Miller, with his cap tucked into his pocket, leaned forward, taking deep gulps of the wonderful air.

"Marvellous!" he exclaimed. "Tallente, you ought to live for ever in such a spot!"

"What does Dartrey want to see me about?" his companion asked, a little abruptly.

Miller coughed, leaned back in his place and became impressive.

"Tallente," he said, "I don't know exactly what Dartrey is going to say to you. I only know this, that it is very possible he may make you, on behalf of all of us—the Democratic Party, that is to say—an offer which you will do well to consider seriously."

"To join your ranks, I suppose?"

"I must not betray a confidence," Miller continued cautiously. "At the same time, you know our power, you have insight enough to guess at our destiny. It is an absolute certainty that Dartrey, if he chooses, may be the next Prime Minister. You might have been in Horlock's Cabinet but for an accident. It may be that you are destined to be in Dartrey's."

Tallente found his thoughts playing strange pranks with him. No man appreciated the greatness of Dartrey more than he. No man, perhaps, had a more profound conviction as to the truth and future of the principles of which he had become the spokesman. He realised the irresistible power of the new democracy. He was perfectly well aware that it was within Dartrey's power to rule the country whenever he chose. Yet there seemed something shadowy about these things, something unpleasantly real and repulsive in the familiarity of his companion, in the thought of association with him, He battled with the idea, treated it as a prejudice, analysed it. From head to foot the man wore the wrong clothes in the wrong manner,—boots of a vivid shade of brown, thick socks without garters, an obviously ready-made suit of grey flannel, a hopeless tie, an unimaginable collar. Even his ready flow of speech suggested the gifts of the tubthumpers his indomitable persistence, a lack of sensibility. He knew his facts, knew all the stock arguments, was brimful of statistics, was argumentative, convincing, in his way sincere. Tallente acknowledged all these things and yet found himself wondering, with a grim sense of irony, how he could call a man "Comrade" with such finger nails!

"It's given you something to think about, eh?" Miller remarked affably.

Tallente came to himself with a little start.

"I'm afraid my mind was wandering," he confessed.

His companion smiled knowingly. He was conscious of Tallente's aloofness, but determined to break through it if he could. After all, this caste feeling was absurd. He was, in his way, a well-known man, a Member of Parliament, a future Cabinet Minister. He was the equal of anybody.

"Don't wonder at it! Pleasant neighbours hereabouts, eh?"

Tallente affected to misunderstand. He glanced around at the few farmhouses dotted in sheltered places amongst the hills.

"There are very few of them," he answered. "That makes this place all the more enjoyable for any one who comes for a real rest."

Miller felt that he was suffering defeat. He opened his lips and closed them again. The jocular reference to Lady Jane remained unspoken. There was something in the calm aloofness of the man by his side which intimidated even while it annoyed him. Soon they commenced the drop from the moorland to where, far away below, the Manor with its lawn and gardens and outbuildings seemed like a child's pleasure palace. Miller leaned forward and pointed downwards.

"There's Dartrey sitting on the terrace," he pointed out. "Dartrey and Nora Miall. You've heard of her, I expect?"

"I know her by repute, of course," Tallente admitted. "She is a very brilliant young woman. It will give me great pleasure to meet her."

CHAPTER IX

Tallente took tea that afternoon with his three guests upon the terrace. Before them towered the wood-embosomed cliffs, with here and there great red gashes of scarred sandstone. Beyond lay the sloping meadow, with its clumps of bracken and grey stone walls, and in the background a more rugged line of rocky cliffs. The sea in the bay flashed and glittered in the long rays of the afternoon sunshine. The scene was extraordinarily peaceful. Stephen Dartrey for the first few minutes certainly justified his reputation for taciturnity. He leaned back in a long wicker chair, his head resting upon his hand, his thoughtful eyes fixed upon vacancy. No man in those days could have resembled less a popular leader of the people. In appearance he was a typical aristocrat, and his expression, notwithstanding his fine forehead and thoughtful eyes, was marked with a certain simplicity which in his younger days had lured many an inexperienced debater on to ridicule and extinction. In an intensely curious age, Dartrey was still a man over whose personality controversy raged fiercely. He was a poet, a dreamer, a writer of elegant prose, an orator, an artist. And behind all these things there was a flame in the man, a perfect passion for justice, for seeing people in their right places, which had led him from the more flowery ways into the world of politics. His enemies called him a dilettante and a poseur. His friends were led into rhapsodies through sheer affection. His supporters hailed him as the one man of genius who held out the scales of justice before the world.

"Of course," Nora Miall observed, looking up at her host pleasantly, "I can see what is going to happen. Mr. Dartrey came out here to talk to you upon most important matters. This place, the beauty of it all, is acting upon him like a soporific. If we don't shake him up presently, he will go away with wonderful mind pictures of your cliffs and sea, and his whole mission unfulfilled."

"Libellous as usual, Nora," Dartrey murmured, without turning his head. "Mr. Tallente is providing me with a few minutes of intense enjoyment. He has assured me that his time is ours. Soon I shall finish my tea, light a cigarette and talk. Just now you may exercise the privilege of your sex unhindered and better your own acquaintance with our host."

The girl laughed up into Tallente's face.

"Very likely Mr. Tallente doesn't wish to improve his acquaintance with me," she said.

Tallente hastened to reassure her. Somehow, the presence of these two did much to soothe the mental irritation which Miller had set up in him. They at least were of the world of understandable things. Miller, slouching in his chair, with a cheap tie-clip showing underneath his waistcoat, a bulging mass of sock descending over the top of his boot, rolling a cigarette with yellow-stained, objectionable fingers, still involved him in introspective speculation as to real values in life.

"I have often felt myself unfortunate in not having met you before, Miss Miall," he said. "Some of your writings have interested me immensely."

"Some of them?" she queried, with a smile.

"Absolute agreement would deny us even the stimulus of an argument," he observed. "Besides, after all, men find it more difficult to get rid of prejudices than women."

She leaned forward to help herself to a cigarette and he studied her for a moment. She was a little under medium height, trimly yet almost squarely built. Her mouth was delightful, humourous and attractive, and her eyes were of the deepest shade of violet, with black, silken eyelashes. Her voice was the voice of a cultivated woman, and Tallente, as he mostly listened to her light ripple of conversation, realised that the charm which was hers by reputation was by no means undeserved. In many ways she astonished him. The stories which had been told of her, even written, were incredible, yet her manners were entirely the manners of one of his own world. The trio—Dartrey, with his silence and occasional monosyllabic remarks—seemed to draw closer together at every moment until Miller, obviously chafing at his isolation, thrust himself into the conversation.

"Mr. Tallente," he said, taking advantage of a moment's pause to direct the conversation into a different channel, "we kept our word at Hellesfield."

"You did," his host acknowledged drily. "You succeeded in cheating me out of the seat. I still don't know why."

He turned as though appealing to Dartrey, and Dartrey accepted the challenge, swinging a little around in his chair and tapping his cigarette against the table, preparatory to lighting it.

"You lost Hellesfield, Mr. Tallente, as you would have lost any seat north of Bedford," he declared.

"Owing to the influence of the Democrats?"

"Certainly."

"But why is that influence exercised against me?" Tallente demanded. "I am thankful to have an opportunity of asking you that question, Dartrey. Surely you would reckon me more of a people's man than these Whigs and Coalitionists?"

"Very much more," Dartrey agreed. "So much more, Mr. Tallente, that we don't wish to see you dancing any longer between two stools. We want you in our camp. You are the first man, Tallente, whom we have sought out in this way. We have come at a busy time, under pretext of a holiday, some two hundred miles from London to suggest to you, temporarily deprived of political standing, that you join us."

"That temporary deprivation," Tallente murmured, "being due to your efforts."

"Precisely!"

"And the alternative?"

"Those who are not with us are against us," Dartrey declared. "If you persist in remaining the doubtful factor in politics, it is our business to see that you have no definite status there."

Tallente laughed a little cynically.

"Your methods are at least modern," he observed. "You invite a man to join your party, and if he refuses you threaten him with political extinction."

"Why not?" Dartrey asked wonderingly. "You do not pause to consider the matter. Government is meant for the million. Where the individual might impede good government, common sense calls for his ostracism. No nation has been more slow to realise this than England. A code of order and morals established two thousand years ago has been accepted by them as incapable of modification or improvement. To take a single instance. Supposing De Valera had been shot the first day he talked treason against the Empire, your troubles with Ireland would have been immensely minimised. And mark this, for it is the crux of the whole matter, the people of Ireland would have attained what they wanted much sooner. You are not one of those, Andrew Tallente, who refuse to see the writing on the wall. You know that in one form or another in this country the democracy must rule. They felt the flame of inspiration when war came and they helped to win the war. What was their reward? The opulent portion of them were saddled with an enormous income tax and high prices of living through bad legislation, which made life a burden. The more poverty-stricken suffered sympathetically in exactly the same way. We won the war and we lost the peace. We fastened upon the shoulders of the deserving, the wage-earning portion of the community, a burden which their shoulders could never carry a burden which, had we lost the war instead of winning it, would have led promptly to a revolution and a measure at least of freedom."

"There is so much of truth in what you say," Tallente declared, "that I am going to speak to you frankly, even though my frankness seems brutal. I am going to speak about your friend Miller here. Throughout the war, Miller was a pacifist. He was dead against killing Germans. He was all for a peace at any price."

"Steady on," Miller interrupted, suddenly sitting up in his chair. "Look here, Tallente—"

"Be quiet until I have finished," Tallente went on. "He was concerned in no end of intrigue with Austrian and German Socialists for embarrassing the Government and bringing the war to an end. I should say that but for the fact that our Government at the time was wholly one of compromise, and was leaning largely upon the Labour vote, he would have been impeached for high treason."

Miller, who had been busy rolling a cigarette, lit it with ostentatious carelessness.

"And what of all this?" he demanded.

"Nothing," Tallente replied, "except that it seems a strange thing to find you now associated with a party who threaten me openly with political extinction unless I choose to join them. I call this junkerdom, not socialism."

"No man's principles can remain stable in an unstable world," Miller pronounced. "I still detest force and compulsion of every sort, but I recognise its necessity in our present civil life far more than I did in a war which was, after all, a war of politicians."

Nora Miall leaned over from her chair and laid her hand on Tallente's arm. After Miller's raucous tones, her voice sounded almost like music.

"Mr. Tallente," she said, "I can understand your feeling aggrieved. You are not a man whom it is easy to threaten, but remember that after all we must go on our fixed way towards the appointed goal. And—consider—isn't the upraised rod for your good? Your place is with us—indeed it is. I fancy that Stephen here forgets that you are not yet fully acquainted with our real principles and aims. A political party cannot be judged from the platform. The views expressed there have to be largely governed by the character of the audience. It is to the textbooks of our creed, Dartrey's textbooks, that you should turn."

"I have read your views on certain social matters, Miss Miall," Tallente observed, turning towards her.

She laughed understandingly. Her eyes twinkled as she looked at him.

"And thoroughly disapproved them, of course! But you know, Mr. Tallente, we are out not to reconstruct Society but to lay the stepping stones for a reconstruction. That is all, I suppose, that any single generation could accomplish. The views which I have advocated in the *Universal Review* are the views which will be accepted as a matter of course in fifty years' time. To-day they seem crude and unmoral, chiefly because the casual reader, especially the British reader, dwells so much upon external effects and thinks so little of the soul that lies below. Even you, Mr. Tallente, with your passion for order and your distrust of all change in established things, can scarcely consider our marriage laws an entire success?"

Tallente winced a little and Dartrey hastily intervened.

"We want you to remember this," he said. "The principles which we advocate are condemned before they are considered by men of inherited principles and academic education such as yourself, because you have associated them always with the disciples of anarchy, bolshevism, and other diseased rituals. You have never stooped to separate the good from the bad. The person who dares to tamper with the laws of King Alfred stands before you prejudged. Granted that our doctrines are extreme, are we—let me be personal and say am I—the class of man whom you have associated with these doctrines? We Democrats have gained great power during the last ten years. We have thrust our influence deep into the hearts of those great, sinister bodies, the trades unions. There is no one except ourselves who realises our numerical and potential strength. We could have created a revolution in this country at any time since the Premier's first gloomy speech in the House of Commons after the signing of peace, had we chosen. I can assure you that we haven't the least fancy for marching through the streets with red flags and letting loose the diseased end of our community upon the palaces and public buildings of London. We are Democrats or Republicans, whichever you choose to call us, who desire to conquer with the brain, as we shall conquer, and where we recognise a man of genius like yourself, who must be for us or against us, if we cannot convert him then we must see that politically he ceases to count."

Robert came out and whispered in his master's ear. Tallente turned to his guests.

"I cannot offer you dinner," he said, "but my servant assures me that he can provide a cold supper. Will you stay? I think that you, Dartrey, would enjoy the view from some of my lookouts."

"I accept your invitation," Dartrey replied eagerly. "I have been sitting here, longing for the chance to watch the sunset from behind your wood."

"It will be delightful," Nora murmured. "I want to go down to the grass pier."

Miller too accepted, a little ungraciously. The little party wandered off down the path which led to the seashore. Miller detained his host for a moment at one of the corners.

"By the by, Tallente," he asked, "what about the disappearance of Palliser?"

"He has disappeared," Tallente answered calmly. "That is all I know about it."

Miller stood with his hands in his pockets, gnawing the end of his moustache, gazing covertly at the man who stood waiting for him to pass on. Tallente's face was immovable.

"Disappeared? Do you mean to say that you don't know where he is?"

"I have no idea."

Again there was a moment's silence. Then Miller leaned a little forward. "Look here, Tallente," he began—Nora turned round and suddenly beckoned her host to her.

"Come quickly," she begged. "I can do nothing with Mr. Dartrey. He has just decided that our whole scheme of life is absurd, that politics and power are shadows, and that work for others is lunacy. All that he wants is your cottage, a fishing rod and a few books."

"Nothing else?" Tallente asked, smiling.

There was a momentary cloud upon her face.

"Nothing else in the world," she answered, her eyes fixed upon the figure of the man who was leaning now over the grey stone wall, gazing seaward.

During the service of the meal, on the terrace afterwards, and even when they strolled down to the edge of the cliff to see the great yellow moon come up from behind the hills, scarcely a word was spoken on political subjects. Dartrey was an Oxford man of Tallente's own college, and, although several years his senior, they discovered many mutual acquaintances and indulged in reminiscences which seemed to afford pleasure to both. Then they drifted into literature, and Tallente found himself amazed at the knowledge of the man whose whole life was supposed to have been given to his labours for the people. Dartrey explained his intimate acquaintance with certain modern writings and his marvellous familiarity with many of the classics, as he and his host walked down together along one of the narrow paths. "You see, Tallente," he said, "I have never been a practical politician. I dare say that accounts for my rather peculiar position to-day. I have evolved a whole series of social laws by which I maintain that the people should be governed, and those laws have been accepted wherever socialism flourishes. They took me some years of my earlier life to elaborate, some years of study before I set pen to paper, some years of my later life to place before the world, and there my task practically ended. There is nothing fresh to say about these great human problems. They are there for any man to whom daylight comes, to see. They are all inevitably bound up with the future of our race, but there is no need to dig further. My work is done."

"How can you say that," Tallente argued, "when day by day your power in the country grows, when everything points to you as the next Premier?"

"Precisely," Dartrey replied quietly. "That is why I am here. The head of the Democratic Party has a right to the government of this country, but you know, at this point I have a very sad confession to make. I am the worst politician who ever sat in the House. I am a poor debater, a worse strategist. Again, Tallente, that is why you and I at this moment walk together through your beautiful grounds and watch the rim of that yellow moon. It is yourself we want."

Tallente felt the thrill of the moment, felt the sincerity of the man whose hand pressed gently upon his arm.

"If you are our man, Tallente," his visitor continued, "if you see eye to eye with us as to the great Things, if you can cast away what remains to you of class and hereditary prejudice and throw in your lot with ours, there is no office of the State which you may not hope to occupy. I had not meant to appeal to your ambitions. I do so now only generally. As a rule, every man connected with a revolution thinks himself able to govern the State. That is not so with us. A man may have the genius for seeing the truth, the genius even for engraving the laws which should govern the world upon tablets of stone, without having the capacity for government."

"But do you mean to say," Tallente asked, "that when Horlock goes down, as go down he must within the next few months, you are not prepared to take his place?"

"I should never accept the task of forming a government," Dartrey said quietly, "unless I am absolutely driven to do so. I have shown the truth to the world. I have shown to the people whom I love their destiny, but I have not the gifts to lead them. I am asking you, Tallente, to join us, to enter Parliament as one of our party and to lead for us in the House of Commons."

"Yours is the offer of a prince," Tallente replied, after a brief, nervous pause. "If I hesitate, you must remember all that it means for me."

Dartrey smiled.

"Now, my friend," he said, "look me in the face and answer me this question. You know little of us Democrats as a party. You see nothing but a hotchpotch of strange people, struggling and striving to attain definite form. Naturally you are full of prejudices. Yet consider your own political position. I am not here to make capital out of a man's disappointment in his friends, but has your great patron used you well? Horlock offers you a grudging and belated place in his Cabinet. What did he say to you when you came hack from Hellesfield?" Tallente was silent. There was, in fact, no answer which he could make. "I do not wish to dwell on that," Dartrey went on. "Ingratitude is the natural sequence of the distorted political ideals which we are out to destroy. You should be in the frame of mind, Tallente, to see things clearly. You must realise the rotten condition of the political party to which Horlock belongs—the Coalitionists, the Whip, or whatever they like to call themselves. The government of this country since the war has been a farce and a mockery. We are dropping behind in the world's race. Labour fattens with sops, develops a spirit of greed and production languishes. You know why. Labour would toil for its country, Labour can feel patriotism with the best, but Labour hates to toil under the earth, upon the earth, and in the factories of the world for the sake of the profiteer. This is the national spirit, that jealousy, that slackness, which the last ten years has developed. There is a new Little Englander abroad and he speaks with the voice of Labour. It is our task to find the soul of the people. And I have come to you for your aid."

Tallente looked for a moment down to the bay and listened to the sound of the incoming tide breaking upon the rocks. Dimmer now, but even more majestic in the twilight, the great, immovable cliffs towered up to the sky. An owl floated up from the grove of trees beneath and with a strange cry circled round for a moment to drop on to the lawn, a shapeless, solemn mass of feathers. At the back of the hills a little rim of gold, no wider than a wedding ring, announced the rising of the moon. He felt a touch upon his sleeve, a very sweet, persuasive voice in his ear. Nora had left Miller in the background and was standing by his side.

"I heard Mr. Dartrey's last words," she said. "Can you refuse such an appeal in such a spot? You turn away to think, turn to the quietness of all these dreaming voices. Believe me, if there is a soul beneath them, it is the same soul which has inspired our creed. You yourself have come here full of bitterness, Andrew Tallente, because it seemed to you that there was no place for you amongst the prophets of democracy. It was you yourself, in a moment of passion, perhaps, who said that democracy, as typified in existing political parties, was soulless. You were right. Hasn't Mr. Dartrey just told you so and doesn't that make our task the clearer? It brings before us those wonderful days written about in the Old Testament—the people must be led into the light."

Her voice had become almost part of the music of the evening. She was looking up at him, her beautiful eyes aglow. Dartrey, a yard or two off, his thoughtful face paler than ever in the faint light, was listening with joyous approval. In the background, Miller, with his hands in his pockets, was smoking mechanically the cigarette which he had just rolled and lit. The thrill of a great moment brought to Tallente a feeling of almost strange exaltation.

"I am your man, Dartrey," he promised. "I will do what I can."

CHAPTER X

The Right Honourable John Augustus Horlock, Prime Minister of England through a most amazing fluke, received Tallente, a few days later, with the air of one desiring to show as much graciousness as possible to a discomfited follower. He extended two fingers and indicated an uncomfortable chair.

"Well, well, Tallente," he said, "sorry I wasn't in town when you passed through from the north. Bad business, that Hellesfield affair."

"It was a very bad business indeed," Tallente agreed, "chiefly because it shows that our agents there must be utterly incapable."

The Prime Minister coughed.

"You think so, Tallente, eh? Now their point of view is that you let Miller make all the running, let him make his points and never got an answer in—never got a grip on the people, eh?"

"That may do for the official explanation," Tallente replied coldly, "but as a plain statement of facts it is entirely beside the mark. If you will forgive my saying so, sir, it has been one of your characteristics in life, born, without doubt," he added, with a little bow, "of your indomitable courage, to minimise difficulties and dangers of a certain type. You did not sympathise with me in my defeat at Hellesfield because you underrated, as you always have underrated, the vastly growing strength and dangerous popularity of the party into whose hands the government of this country will shortly pass."

Mr. Horlock frowned portentously. This was not at all the way in which he should have been addressed by an unsuccessful follower. But underneath that frown was anxiety.

"You refer to the Democrats?"

"Naturally."

"Do I understand you to attribute your defeat, then, to the tactics of the Democratic Party?"

"It is no question of supposition," Tallente replied. "It is a certainty."

"You believe that they have a greater hold upon the country than we imagine, then?"

"I am sure of it," was the confident answer. "They occupy a position no other political party has aimed at occupying in the history of this country. They aid and support themselves by means of direct and logical propaganda, carried to the very heart and understanding of their possible supporters. Their methods are absolutely unique and personally I am convinced that it is their destiny to bring into one composite body what has been erroneously termed the Labour vote."

Horlock smiled indulgently. He preferred to assume a confidence which he could not wholly feel.

"I am glad to hear your opinion, Tallente," he said. "I have to remember, however, that you are still smarting under a defeat inflicted by these people. What I cannot altogether understand is this: How was it that you were entirely deprived of their support at Hellesfield. You yourself are supposed to be practically a Socialist, at any rate from the point of view of the staider of my party. Yet these fellows down at Hellesfield preferred to support Bloxham, who twenty years ago would have been called a Tory."

"I can quite understand your being puzzled at that," Tallente acknowledged. "I was myself at first. Since then I have received an explanation."

"Well, well," Mr. Horlock interjected, with a return of his official genial manner, "we'll let sleeping dogs lie. Have you made any plans, Tallente?"

"A week ago I thought of going to Samoa," was the grim reply. "You don't want me, the country didn't seem to want me. I have worked for other people for thirty years. I rather thought of resting, living the life of a lotus eater for a time."

"An extremist as ever," the Prime Minister remarked tolerantly. "Even a politician who has worked as hard as you have can find many pleasurable paths in life open to him in this country. However, the necessity for such an extreme course of action on your part is done away with. I am very pleased to be able to tell you that the affair concerning which I have been in communication with your secretary for the last two months has taken an unexpectedly favourable turn."

"What the mischief do you mean?" Tallente enquired, puzzled.

"I mean," Mr. Horlock announced, with a friendly smile, "that sooner than be deprived of your valuable services, His Majesty has consented that you should go to the Upper House. You will be offered a peerage within the next fortnight."

Tallente stared at the speaker as though he had suddenly been bereft of his senses.

"What on earth are you talking about, sir?" he demanded.

Mr. Horlock somewhat resented his visitor's tone.

"Surely my statement was sufficiently explicit?" he said, a little stiffly. "The peerage concerning which at first, I admit, I saw difficulties, is yours. You can, without doubt, be of great service to us in the Upper House and—"

"But I'd sooner turn shopkeeper!" Tallente interrupted. "If I understand that it is your intention to offer me a peerage, let us have no misunderstanding about the matter. It is refused, absolutely and finally."

The Prime Minister stared at his visitor for a moment in amazement. Then he unlocked a drawer in his desk, drew out several letters and threw them over to Tallente.

"And will you tell me what the devil you mean by authorising your secretary to write these letters?" he demanded.

Tallente picked them up, read them through and gasped.

"Written by Palliser, aren't they?" Mr. Horlock demanded.

"Without a doubt," Tallente acknowledged. "The amazing thing, however, is that they are entirely unauthorised. The subject has never even been discussed between Palliser and myself. I am exceedingly sorry, sir," he went on, "that you should have been misled in this fashion, but I can only give you my word of honour that these letters are entirely and absolutely unauthorised."

"God bless my soul!" the Prime Minister exclaimed.
"Where is Palliser?
Better telephone."

"Palliser left my service a week or more ago," Tallente replied. "He left it at a moment's notice, in consequence of a personal disagreement concerning which I beg that you will ask no questions I can only assure you that it was not political. Since he left no word has been heard of him. The papers, even, have been making capital of his disappearance."

"It is the most extraordinary thing I ever heard in my life," Horlock declared, a little irritably. "Why, I've spent hours of my time trying to get this matter through."

"Dealing seriously with Palliser, thinking that he represented me in this matter?"

"Without a doubt."

"Will you lend me the letters?" Tallente asked.

Mr. Horlock threw them across the table.

"Here they are. My secretary wrote twice to Palliser last week and received no reply. That is why I sent you a telegram."

"I was on my way to see you, anyway," Tallente observed. "I thought that you were going to offer me a seat."

Mr. Horlock shook his head.

"We simply haven't a safe one," he confided, "and there isn't a soul I could ask to give up, especially, to speak plainly, for you, Tallente. They look upon you as dangerous, and although it would have been a nine days' wonder, most of my people would have been relieved to have heard of your going to the Upper House."

"I see," Tallente murmured. "In plain words, you've no use for me in the Cabinet?"

"My dear fellow," the Prime Minister expostulated, "you have no right to talk like that. I offered you a post of great responsibility and a seat which we believed to be perfectly safe. You lost the election, bringing a considerable amount of discredit, if you will forgive my saying so, upon the Government. What more can I do?"

Tallente was watching the speaker curiously. He had thought over this interview all the way up on the train, thought it out on very different lines.

"Nothing, I suppose," he admitted, "yet there's a certain risk about dropping me, isn't there? You might drive me into the arms of the enemy."

"What, the old Whig lot? Not a chance! I know you too well for that."

"No, the Democrats."

Horlock moved restlessly in his chair. He was eyeing his visitor steadfastly.

"What, the people who have just voted solidly against you?"

"Hasn't it occurred to you that that might have been political strategy?" Tallente suggested. "They might have maneuvered for the very situation which has arisen—that is, if I am really worth anything to anybody."

Horlock shook his head.

"Oil and water won't mix, Tallente, and you don't belong to that crowd. All the same," he confessed, "I shouldn't like you with them. I cannot believe that such a thing would ever come to pass, but the thought isn't a pleasant one."

"Now that you have made up your mind that I don't want to go to the House of Lords and wouldn't under any possible consideration," Tallente asked, "have you anything else to suggest?"

Mr. Horlock was a little annoyed. He considered that he had shown remarkable patience with a somewhat troublesome visitor.

"Tallente," he said, "it is of no use your being unreasonable. You had your chance at Hellesfield and you lost it; your chance in my Cabinet and lost that too. You know for yourself how many rising politicians I have to satisfy. You'll be back again with us before long, of course, but for the present you must be content to take a rest. We can make use of you on the platform and there are always the reviews."

"I see," Tallente murmured.

"The fact is," his host concluded, as his fingers strayed towards the dismissal bell, "you made rather a mistake, Tallente, years ago, in dabbling at all with the Labour Party. At first, I must admit that I was glad. I felt that you created, as it were, a link between my Government and a very troublesome Opposition. To-day things have altered. Labour has shown its hand and it demands what no sane man could give. We've finished with compromise. We have to fight Socialism or go under."

Tallente nodded.

"One moment," he begged, as the Prime Minister's forefinger rested upon the button of the bell. "Now may I tell you just why I came to pay you this visit?"

"If there is anything more left to be said," Mr. Horlock conceded, with an air of exaggerated patience.

"There is just this," Tallente declared. "If you had had a seat to offer me or a post in your Cabinet, I should have been compelled to decline it, just as I have declined that ridiculous offer of a peerage. I have consented to lead the Democratic Party in the House of Commons."

The Prime Minister's fingers slipped slowly from the knob of the bell. He was a person of studied deportment. A journalist who had once written of his courtly manners had found himself before long the sub-editor of a Government journal. At that moment he was possessed of neither manners nor presence. He sat gazing at Tallente with his mouth open. The latter rose to his feet.

"I ask you to believe, sir," he said, "that the step which I am taking is in no way due to my feeling of pique or dissatisfaction with your treatment. I go where I think I can do the best work for my country and employ such gifts as I have to their best advantage."

"But you are out to ruin the country!" Horlock faltered. "The Democrats are Socialists."

"From one point of view," Tallente rejoined, "every Christian is a Socialist. The term means nothing. The programme of my new party aims at the destruction of all artificial barriers which make prosperity easy to one and difficult to another. It aims not only at the abolition of great fortunes and trusts, but at the abolition of the conditions which make them possible. It embraces a scheme for national service and a reasonable imperialism. It has a sane programme, and that is more than any Government which has been in office since the war has had."

Mr. Horlock rose to his feet.

"Tallente," he pronounced, "you are a traitor to your class and to your country."

He struck the bell viciously. His visitor turned away with a faint smile.

> "Don't annoy me," he begged, "or I may some day have to send you to the House of Lords!"

CHAPTER XI

Tallente, obeying an urgent telephone message, made his way to Claridge's and sent his card up to his wife. Her maid came down and invited him to her suite, an invitation which he promptly declined. In about a quarter of an hour she descended to the lounge, dressed for the street. She showed no signs of confusion or nervousness at his visit. She was hard and cold and fair, with a fraudulent smile upon her lips, dressed to perfection, her maid hovering in the background with a Pekinese under one arm and a jewel case in her other hand.

"Thank goodness," she said, as she fluttered into a chair by his side, "that you hate scenes even more than I do! You have the air of a man who has found out no end of disagreeable things!"

"You are observant," he answered drily. "I have just come from the Prime Minister."

"Well?"

"I find that Palliser has been conducting a regular conspiracy behind my back, with reference to this wretched peerage. He has practically forged my name and has placed me in a most humiliating position. You, I suppose, were his instigator in this matter?"

"I suppose I was," she admitted.

"What was to be his reward—his ulterior reward, I mean?"

"I promised him twenty thousand pounds," she answered, with cold fury. "It appears that I overvalued your importance to your party. Tony apparently did the same. He thought that you had only to intimate your readiness to accept a peerage and the thing would be arranged. It seems that we were wrong."

"You were doubly wrong," he replied. "In the first place, there were difficulties, and in the second, nothing would have induced me to accept such a humiliating offer."

"How did you find this out?" she enquired.

"The Prime Minister offered me the peerage less than an hour ago," he answered. "I need not say that I unhesitatingly refused it."

Stella ceased buttoning her gloves. There was a cold glitter in her eyes.

"You refused it?"

"Of course!"

She was silent for a moment.

"Andrew," she said, "you have scarcely kept your bargain with me."

"I am not prepared to admit that," he replied. "You had a very considerable social position at the time when I was in office. It was up to you to make that good."

"I am tired of political society," she answered. "It isn't the real thing. Now you are out of Parliament, though, even that has vanished. Andrew!"

"Well?"

She leaned a little towards him. She began to regret that he had not accepted her invitation to visit her in her suite. Years ago she had been able to bend him sometimes to her will. Why should she take it for granted that she had lost her power? Here, however, even persuasions were difficult. He sat upon a straight, high-backed chair by her side and his face seemed as though it were carved out of stone.

"You have always declined, Andrew, to make very much use of my money," she said. "Could we not make a bargain now? I will give you a hundred thousand pounds and settle five million dollars on the holder of the title forever, if you will accept this peerage. I wouldn't mind a present to the party funds, either, if that helped matters."

Tallente shook his head.

"I am sorry for your disappointment," he said, "but nothing would induce me to accept a seat in the Upper House. I have other plans."

"They could be changed."

"Impossible!"

"You might be forced to change them."

"By whom?"

The smile maddened her. She had meant to be subtle. She became flamboyant. She leaned forward in her chair.

"What have you done with Tony Palliser?" she demanded.

Tallente remained absolutely unruffled. He had been expecting something of this sort. The only wonder was that it had been delayed so long.

"A threat?" he asked pleasantly.

"Call it what you like. Men don't disappear like that. What did you do with him?"

"What do you think he deserved?"

She bit her lip.

"I think you are the most detestable human being who ever breathed," she faltered. "Supposing I go to the police?"

"Don't be melodramatic," he begged. "In the first place, what have you to tell? In the second place, in this country, at any rate, a wife cannot give evidence against her husband."

"You admit that something has happened?" she asked eagerly.

"I admit nothing," he replied, "except that Anthony Palliser has disappeared under circumstances which you and I know about, that he has forged my name and entered into a disgraceful conspiracy with you, and that he has stolen from my wife a political document of great importance to me."

"I knew nothing about the political document," she said quickly.

"Possibly not," he agreed. "Still, the fact remains that Tony was a thoroughly bad lot. I find myself able to regard the possibility of an accident having happened to him with equanimity. Have you anything further to say?"

She sat looking down on the floor for several minutes. She had probably, Tallente decided as he watched her, some way of suffering in secret, all the more terrible because of its repression. When she looked up, her face seemed pinched and older. Her voice, however, was steady.

"Let us have an understanding," she said. "You do not desire my return to Martinhoe?"

"I do not," he agreed.

"And what about Cheverton House here?"

"I have nothing to do with it," he replied. "You persuaded me to allow you to take it and I have lived with you there. I never pretended, however, to be able to contribute to its upkeep. You can live there, if you choose, or wherever else you please."

"Alone?"

"It would be more reputable."

"You mean that you will not return there?"

"I do mean that."

His cold firmness daunted her. She was, besides, at a disadvantage; she had no idea how much he knew.

"I can make you come back to me if I choose," she threatened.

"The attempt would cost you a great deal of money," he told her, "and the result would be the same. Frankly, Stella," he went on, striving to impart a note of friendliness into his tone, "we made a bad bargain and it is no use clinging to the impossible. I have tried to keep my end of it. Technically I have kept it. If I have failed in other ways, I am very sorry. The whole thing was a mistake. We have been frank about it more than once, so we may just as well be frank about it now. I married for money and you for position. I have not found your money any particular advantage, and I have realised that as a man gets on in life there are other and more vital things which he misses though making such a bargain. You are not satisfied with your position, and perhaps you, too, have something of the same feeling that I have. You are your own mistress and you are a very rich woman, and in whichever direction you may decide to seek for a larger measure of content, you will not find me in the Way."

"I am not sentimental," she said coldly. "I know what I want and I am not afraid to own it. I want to be a Peeress."

"In that respect I am unable to help you," he replied. "And in case I have not made myself sufficiently clear upon the subject, let me tell you that I deeply resent the plot by which you endeavoured to foist such an indignity upon me."

"This is your last word?" she demanded.

"Absolutely!"

"Then I demand that you set me free."

He was a little staggered.

"How on earth can I do that?"

"You can allow me to divorce you."

"And spoil any chance I might have of reentering political life," he remarked quietly.

"I have no further interest in your political life," she retorted.

He looked at her steadfastly.

"There is another way," he suggested. "I might divorce you."

Her eyes fell before the steely light in his. She did her best, however, to keep her voice steady.

"That would not suit me," she admitted. "I could not be received at Court, and there are other social penalties which I am not inclined to face. In the case of a disagreement like ours, if the man realises his duty, it is he who is willing to bear the sacrifice."

"Under some circumstances, yes," he agreed. "In our case, however, there is a certain consideration upon which I have forborne to touch—"

It was as much her anger as anything else which induced her lack of self-control. She gave a little cry.

"Andrew, you are detestable!" she exclaimed. "Let us end this conversation. You have said all that you wish to say?"

"Everything."

"Please go away, then," she begged. "I am expecting visitors. I think that we understand each other."

He rose to his feet.

"I am sorry for our failure, Stella," he said. "Pray do not hesitate to write to me at any time if my advice or assistance can be of service."

He passed down the lounge, more crowded now than when he had entered. A very fashionably dressed young woman, one of a smart tea party, leaned back in her chair as he passed and held out her hand.

"And how does town seem, Mr. Tallente, after your sylvan solitude?" she asked.

Tallente for a moment was almost at a loss. Then a glance into her really very wonderful eyes, and the curve of her lips as she smiled convinced him of the truth which he had at first discarded.

"Miss Miall!" he exclaimed.

"Please don't look so surprised," she laughed. "I suppose you think I have no right to be frivolling in these very serious times, but I am afraid I am rather an offender when the humour takes me. You kept your word to Mr. Dartrey, I see?"

Tallente nodded.

"I came to town yesterday."

"I must hear all the news, please," she insisted. "Will you come and see me to-morrow afternoon? I share a flat with another girl in Westminster—Number 13, Brown Square."

"I shall be delighted," he answered. "I think your hostess wants to speak to me. She is an old friend of my aunt."

He moved on a few steps and bowed over the thin, over-bejewelled fingers of the Countess of Clanarton, an old lady whose vogue still remained unchallenged, although the publication of her memoirs had very nearly sent a highly respected publisher into prison.

"Andrew," she exclaimed, "we are all so distressed about you! How dared you lose your election! You know my little fire-eating friend, I see. I keep in with her because when the revolution comes she is going to save me from the guillotine, aren't you, Nora?"

"My revolution won't have anything to do with guillotines," the girl laughed back, "and if you really want to have a powerful friend at court, pin your faith on Mr. Tallente."

Lady Clanarton shook her head.

"I have known Andrew, my dear, since he was in his cradle," she said. "I have heard him spout Socialism, and I know he has written about revolutions, but, believe me, he's a good old-fashioned Whig at heart. He'll never carry the red flag. I see your wife has bought the Maharajaim of Sapong's pearls, Andrew. Do you think she'd leave them to me if I were to call on her?"

"Why not ask her?" Tallente suggested. "She is over there."

"Dear me, so she is!" she exclaimed. "How smart, too! I thought when she came in she must be some one not quite respectable, she was so well-dressed. Going, Andrew? Well, come and see me before you return to the country. And I wouldn't go and have tea with that little hussy, if I were you. She'll burn the good old-fashioned principles out of you, if anything could."

"Not later than five, please," Nora called out. "You shall have muffins, if I can get them."

"She's got her eye on you," the old lady chuckled. "Most dangerous child in London, they all tell me. You're warned, Andrew."

He smiled as he raised her fingers to his lips.

"Is my danger political or otherwise?" he whispered.

"Otherwise, I should think," was the prompt retort. "You are too British to change our politics, but thank goodness infidelity is one of the cosmopolitan virtues. You were never the man to marry a plaster-cast type of wife, Andrew, for all her millions. I could have done better for you than that. What's this they are telling me about Tony Palliser?"

Tallente stiffened a little.

"A good many people seem to be talking about Tony Palliser," he observed.

"You shouldn't have let your wife make such an idiot of herself with him—lunching and dining and theatring all the time. And now they say he has disappeared. Poor little man! What have you done to him, Andrew?"

Tallente sighed.

"I can see that I shall have to take you into my confidence," he murmured.

"You needn't tell me a single word, because I shouldn't believe you if you did. Are you staying here with your wife?"

"No," Tallente answered. "I am back at my old rooms in Charges Street."

The old lady patted him on the arm and dismissed him.

"You see, I've found out all I wanted to know!" she chuckled.

CHAPTER XII

Dartrey had been called unexpectedly to the north, to a great Labour conference, and Tallente, waiting for his return, promised within the next forty-eight hours, found himself rather at a loose end. He avoided the club, where he would have been likely to meet his late political associates, and spent the morning after his visit to the Prime Minister strolling around the Park, paying visits to his tailor and hosier, and lunched by himself a little sadly in a fashionable restaurant. At five o'clock he found his way to Westminster and discovered Nora Miall's flat. A busy young person in pince-nez and a long overall, who announced herself as Miss Miall's secretary, was in the act of showing out James Miller as he rang the bell. "Any news?" the latter asked, after Tallente had found it impossible to avoid shaking hands. "I am waiting for Mr. Dartrey's return. No, there is no particular news that I know of."

"Dartrey's had to go north for a few days," Miller confided officiously. "I ought to have gone too, but some one had to stay and look after things in the House. Rather a nuisance his being called away just now."

Tallente preserved a noncommittal silence. Miller rolled a cigarette hastily, took up his unwrapped umbrella and an ill-brushed bowler hat.

"Well, I must be going," he concluded. "If there is anything I can do for you during the chief's absence, look me up, Mr. Tallente. It's all the same, you know—Dartrey or me—Demos House in Parliament Street, or the House. You haven't forgotten your way there yet, I expect?"

With which parting shaft Mr. James Miller departed, and the secretary,
Opening the door of Nora's sitting room, ushered Tallente in.

"Mr. Tallente," she announced, with a subdued smile, "fresh from a most engaging but rather one-sided conversation with Mr. Miller."

Nora was evidently neither attired nor equipped this afternoon for a tea party at Claridge's. She wore a dark blue princess frock, buttoned right up to the throat. Her hair was brushed straight back from her head, revealing a little more completely her finely shaped forehead. She was seated before a round table covered with papers, and Tallente fancied, even as he crossed the threshold, that there was an electric atmosphere in the little apartment, an impression which the smouldering fire in her eyes, as she glanced up, confirmed. The change in her expression, however, as she recognised her visitor, was instantaneous. A delightful smile of welcome chased away the sombreness of her face.

"My dear man," she exclaimed, "come and sit down and help me to forget that annoying person who has just gone out!"

Tallente smiled.

"Miller is not one of your favorites, then?"

"Isn't he the most impossible person who ever breathed." she replied. "He was a conscientious objector during the war, a sex fanatic since—Mr. Dartrey had to use all his influence to keep him out of prison for writing those scurrilous articles in the Comet—and I think he is one of the smallest-minded, most untrustworthy persons I ever met. For some reason or other, Stephen Dartrey believes in him. He has a wonderful talent for organization and a good deal of influence with the trades unions.—By the by, it's all right about the muffins."

She rang the bell and ordered tea. Tallente glanced for a moment about the room. The four walls were lined with well-filled bookcases, but the mural decorations consisted—except for one wonderful nude figure, copy of a well-known Rodin—of statistical charts and shaded maps. There were only two signs of feminine occupation: an immense bowl of red roses, rising with strange effect from the sea of manuscript, pamphlets, and volumes of reference, and a wide, luxurious couch, drawn up to the window, through which the tops of a little clump of lime trees were just visible. As she turned back to him, he noticed with more complete appreciation the lines of her ample but graceful figure, the more remarkable because she was neither tall nor slim.

"So that was your wife at Claridge's yesterday afternoon?" she remarked, a little abruptly.

He assented in silence. Her eyes sought his speculatively.

"I know that Lady Clanarton is a terrible gossip," she went on. "Was she telling me the truth when she said that your married life was not an entire success?"

"She was telling you the truth," Tallente admitted.

"I like to know everything," she suggested quietly. "You must remember that we shall probably become intimates."

"I did my wife the injustice of marrying her for money," Tallente explained. "She married me because she thought that I could provide her with a social position such as she desired. Our marriage was a double failure. I found no opportunity of making use of her money, and she was discontented with the value she received for it. We have within the last few days agreed to separate. Now you know everything," he added, with a little smile, "and curiously enough, considering the brevity of our acquaintance, you know it before anybody else in the world except one person."

She smiled.

"I like to know everything about the people I am interested in," she admitted. "Besides, your story sounds so quaint. It seems to belong, somehow or other, to the days of Anthony Trollope and Jane Austen. I suppose that is because I always feel that I am living a little way in the future."

Tea was brought in, and a place cleared for the tray upon a crowded table. Afterwards she lit a cigarette and threw herself upon the lounge.

"Turn your chair around towards me," she invited. "This is the hour I like best of any during the day. Do you see what a beautiful view I have of the Houses of Parliament? And there across the river, behind that mist, the cesspool begins. Sometimes I lie here and think. I see right into Bermondsey and Rotherhithe and all those places and think out the lives of the people as they are being lived. Then I look through those wonderful windows there—how they glitter in the sunshine, don't they!—and I think I hear the men speak whom they have sent to plead their cause. Some Demosthenes from Tower Hill exhausts himself with phrase-making, shouts himself into a perspiration, drawing lurid, pictures of hideous and apparent wrongs, and a hundred or so well-dressed legislators whisper behind the palms of their hands, make their plans for the evening and trot into their appointed lobbies like sheep when the division bell rings. It is the most tragical epitome of inadequacy the world has ever known."

"Have you Democrats any fresh inspiration, then?" he asked.

"Of course we have," she rapped out sharply. "It isn't like you to ask such a question. The principles for which we stand never existed before, except academically. No party has ever been able to preach them within the realm of practical politics, because no party has been comprehensive enough. The Labour Party, as it was understood ten years ago, was a pitiful conglomeration of selfish atoms without the faintest idea of coordination. It is for the souls of the people we stand, we Democrats, whether they belong to trades unions or not, whether they till the fields or sweat in the factories, whether they bend over a desk or go back and forth across the sea, whether they live in small houses or large, whether they belong to the respectable middle classes whom the after-the-war legislation did its best to break, or to the class of actual manual laborers."

"I don't see what place a man like Miller has in your scheme of things," he observed, a little restlessly.

She shrugged her shoulders.

"Miller is a limpet," she said. "He has posed as a man of brains for half a generation. His only real cleverness is an unerring but selfish capacity for attaching himself to the right cause. We can't ignore him. He has a following. On the other hand, he does not represent our principles any more than Pitt would if he were still alive."

"What will be your position really as regards the two main sections of the Labour Party?" he asked. "We are absorbing the best of them, day by day," she answered quickly. "What is left of either will be merely the scum. The people will come to us. Their discarded leaders can crawl back to obscurity. The people may follow false gods for a very long time, but they have the knack of recognising the truth when it is shown them."

"You have the gift of conviction," he said thoughtfully.

She shrugged her shoulders.

"Our cause speaks, not I," she declared. "Every word I utter is a waste of breath, a task of supererogation. You can't associate with Stephen Dartrey for a month without realising for yourself what our party means and stands for. So—enough. I didn't ask you here to undertake any missionary work. I asked you, as a matter of fact, for my own pleasure. Take another cigarette and pass me one, please. And here's another cushion," she added, throwing it to him. "You look as though you needed it." He settled down more comfortably. He had the pleasant feeling of being completely at his ease.

"So far as entertaining you is concerned," he confessed, "I fear I am likely to be a failure. I am beginning to feel like a constant note of interrogation. There is so much I want to know."

"Proceed, then. I am resigned," she said with a smile. "About yourself. I just knew of you as the writer of one or two articles in the reviews. Why have I never heard more of you?"

"One reason," she confided, "is because I am so painfully young. I haven't had time yet to become a wonderful woman. You see, I have the tremendous advantage of not having known the world except from underneath a pigtail, while the war was on. I was able to bring to these new conditions an absolutely unbiassed understanding."

"But what was your upbringing?" he asked. "Your father, for instance?"

"Is this going to be a pill for you?" she enquired, with slightly wrinkled forehead. "He was professor of English at Dresden University. We were all living there when the war broke out, but he was such a favourite that they let us go to Paris. He died there, the week after peace was declared. My mother still lives at Versailles. She was governess to Lady Clanarton's grandchildren, hence my presence yesterday in those aristocratic circles."

"And you live here alone?"

"With my secretary—the fuzzyhaired young person who was just getting rid of Mr. Miller for me when you arrived. We are a terribly advanced couple, in our ideas, but we lead a thoroughly reputable life. I sometimes think," she went on, with a sigh, "that all one's tendencies towards the unusual can be got rid of in opinions. Susan, for instance—that is my secretary's name—pronounces herself unblushingly in favour of free love, but I don't think she has ever allowed a man to kiss her in her life."

"Your own opinions?" he asked curiously. "I suppose they, too, are a little revolutionary, so far as regards our social laws?"

"I dare not even define them," she acknowledged, "they are so entirely negative. Somehow or other, I can't help thinking that the present system will die out through the sheer absurdity of it. We really shan't need a crusade against the marriage laws. The whole system is committing suicide as fast as it can."

"How old are you?" he asked.

"Twenty-four," she answered promptly.

"And supposing you fell in love—taking it for granted that you have not done so already—should you marry?"

Her eyes rested upon his, a little narrowed, curiously and pleasantly reflective. All the time the corners of her sensitive mouth twitched a little.

"To tell you the truth," she confided, with a somewhat evasive air, "I have been so busy thinking out life for other people that I have never stopped to apply its general principles to myself."

"You are a sophist," he declared.

"I have not your remarkable insight," she laughed mockingly.

CHAPTER XIII

"How this came about I don't even quite know," Tallente remarked, an hour or so later, as he laid down the menu and smiled across the corner table in the little Soho restaurant at his two companions.

"I can tell you exactly," Nora declared. "You are in town for a few days only, and I want to see as much of you as I can; Susan here is deserting me at nine o'clock to go to a musical comedy; I particularly wanted a sole Georges, and I knew, if Susan and I came here alone, a person whom we neither of us like would come and share our table. Therefore, I made artless enquiries as to your engagements for the evening. When I found that you proposed to dine alone in some hidden place rather than run the risk of meeting any of your political acquaintances at the club, I went in for a little mental suggestion."

"I see," he murmured. "Then my invitation wasn't a spontaneous one?"

"Not at all," she agreed. "I put the idea into your head."

"And now that we are here, are you going to stretch me on the rack and delve for my opinions on all sorts of subjects? is Miss Susan there going to take them down in shorthand on her cuff and you make a report to Dartrey when he comes back to-morrow?"

She laughed at him from underneath her close-fitting, becoming little hat. She was biting an olive with firm white teeth.

"After hours," she reassured him. "Susan and I are going to talk a little nonsense after the day's work. You may join in if you can unbend so far. We shall probably eat more than is good for us—I had a cup of coffee for lunch—and if you decide to be magnificent and offer us wine, we shall drink it and talk more nonsense than ever."

He called for the wine list.

"I thought we were going to discuss the effect of Grecian philosophy upon the Roman system of government."

She shook her head.

"You're a long way out," she declared, "Our conversation will skirt the edges of many subjects. We shall speak of the Russian Ballet, Susan and I will exchange a few whispered confidences about our admirers, we shall discuss even one who comes in and goes out, with subtle references to their clothes and morals, and when you and I are left alone we may even indulge in the wholesome, sentimental exercise of a little flirtation."

"There you have me," he confessed. "I know a little about everything else you have mentioned."

"A very good opening," she approved. "Keep it till Susan has gone and then propose yourself as a disciple. There is only one drawback about this place," she went on, nodding curtly across the room to Miller. "So many of our own people come here. Mr. Miller must be pleased to see us together."

"Why?" Tallente asked. "Is he an admirer?"

Nora's face was almost ludicrously expressive.

"He would like to he," she admitted, "but, thick-skinned though he is, I have managed to make him understand pretty well how I feel about him. You'll find him a thorn in your side," she went on reflectively.

"You see, if our party has a fault, it is in a certain lack of system. We have only a titular chief and no real leader. Miller thinks that post is his by predestination. Your coming is beginning to worry him already. It was entirely on your account he paid me that visit this afternoon."

"To be perfectly frank with you," Tallente sighed, "I should find Miller a loathsome coadjutor."

"There are drawbacks to everything in life," Nora replied. "Long before Miller has become anything except a nuisance to you, you will have realised that the only political party worth considering, during the next fifty years, at any rate, will be the Democrats. After that, I shouldn't be at all surprised if the aristocrats didn't engineer a revolution, especially if we disenfranchise them.—Susan, you have a new hat on. Tell me at once with whom you are going to Daly's?"

"No one who counts," the girl declared, with a little grimace. "I am going with my brother and a very sober married friend of his."

"After working hours," Nora confessed, glancing critically at the sole which had just been tendered for Tallente's examination, "the chief interest of Susan and myself, as you may have observed, lies in food and in your sex. I think we must have what some nasty German woman once called the man-hunger."

"It sounds cannibalistic," Tallente rejoined. "Have I any cause for alarm?"

"Not so far as I am concerned," Susan assured him. "I have really found my man, only he doesn't know it yet. I am trying to get it into his brain by mental suggestion."

"You wouldn't think Susan would be so much luckier than I, would you?" Nora observed, studying her friend reflectively. "I am really much better-looking, but I think she must have more taking ways. You needn't be nervous, Mr. Tallente. You are outside the range of our ambitions. I shall have to be content with some one in a humbler walk of life."

"Aren't you a little over-modest?" he asked. "You haven't told me much about the social side of this new era which you propose to inaugurate, but I imagine that intellect will be the only aristocracy."

"Even then," Norah sighed, "I am lacking in confidence. To tell you the truth, I am not a great believer in my own sex. I don't see us occupying a very prominent place in the politics of the next few decades. The functions of woman were decided for her by nature and a million years of revolt will never alter them."

Tallente was a little surprised.

"You mean that you don't believe in woman Member of Parliament, doctors and lawyers, and that sort of thing?"

"In a general way, certainly not," she replied. "Women doctors for women and children, yes! Lawyers—no! Members of Parliament—certainly not! Women were made for one thing and to do that properly should take all the energy they possess."

"You are full of surprises," Tallente declared. "I expected a miracle of complexity and I find you almost primitive." She laughed. "Then considering the sort of man you are, I ought to have gone up a lot in your estimation."

"There are a very few higher notches," he assured her, smiling, "than the one where you now sit enthroned."

Nora glanced at her wrist watch.

"Susan dear, what time do you have to join your friends?" she asked.

Susan shook her head.

"Nothing doing. I've got my seat. I am going when I've had my dinner comfortably. There's fried chicken coming and no considerations of friendship would induce me to hurry away from it."

Nora sighed plaintively.

"There is no doubt about it, women do lack the sporting instinct," she lamented. "Now if we'd both been men, and Mr. Tallente a charming woman, I should have just given you a wink, you would have muttered something clumsy about an appointment, shuffled off and finished your dinner elsewhere."

"Our sex isn't capable of such sacrifices," Susan declared, leaning back to enable the waiter to fill her glass. "There's the champagne, too."

The meal came to a conclusion with scarcely another serious word. Susan departed in due course, and Tallente called for his bill, a short time afterwards, with a feeling of absolute reluctance.

"Shall we try and get in at a show somewhere?" he suggested.

She shook her head.

"Not to-night. Four nights a week I go to bed early and this is one of them. Let's escape, if we can, before Mr. Miller can make his way over here. I know he'll try and have coffee with us or something."

Tallente was adroit and they left the restaurant just as Miller was rising to his feet. Nora sprang into the waiting taxi with a little laugh of triumph and drew her skirts on one side to make room for her escort. They drove slowly off along the hot and crowded street, with its long-drawn-out tangle of polyglot shops, foreign-looking restaurants and delicatessen establishments. Every one who was not feverishly busy was seated either at the open windows of the second or third floor, or out on the pavement below. The city seemed to be exuding the soaked-in heat of the long summer's day. The women who floated by were dressed in the lightest of muslins; even the plainest of them gained a new charm in their airy and butterfly-looking costumes. The men walked bareheaded, waistcoatless, fanning themselves with straw hats. Here and there, as they turned into Shaftesbury Avenue, an immaculately turned-out young man in evening dress passed along the baked pavements and dived into one of the theatres. Notwithstanding the heat, there seemed to be a sort of voluptuous atmosphere brooding over the crowded streets. The sky over Piccadilly Circus was almost violet and the luminous, unneeded lamps had a festive effect. The strain of a long day had passed. It was the pleasure-seekers alone who thronged the thoroughfares. Tallente turned and looked into the corner of the cab, to meet a soft, reflective gleam in Nora's eyes.

"Isn't London wonderful!" she murmured dreamily. "On a night like this it always seems to me like a great human being whose pulses you can see heating, beating all the time."

Tallente, a person very little given to self-analysis, never really understood the impulse which prompted him to lean towards her, the slightly quickening sense of excitement with which he sought for the kindness of her eyes. Suddenly he felt his fingers clasped in hers, a warm, pleasant grasp, yet which somehow or other seemed to have the effect of a barrier.

"You asked me a question at dinner-time," she said, "winch I did not answer at the time. You asked me why I disliked James Miller so much."

"Don't tell me unless you like," he begged. "Don't talk about that sort of person at all just now, unless you want to."

"I must tell you why I dislike him so much," she insisted. "It is because he once tried to kiss me."

"Was that so terrible a sin?" he asked, a little thickly.

She smiled up at him with the candour of a child.

"To me it was," she acknowledged, "because it was just the casual caress of a man seeking for a momentary emotion. Sometimes you have wondered—or you have looked as though you were wondering—what my ideas about men and women and the future and the marriage laws, and all that sort of thing really are. Perhaps I haven't altogether made up my mind myself, but I do know this, because it is part of myself and my life. The one desire I have is for children—sons for the State, or daughters who may bear sons. There isn't anything else which it is worth while for a woman thinking about for a moment. And yet, do you know, I never actually think of marrying. I never think about whether love is right or wrong. I simply think that no man shall ever kiss me, or hold me in his arms, unless it is the man who is sent to me for my desire, and when he comes, just whoever he may be, or whenever it may be, and whether St. George's opens its doors to us or whether we go through some tangle of words at a registry office, or whether neither of these things happens, I really do not mind. When he comes, he will give me what I want—that is just all that counts. And until he comes, I shall stay just as I have been ever since my pigtail went up and my skirts came down."

She gave his hand a final little pressure, patted and released it. He felt, somehow or other, immeasurably grateful to her, flattered by her confidence, curiously exalted by her hesitating words. Speech, however, he found an impossibility.

"So you see," she concluded, sitting up and speaking once more in her conversational manner, "I am not a bit modern really, am I? I am just as primitive as I can be, longing for the things all women long for and unashamed to confess my longing to any one who has the gift of understanding, any one who walks with his eyes turned towards the clouds."

Their taxicab stopped outside the building in which her little flat was situated. She handed him the door key. "Please turn this for me," she begged. "I am at home every afternoon between five and seven. Come and see me whenever you can." He opened the door and she passed in, looking back at him with a little wave of the hand before she vanished lightly into the shadows. Tallente dismissed the cab and walked back towards his rooms. His light-heartedness was passing away with every step he took. The cheerful little groups of pleasure-seekers he encountered seemed like an affront to his increasing melancholy. Once more he had to reckon with this strange new feeling of loneliness which had made its disturbing entrance into his thoughts within the last few years. It was as though a certain weariness of life and its prospects had come with the temporary cessation of his day-by-day political work, and as though an unsuspected desire, terrified at the passing years, was tugging at his heartstrings in the desperate call for some tardy realisation.

CHAPTER XIV

Tallente met the Prime Minister walking in the Park early on the following morning. The latter had established the custom of walking from Knightsbridge Barracks, where his car deposited him, to Marble Arch and back every morning, and it had come to be recognised as his desire, and a part of the etiquette of the place, that he should be allowed this exercise without receiving even the recognition of passersby. On this occasion, however, he took the initiative, stopped Tallente and invited him to talk with him.

"I thought of writing to you, Tallente," he said. "I cannot bring myself to believe that you were in earnest on Wednesday morning."

"Absolutely," the other assured him. "I have an appointment with Dartrey in an hour's time to close the matter."

The Prime Minister was shocked and pained.

"You will dig your own grave," he declared. "The idea is perfectly scandalous. You propose to sell your political birthright for a mess of pottage."

"I am afraid I can't agree with you, sir," Tallente regretted. "I am at least as much in sympathy with the programme of the Democratic Party as I am with yours."

"In that case," was the somewhat stiff rejoinder, "there is, I fear, nothing more to be said."

There was a brief silence. Tallente would have been glad to make his escape, but found no excuse.

"When we beat Germany," Horlock ruminated, "the man in the street thought that we had ensured the peace of the world. Who could have dreamed that a nation who had played such an heroic part, which had imperiled its very existence for the sake of a principle, was all the time rotten at the core!"

"I will challenge you to repeat that statement in the House or on any public platform, sir," Tallente objected. "The present state of discontent throughout the country is solely owing to the shocking financial mismanagement of every Chancellor of the Exchequer and lawmaker since peace was signed. We won the war and the people who had been asked to make heroic sacrifices were simply expected to continue them afterwards as a matter of course. What chance has the man of moderate means had to improve his position, to save a little for his old age, during the last ten years? A third of his income has gone in taxation and the cost of everything is fifty per cent, more than it was before the war. And we won it, mind. That is what he can't understand. We won the war and found ruin."

"Legislation has done its best," the Prime Minister said, "to assist in the distribution of capital."

"Legislation was too slow," Tallente answered bluntly. "Legislation is only playing with the subject now. You sneer at the Democratic Party, but they have a perfectly sound scheme of financial reform and they undertake to bring the income tax down to two shillings in the pound within the next three years."

"They'll ruin half the merchants and the manufacturers in the country if they attempt it."

"How can they ruin them?" Tallente replied. "The factories will be there, the trade will be there, the money will still be there. The financial legislation of the last few years has simply been a blatant nursing of the profiteer."

"I need not say, Tallente, that I disagree with you entirely," his companion declared. "At the same time, I am not going to argue with you. To tell you the truth, I spent a great part of last night with you in my thoughts. We cannot afford to let you go. Supposing, now, that I could induce Watkinson to give up Kendal? His seat is quite safe and with a little reshuffling you would be able to slip back gradually to your place amongst us?"

Tallente shook his head.

"I am very sorry, sir," he said, "but my decision is taken. I have come to the conclusion that, with proper handling and amalgamation, the Democrats are capable of becoming the only sound political party at present possible. If Stephen Dartrey is still of the same mind when I see him this morning, I shall throw in my lot with theirs."

The Prime Minister frowned. He recognised bitterly an error in tactics. The ranks of his own party were filled with brilliant men without executive gifts. It was for that reason he had for the moment ignored Tallente. He realised, however, that in the opposite camp no man could be more dangerous.

"This thing seems to me really terrible, Tallente," he protested gravely. "After all, however much we may ignore it, there is what we might call a clannishness amongst Englishmen of a certain order which has helped this country through many troubles. You are going to leave behind entirely the companionship of your class. You are going to cast in your lot with the riffraff of politics, the mealy-mouthed anarchist only biding his time, the blatant Bolshevist talking of compromise with his tongue in his cheek, the tub-thumper out to confiscate every one's wealth and start a public house. You won't know yourself in this gallery."

Tallente shook his head.

"These people," he admitted, "are full of their extravagances, although I think that the types you mention are as extinct as the dodo, but I will admit their extravagances, only to pass on to tell you this. I claim for them that they are the only political party, even with their strange conglomeration of material, which possesses the least spark of spirituality. I think, and their programme proves it, that they are trying to look beyond the crying needs of the moment, trying to frame laws which will be lasting and just without pandering to capital or factions of any sort. I think that when their time comes, they will try at least to govern this country from the loftiest possible standard."

The Prime Minister completed his walk, the enjoyment of which Tallente had entirely spoilt. He held out his hand a little pettishly.

"Politics," he said, "is the one career in which men seldom recover from their mistakes. I hope that even at the eleventh hour you will relent. It will be a grief to all of us to see you slip away from the reputable places."

The Right Honourable John Augustus Horlock stepped into his motor-car and drove away. Tallente, after a glance at his watch, called a taxi and proceeded to keep his appointment at Demos House, the great block of buildings where Dartrey had established his headquarters. In the large, open waiting room where he was invited to take a seat he watched with interest the faces of the passers-by. There seemed to be visitors from every class of the community. A Board of Trade official was there to present some figures connected with the industry which he represented. Half a dozen operatives, personally conducted by a local leader, had travelled up that morning from one of the great manufacturing centres. A well-known writer was there, waiting to see the chief of the literary section. Tallente found his period of detention all too short. He was summoned in to see Dartrey, who welcomed him warmly.

"Sit down, Tallente," he invited. "We are both of us men who believe in simple things and direct action. Have you made up your mind?"

"I have," Tallente announced. "I have broken finally with Horlock. I have told him that I am coming to you."

Dartrey leaned over and held out both his hands. The spiritual side of his face seemed at that moment altogether in the ascendant. He welcomed Tallente as the head of a great religious order might have welcomed a novice. He was full of dignity and kindliness as well as joy.

"You will help us to set the world to rights," he said. "Alas! that is only a phrase, but you will help us to let in the light. Remember," he went on, "that there may be moments of discouragement. Much of the material we have to use, the people we have to influence, the way we have to travel, may seem sordid, but the light is shining there all the time, Tallente. We are not politicians. We are deliverers."

It was one of Dartrey's rare moments of genuine enthusiasm. His visitor forgot for a moment the businesslike office with its row of telephones, its shelves of blue books and masses of papers. He seemed to be breathing a new and wonderful atmosphere.

"I am your man, Dartrey," he promised simply. "Make what use of me you will."

Dartrey smiled, once more the plain, kindly man of affairs.

"To descend, then, very much to the earth," he said, "to-night you must go to Bradford. Odames will resign to-morrow. This time," he added, with a little smile, "I think I can promise you the Democratic support and a very certain election."

BOOK TWO

CHAPTER I

Tallente found himself possessed of a haunting, almost a morbid feeling that a lifetime had passed since last his car had turned out of the station gates and he had seen the moorland unroll itself before his eyes. There was a new pungency in the autumn air, an unaccustomed scantiness in the herbage of the moor and the low hedges growing from the top of the stone walls. The glory of the heather had passed, though here and there a clump of brilliant yellow gorse remained. The telegraph posts, leaning away from the wind, seemed somehow scantier; the road stretched between them, lonely and desolate. From a farmhouse in the bosom of the tree-hung hills lights were already twinkling, and when he reached the edge of the moor, and the sea spread itself out almost at his feet, the shapes of the passing steamers, with their long trail of smoke, were blurred and uncertain. Below, his home field, his wall-enclosed patch of kitchen garden, the long, low house itself lay like pieces from a child's play-box stretched out upon the carpet. Only to-night there was no mist. They made their cautious way downwards through the clearest of darkening atmospheres. On the hillsides, as they dropped down, they could hear the music of an occasional sheep bell. Rabbits scurried away from the headlights of the car, an early owl flew hooting over their heads. Tallente, tired with his journey, perhaps a little worn with the excitement of the last two months, found something dark and a little lonely about the unoccupied house, something a little dreary in his solitary dinner and the long evening spent with no company save his books and his pipe. Later on, he lay for long awake, watching the twin lights flash out across the Channel and listening to the melancholy call of the owls as they swept back and forth across the lawn to their secret abodes in the cliffs. When at last he slept, however, he slept soundly. An unlooked-for gleam of sunshine and the dull roar of the incoming tide breaking upon the beach below woke him the next morning long after his usual hour. He bathed, shaved in front of the open window, and breakfasted with an absolute renewal of his fuller interest in life. It was not until he had sent back the car in which he had driven as far as the station, and was swinging on foot across Woolhanger

Moor, that he realised fully why he had come, why he had schemed for these two days out of a life packed with multifarious tasks. Then he laughed at himself, heartily yet a little self-consciously. A fool's errand might yet be a pleasant one, even though his immediate surroundings seemed to mock the sound of his mirth. Woolhanger Moor in November was a drear enough sight. There were many patches of black mud and stagnant water, carpets of treacherous-looking green moss, bare clumps of bushes bent all one way by the northwest wind, masses of rock, gaunter and sterner now that their summer covering of creeping shrubs and bracken had lost their foliage. It was indeed the month of desolation. Every scrap of colour seemed to have faded from the dripping wet landscape. Phantasmal clouds of grey mist brooded here and there in the hollows. The distant hills were wreathed in vapour, so that even the green of the pastures was invisible. Every now and then a snipe started up from one of the weedy places with his shrill, mournful cry, and more than once a solitary hawk hovered for a few minutes above his head. The only other sign of life was a black speck in the distance, a speck which came nearer and nearer until he paused to watch it, standing upon a little incline and looking steadily along the rude cart track. The speck grew in size. A person on horseback,—a woman! Soon she swung her horse around as though she recognised him, jumped a little dike to reach him the quicker and reined up her horse by his side, holding one hand down to him. "Mr. Tallente!" she exclaimed. "How wonderful!" He held her hand, looking steadfastly, almost eagerly, up into her flushed face. Her eyes were filled with pleasure. His errand, in those few breathless moments, seemed no longer the errand of a fool.

"I can't realise it, even now," she went on, drawing her hand away at last. "I pictured you at Westminster, in committee rooms and all sorts of places. Aren't you forging weapons to drive us from our homes and portion out our savings?"

"I have left the thunderbolts alone for one short week-end," he answered. "I felt a hunger for this moorland air. London becomes so enveloping." Jane sat upright upon her horse and looked at him with a mocking smile. "How ungallant! I hoped you had come to atone for your neglect."

"Have I neglected you?" he asked quietly, turning and walking by her side.

"Shockingly! You lunched with me on the seventh of August. I see you again on the second of November, and I do believe that I shall have to save you from starvation again."

"It's quite true," he admitted. "I have a sandwich in my pocket, though, in case you were away from home."

"Worse than ever," she sighed. "You didn't even trouble to make enquiries."

"From whom should I? Robert—my servant—his wife, and a boy to help in the garden are all my present staff at the Manor. Robert drives the car and waits on me, and his wife cooks. They are estimable people, but I don't think they are up in local news."

"You were quite safe," she said, looking ahead of her. "I am never away." The tail end of a scat of rain beat on their faces. From the hollow on their left, the wind came booming up.

"I should have thought that for these few months just now," he suggested, "you might have cared for a change."

"I have my work here, such as it is," she answered, a little listlessly. "If I were in town, for instance, I should have nothing to do."

"You would meet people. You must sometimes feel the need of society down here."

"I doubt whether I should meet the people who would interest me," she replied, "and in any case I have my work here. That keeps me occupied."

They turned into the avenue and soon the long front of the house spread itself out before them. Jane, who had been momentarily absorbed, looked down at her companion.

"You are alone at the Manor?" she asked.

"Quite alone."

She became the hostess directly they had passed the portals of the house. She led him across the hall into her little sanctum.

"This is the room," she told him, "in which I never do a stroke of work—sacred to the frivolities alone. I shall send Morton in to see what you will have to drink, while I change my habit. You must have something after that walk. I shan't be long."

For the second time she avoided meeting his eyes as she left the room. Tallente stood on the hearth-rug, still looking at the closed door through which she had vanished, puzzled, a little chilled. He gave his order to the attentive butler who presently appeared and who looked at him with covert interest,—the Press had been almost hysterically prodigal of his name during the last few weeks. Then he settled down to wait for her return with an impatience which became almost uncontrollable. It seemed to him, as he paced restlessly about, that this little apartment, which he remembered so well, had in a measure changed, was revealing a different atmosphere, as though in sympathy with some corresponding change in its presiding spirit. There was a huge and well-worn couch, smothered with cushions and suggestive of a comfort almost voluptuous; a large easy-chair, into which he presently sank, of the same character. The wood logs burning in the grate gave out a pleasant sense of warmth. He took more particular note of the volumes in the well-filled bookcases,—volumes of poetry, French novels, with a fair sprinkling of modern English fiction. There was a plaster cast of the Paris Magdalene over the door and one or two fine point etchings, after the style of Heillieu, upon the walls. There was no writing table in the room, nor any signs of industry, but a black oak gate-table was laden with magazines and fashion papers. Against the brown walls, a clump of flaming yellow gorse leaned from a distant corner, its faint almond-like fragrance mingling aromatically with the perfume of burning logs and a great bowl of dried lavender. More than ever it seemed to Tallente that the atmosphere of the room had changed, had become in some subtle way at the same time more enervating and more exciting. It was like a revelation of a hidden side of the woman, who might indeed have had some purpose of her own in leaving him here. He set down his empty glass with the feeling that vermouth was a heavier drink than he had fancied. Then a streak of watery sunshine filtered its way through the plantation and crept across the worn, handsome carpet. He felt a queer exultation at the sound of her footsteps outside. She entered, as she had departed, without directly meeting his earnest gaze.

"I hope you have made yourself at home," she said. "Dear me, how untidy everything is!"

She moved about, altering the furniture a little, making little piles of the magazines, a graceful, elegant figure in her dark velvet house dress, with a thin band of fur at the neck. She turned suddenly around and found him watching her. This time she laughed at him frankly.

"Sit down at once," she ordered, motioning him back to his easy-chair and coming herself to a corner of the lounge. "Remember that you have a great deal to tell me and explain. The newspapers say such queer things. Is it true that I really am entertaining a possible future Prime Minister?"

"I suppose that might be," he answered, a little vaguely, his eyes still fixed upon her. "So this is your room. I like it. And I like—"

"Well, go on, please," she begged.

"I like the softness of your gown, and I like the fur against your throat and neck, and I like those buckles on your shoes, and the way you do your hair."

She laughed, gracefully enough, yet with some return to that note of uneasiness.

"You mustn't turn my head!" she protested. "You, fresh from London, which they tell me is terribly gay just now! I want to understand just what it means, your throwing in your lot with the Democrats. My uncle says, for instance, that you have abandoned respectable politics to become a Tower Hill pedagogue."

"Respectable politics," he replied, "if by that you mean the present government of the country, have been in the wrong hands for so long that people scarcely realise what is undoubtedly the fact—that the country isn't being governed at all. A Government with an Opposition Party almost as powerful as itself, all made up of separate parties which are continually demanding sops, can scarcely progress very far, can it?"

"But the Democrats," she ventured, "are surely only one of these isolated parties?"

"I have formed a different idea of their strength," he answered. "I believe that if a general election took place to-morrow, the Democrats would sweep the country. I believe that we should have the largest working majority any Government has had since the war."

"How terrible!" she murmured, involuntarily truthful.

"Your tame socialism isn't equal to the prospect," he remarked, a little bitterly.

"My tame socialism, as you call it," she replied, "draws the line at seeing the country governed by one class of person only, and that class the one who has the least at stake in it."

"Lady Jane," he said earnestly, "I am glad that I am here to point out to you a colossal mistake from which you and many others are suffering. The Democrats do not represent Labour only."

"The small shopkeepers?" she suggested.

"Nothing of the sort," he replied. "The influence of my party has spread far deeper and further. We number amongst our adherents the majority of the professional classes and the majority of the thinking people amongst the community of moderate means. Why, if you consider the legislation of the last seven or eight years, you will see how they have been driven to embrace some sort of socialism. Nothing so detestable and short-sighted as our financial policy has ever been known in the history of the world. The middle classes, meaning by the middle classes professional men and men of moderate means, bore the chief burden of the war. They submitted to terrible taxation, to many privations, besides the universal gift of their young blood. We won the war and what was the result? The wealth of the country, through ghastly legislation, drifted into the hands of the profiteering classes, the wholesale shopkeepers, the ship owners, the factory owners, the mine owners. The professional man with two thousand a year was able to save a quarter of that before the war. After the war, taxation demanded that quarter and more for income tax, thrust upon him an increased cost of living, cut the ground from beneath his feet. It isn't either of the two extremes—the aristocrat or the labouring man—where you must look for the pulse of a country's prosperity. It is to the classes in between, and, Lady Jane, they are flocking to our camp just as fast as they can, just as fast as the country is heading for ruin under its present Government."

"You are very convincing," she admitted. "Why have you not spoken so plainly in the House?"

"The moment hasn't arrived," Tallente replied. "There will be a General Election before many months have passed and that will be the end of the present fools' paradise at St. Stephen's."

"And then?"

"We shan't abuse our power," he assured her. "What we aim at is a National Party which will consider the interests of every class. That is our reading of the term 'Democrat.' Our programme is not nearly so revolutionary as you are probably led to believe, but we do mean to smooth away, so far as we can from a practical point of view, the inequalities of life. We want to sweep away the last remnants of feudalism."

"Tell me why they were so anxious to gather you into the fold?" she asked.

"I think for this reason," he explained. "Stephen Dartrey is a brilliant writer, a great orator, and an inspired lawmaker. The whole world recognises him as a statesman. It is his name and genius which have made the Democratic Party possible. On the other hand, he is not in the least a politician. He doesn't understand the game as it is played in the House of

Commons. He lives above those things. That is why I suppose they wanted me. I have learnt the knack of apt debating and I understand the tricks. Even if ever I become the titular head of the party, Dartrey will remain the soul and spirit of it. If they were not able to lay their hands upon some person like myself, I believe that Miller was supposed to have the next claim, and I should think that Miller is the one man in the world who might disunite the strongest party on earth."

"Disunite it? I should think he would disperse it to the four corners of the world!" she exclaimed.

The butler announced luncheon. She rose to her feet.

"I cannot tell you," he said, with a little sigh of relief, as he held open the door for her, "how thankful I am that I happened to find you alone."

CHAPTER II

Luncheon was a pleasant, even a luxurious meal, for the Woolhanger chef had come from the ducal household, but it was hedged about with restraints which fretted Tallente and rendered conversation monosyllabic. It was served, too, in the larger dining room, where the table, reduced to its smallest dimensions, still seemed to place a formidable distance between himself and his hostess. A manservant stood behind Lady Jane's chair, and the butler was in constant attendance at the sideboard. Under such circumstances, conversation became precarious and was confined chiefly to local topics. When they left the room for their coffee, they found it served in the hall. Tallente, however, protested vigorously.

"Can't we have it served in your sitting room, please?" he begged. "It is impossible to talk to you here. There are people in the background all the time, and you might have callers."

She hesitated for a moment but yielded the point. With the door closed and the coffee tray between them, Tallente drew a sigh of relief.

"I hope you don't think I am a nuisance," he said bluntly, "but, after all, I came down from London purposely to see you."

"I am not so vain as to believe that," she answered.

> "It is nevertheless true and I think that you do believe it. What have I done that you should all of a sudden build a fence around yourself?"

"That may be," she replied, smiling, "for my own protection. I can assure you that I am not used to tête-a-tête luncheons with guests who insist upon having their own way in everything."

"I wonder if it is a good thing for you to be so much your own mistress," he reflected.

"You must judge by results. I always have been—at least since I decided to lead this sort of life."

"Why have you never married?" he asked her, a little abruptly.

"We discussed that before, didn't we? I suppose because the right man has never asked me."

"Perhaps," he ventured, "the right man isn't able to."

"Perhaps there isn't any right man at all—perhaps there never will be."

The minutes ticked away. The room, with its mingled perfumes and pleasant warmth, its manifold associations with her wholesome and orderly life, seemed to have laid a sort of spell upon him. She was leaning back in her corner of the lounge, her hands hanging over the sides, her eyes fixed upon the burning log. She herself was so abstracted that he ventured to let his eyes dwell upon her, to trace the outline of her slim but powerful limbs, to admire her long, delicate feet and hands, the strong womanly face, with its kindly mouth and soft, almost affectionate eyes. Tallente, who for the last ten years had looked upon the other sex as non-existent, crushed into an uninteresting negation for him owing to his wife's cold and shadowy existence, twice within the last few months found himself pass in a different way under the greatest spell in life. Nora Miall had provoked his curiosity, had reawakened a dormant sense of sex without attracting it towards herself. Jane brought to him again, from the first moment he had seen her, that half-wistful recrudescence of the sentiment of his earlier days. He was amazed to find how once more in her presence that sentiment had taken to itself fire and life, how different a thing it was from those first dreams of her, which had seemed like an echo from the period of his poetry-reading youth. Of all women in the world she seemed to him now the most desirable. That she was unattainable he was perfectly willing to admit. Even then he had not the strength to deny himself the doubtful joys of imagination with regard to her. He revelled in her proximity because of the pleasure it gave him, heedless or reckless of consequences. Between them, in vastly different degrees, these two women seemed to have brought him back something of his youth.

The silence became noticeable, led him at last into a certain measure of alarm.

"Lady Jane," he ventured, "have I said anything to offend you?"

"Of course not," she answered, looking at him kindly.

"You are very silent. Are you afraid that I am going to attempt to make love to you?"

She was startled in earnest this time. She sat up and looked at him disapprovingly. There was a touch of the old hauteur in her tone.

"How can you be so ridiculous!" she exclaimed.

"Would it be ridiculous of me?"

"Does it occur to you," she asked, "that I am the sort of person to encourage attentions from a man who is not free to offer them?"

"I had forgotten that," he admitted, quite frankly. "Of course, I see the point. I have a wife, even though of her own choosing she does not count."

"She exists."

"So do I."

Jane broke into a little laugh.

"Now we are both being absurd," she declared, "and I don't want to be and I don't want you to be. Of course, you can't look at things just as I do. You belong to a very large world. You spend your life destroying obstacles. All my people, you know," she went on, "look upon me as terribly emancipated. They think my mild socialism and my refusal to listen to such a thing as a chaperon most terribly improper, but at heart, you know, I am still a very conventional person. I have torn down a great many conventions, but there are some upon which I cannot bring myself even to lay my fingers."

"Perhaps it wouldn't be you if you did," he reflected.

"Perhaps not."

"And yet," he went on, "tell me, are you wholly content here? Your life, in its way, is splendid. You live as much for the benefit of others as for yourself. You are encouraging the right principle amongst your yeomen and your farmers. You are setting your heel upon feudalism—you, the daughter of a race who have always demanded it. You live amongst these wonderful surroundings, you grow into the bigness of them, nature becomes almost your friend. It is one of the most dignified and beautiful lives I ever knew for a woman, and yet—are you wholly content?"

"I am not," she admitted frankly. "And listen," she went on, after a moment's pause, "I will show you how much I trust you, how much I really want you to understand me. I am not completely happy because I know perfectly well that it is unnatural to live as I do. If I met the man I could care for and who cared for me, I should prefer to be married." She had commenced her speech with the faintest tinge of colour burning underneath the wholesome sunburn of her cheeks. She had spoken boldly enough, even though towards the end of her sentence her voice had grown very low. When she had finished, however, it seemed as though the memory of her words were haunting her, as though she suddenly realised the nakedness of them. She buried her face in her hands, and he saw her shoulders heave as though she were sobbing. He stood very close and for the first time he touched her. He held the fingers of her hand gently in his. "Dear Lady Jane," he begged, "don't regret even for a moment that you have spoken naturally. If we are to be friends, to be anything at all to one another, it is wonderful of you to tell me so sweetly what women take such absurd pains to conceal.... When you look up, let us start our friendship all over again, only before you do, listen to my confession. If fifteen years could be rolled off my back and I were free, it isn't political ambition I should look to for my guiding star. I should have one far greater, far more wonderful desire." The fingers he held were gently withdrawn. She drew herself up. Her forehead was wrinkled questioningly. She forced a smile. "You would be very foolish," she said, "if you tried to part with one of those fifteen years. Every one has brought you experiences Every one has helped to make you what you are."

"And yet—" he began.

He broke off abruptly in his speech. The hall seemed suddenly full of voices. Jane rose to her feet at the sound of approaching footsteps. She made the slightest possible grimace, but Tallente was oppressed with a suspicion that the interruption was not altogether unwelcome to her.

"Some of my cousins and their friends from Minehead," she said. "I am so sorry. I expect they have lost the hunt and come here for tea."

The room was almost instantly invaded by a company of light-hearted, noisy young people, flushed with exercise and calling aloud for tea, intimates all of them, calling one another by their Christian names, speaking a jargon which sounded to Tallente like another language. He stayed for a quarter of an hour and then took his leave. Of the newcomers, no one seemed to have an idea who he was, no one seemed to care in the least whether he remained or went, He was only able to snatch a word of farewell with Jane at the door. She shook her head at his whispered request.

"I am afraid not," she answered. "How could I? Besides, there is no telling when this crowd will go. You are sure you won't let me send you home?"

Tallente shook his head.

"The walk will do me good," he said. "I get lazy in town. But you are sure—"

The butler was holding open the door. Two of the girls had suddenly taken possession of Jane. She shook her head slightly.

"Good-by," she called out. "Come and see me next time you are down."

Tallente was suddenly his old self, grave and severe. He bowed stiffly in response to the little chorus of farewells and followed the butler down the hall. The latter, who was something of a politician, did his best to indicate by his manner his appreciation of Tallente's position.

"You are sure you won't allow me to order a car, sir?" he said, with his hand upon the door. "I know her ladyship would be only too pleased. It's a long step to the Manor, and if you'll forgive my saying so, sir, you've a good deal on your shoulders just now."

Tallente caught a glimpse of the bleak moorland and of the distant hills, wrapped in mist. The idea of vigorous exercise, however, appealed to him. He shook his head.

"I'd rather walk, thanks," he said.

"It's a matter of five miles, sir."

Tallente smiled. There was something in the fresh, cold air wonderfully alluring after the atmosphere of the room he had quitted. He turned his coat collar up and strode down the avenue.

CHAPTER III

Tallente reached the Manor about an hour and a half later, mud-splashed, wet and weary. Robert followed him into the study and mixed him a whisky and soda.

"You've walked all the way back, sir?" he remarked, with a note of protest in his tone.

"They offered me a car," Tallente admitted. "I didn't want it. I came down for fresh air and exercise."

"Two very good things in their way, sir, but easily overdone," was the mild rejoinder. "These hills are terrible unless you're at them all the time."

Tallente drank his whisky and soda almost greedily and felt the benefit of it, although he was still weary. He had walked for five miles in the company of ghosts and their faces had been grey. Perhaps, too, it was the passing of his youth which brought this tiredness to his limbs.

"Robert," he confessed abruptly, "I was a fool to come down here at all."

"It's dreary at this time of the year unless you've time to shoot or hunt, sir. Why not motor to Bath to-morrow? I could wire for rooms, and I could drive you up to London the next day. Motoring's a good way of getting the air, sir, and you won't overtire yourself."

"I'll think of it in the morning," his master promised.

"My wife has found the silver, sir," Robert announced, as he turned to leave the room, "and I managed to get a little fish. That, with some soup, a pheasant, and a fruit tart, we thought—"

"I shall be alone, Robert," Tallente interrupted. "There is no one coming for dinner."

The man's disappointment was barely concealed. He sighed as he took up the tray.

"Very good, sir. Your clothes are all out. I'll turn on the hot water in the bathroom."

Tallente threw off his rain and mud-soaked clothes, bathed, changed and descended to the dining room just as the gong sounded. Robert was in the act of moving the additional place from the little round dining table which he had drawn up closer to the wood fire, but his master stopped him.

"You can let those things be," he directed. "Take away the champagne, though. I shan't want that."

Robert bowed in silent appreciation of his master's humour and began ladling out soup at the sideboard. Tallente's lips were curled a little, partly in self-contempt, with perhaps just a dash of self-pity. It had come to this, then, that he must dine with fancies rather than alone, that this tardily developed streak of sentimentality must be ministered to or would drag him into the depths of dejection. He began to understand the psychology of its late appearance. Stella's artificial companionship had kept his thoughts imprisoned, fettered with the meshes of an instinctive fidelity, and had driven him sedulously to the solace of work and books. Now that it was removed and he was to all practical purposes a free man, they took their own course. His life had suddenly become a natural one, and all that was human in him responded to the possibilities of his solitude, He had had as yet no time to experience the relief, to appreciate his liberty, before he was face to face with this new loneliness. To-night, he thought, as he looked at the empty place and remembered his wistful, almost diffident invitation, the solitude was almost unendurable. If she had only understood how much it meant, surely she would have made some effort, would not have been content with that half-embarrassed, half-doubtful shake of the head! In the darkened room, with the throb of the sea and the crackling of the lop in his ears, and only Robert's silent form for company, he felt a sudden craving for the things of his youth, for another side of life, the restaurants, the bright eyes of women, the whispered words of pleasant sentiment, the perfume shaken into the atmosphere they created, the low music in the background "I beg your pardon, sir," Robert said in his ear, "your soup. Gertrude has taken such pains with the dinner, sir," he added diffidently. "If I might take the liberty of suggesting it, it would be as well if you could eat something." Tallente took up his spoon. Then they both started, they both turned to the window. A light had flashed into the room, a low, purring sound came from outside.

"A car, sir!" Robert exclaimed, his face full of pleasurable anticipation. "If you'll excuse me, I'll answer the door. Might it be the lady, after all, sir?" He hurried out. Tallente rose slowly to his feet. He was listening intently. The thing wasn't possible, he told himself. It wasn't possible! Then he heard a voice in the hall. Robert threw the door open and announced in a tone of triumph—

"Lady Jane Partington, sir."

She came towards him, smiling, self-possessed, but a little interrogative. He had a lightning-like impression of her beautiful shoulders rising from her plain black gown, her delightfully easy walk, the slimness and comeliness and stateliness of her.

"I know that I ought to be ashamed of myself for coming after I had told you I couldn't," she said. "It will serve me right if you've eaten all the dinner, but I do hope you haven't."

"I had only just sat down," he told her, as he and Robert held her chair, "and I think that this is the kindest action you ever performed in your life."

Robert, his face glowing with satisfaction, had become ubiquitous. She had scarcely subsided into her chair before he was offering her a cocktail on a silver tray, serving Tallente with his forgotten glass, at the sideboard ladling out soup, out of the room and in again, bringing back the rejected bottle of champagne.

"You will never believe that I am a sane person again," she laughed. "After you had gone, and all those foolish children had departed, I felt it was quite impossible to sit down and dine alone. I wanted so much to come and I realised how ridiculous it was of me not to have accepted at once. At the last moment I couldn't bear it any longer, so I rushed into the first gown I could find, ordered out my little coupé and here I am."

"The most welcome guest who ever came to a lonely man," he assured her. "A moment ago, Robert was complaining because I was sending my soup away. Now I shall show him what Devon air can do."

The champagne was excellent, and the dinner over which Gertrude had taken so much care was after all thoroughly appreciated. Tallente, suddenly and unexpectedly light-hearted, felt a keen desire to entertain his welcome guest, and remembered his former successes as a raconteur. They pushed politics and all personal matters far away. He dug up reminiscences of his class in foreign capitals, when he had first entered the Diplomatic Service, betrayed his intimate knowledge of the Florence which they both loved, of Paris, where she had studied and which he had seen under so many aspects,—Paris, the home of beauty and fashion before the war; torn with anguish and horror during its earlier stages; grim, steadfast and sombre in the clays of Verdun; wildly, madly exultant when wreathed and decorated with victory. There were so many things to talk about for two people of agile brains come together late in life. They had moved into the study and Lady Jane was sealed in his favourite easy-chair, sipping her coffee and some wonderful green chartreuse, before a single personal note had crept into the flow of their conversation.

"It can't be that I am in Devonshire," she said. "I never realised how much like a succession of pictures conversation can be. You seem to remind me so much of things which I have kept locked away just because I have had no one to share them with."

"You are in Devonshire all right," he answered, smiling. "You will realise it when you turn out of my avenue and face the hills. You see, you've dropped down from the fairyland of 'up over' to the nesting place of the owls and the gulls."

"Nine hundred feet," she murmured. "Thank heavens for my forty horsepower engine! I want to see the sea break against your rocks," she went on, as she took the cigarette which he passed her. "There used to be a little path through your plantation to a place where you look sheer down. Don't you remember, you took me there the first time I came to see you, in August, and I have never forgotten it."

He rang the bell for her coat. The night, though windy and dark, was warm. Stars shone out from unexpected places, pencil-like streaks of inky-black clouds stretched menacingly across the sky. The wind came down from the moors above with a dull boom which seemed echoed by the waves beating against the giant rocks. The beads of the bare trees among which they passed were bent this way and that, and the few remaining leaves rustled in vain resistance, or, yielding to the irresistible gusts, sailed for a moment towards the skies, to be dashed down into the ever-growing carpet. The path was narrow and they walked in single file, but at the bend he drew level with her, walking on the seaward side and guiding her with his fingers upon her arm. Presently they reached the little circular space where rustic seats had been placed, and leaned over a grey stone wall.

There was nothing of the midsummer charm about the scene to-night. Sheer below them the sea, driven by tide and wind, rushed upon the huge masses of rock or beat direct upon the cave-indented cliffs. The spray leapt high into the air, to be caught up by the wind in whirlpools, little ghostly flecks, luminous one moment and gone forever the next. Far away across the pitchy waters they could see at regular intervals a line of white where the breakers came rushing in, here and there the agitated lights of passing steamers; opposite, the twin flares on the Welsh coast, and every sixty seconds the swinging white illumination from the Lynmouth Lighthouse, shining up from behind the headland. Jane slipped one hand through his arm and stood there, breathless, rapturously watchful. "This is wonderful," she murmured. "It is the one thing we have always lacked at Woolhanger. We get the booming of the wind—wonderful it is, too, like the hollow thunder of guns or the quick passing of an underground army—but we miss this. I feel, somehow, as though I knew now why it tears past us, uprooting the very trees that stand in its way. It rushes to the sea. What a meeting!" Her hand tightened upon his arm as a great wave broke direct upon the cliff below and a torrent of wind, rushing through the trees and downwards, caught the spray and scattered it around them and high over their heads.

"We humans," he whispered, "are taught our lesson."

"Do we need it?" she asked, with sudden fierceness. "Do you believe that because some mysterious power imposes restraint upon us, the passion isn't there all the while?"

She was suddenly in his arms, the warm wind shrieking about them, the darkness thick and soft as a mantle. Only he saw the anguished happiness in her eyes as they closed beneath his kisses.

"One moment out of life," she faltered, "one moment!"

Another great wave shook the ground beneath them, but she had drawn away. She struggled for breath. Then once more her hand was thrust through his arm. He knew so well that his hour was over and he submitted.

"Back, please," she whispered, "back through the plantation—quietly."

An almost supernatural instinct divined and acceded to her desire for silence. So they walked slowly back towards the long, low house whose faint lights flickered through the trees. She leaned a little upon him, the hand which she had passed through his arm was clasped in his. Only the wind spoke. When at last they were en the terraces she drew a long breath.

"Dear friend," she said softly, "see how I trust you. I leave in your keeping the most precious few minutes of my life."

"This is to be the end, then?" he faltered.

"It is not we who have decided that," she answered. "It is just what must be. You go to a very difficult life, a very splendid one. I have my smaller task. Don't unfit me for it. We will each do our best."

Her servant was waiting by the car. His figure loomed up through the darkness. "You will come into the house for a few minutes?" he begged hoarsely. She shook her head.

"Why? Our farewells have been spoken. I leave you—so."

The man had disappeared behind the bonnet of the car. She grasped his hand with both of hers and brushed it lightly with her lips. Then she gilded away. A moment later he was listening to her polite speeches as she leaned out of the coupé. "My dinner was too wonderful," she said. "Do make my compliments to that dear Robert and his wife. Good luck to you, and don't rob us poor landowners of every penny we possess in life."

The car was gone in the midst of his vague little response. He watched the lights go flashing up the hillside, crawling around the hairpin corners, up until it seemed that they had reached the black clouds and were climbing into the heavens. Then he turned back into the house. The world was still a place for dreams.

CHAPTER IV

Tallente sat in the morning train, on his way to town, and on the other side of the bare ridge at which he gazed so earnestly Lady Jane and Segerson had brought their horses to a standstill half way along a rude cart track which led up to a farmhouse tucked away in the valley.

"This is where James Crockford's land commences," Segerson remarked, riding up to his companion's side. "Look around you. I think you will admit that I have not exaggerated."

She frowned thoughtfully. On every side were evidences of poor farming and neglect. The untrimmed hedges had been broken down in many places by cattle. A plough which seemed as though it had been embedded there for ages, stood in the middle of a half-ploughed field. Several tracts of land which seemed prepared for winter sowing were covered with stones. The farmhouse yard, into which they presently passed, was dirty and untidy. Segerson leaned down and knocked on the door with his whip. After a short delay, a slatternly-looking woman, with tousled fair hair, answered the summons.

"Mr. Crockford in?" Segerson asked.

"You'll find him in the living room," the woman answered curtly, with a stare at Lady Jane. "Here's himself."

She retreated into the background. A man with flushed face, without collar or tie, clad in trousers and shirt only, had stepped out of the parlour. He stared at his visitors in embarrassment.

"I came over to have a word or two with you on business, Mr. Crockford," Jane said coldly. "I rather expected to find you on the land."

The man mumbled something and threw open the door of the sitting room.

"Won't you come in?" he invited. "There's just Mr. Pettigrew here—the vet from Barnstaple. He's come over to look at one of my cows."

Mr. Pettigrew, also flushed, rose to his feet. Jane acknowledged his greeting and glanced around the room. It was untidy, dirty and close, smelling strongly of tobacco and beer. On the table was a bottle of whisky, half empty, and two glasses.

"There is really no reason why I should disturb you," Jane said, turning back upon the threshold. "A letter from Mr. Segerson will do."

Crockford, however, had pulled himself together. A premonition of his impending fate had already produced a certain sullenness.

"Pettigrew," he directed, "you get out and have another look at the cow. If you've any business word to say to me, your ladyship, I'm here."

Jane looked once more around the squalid room, watched the unsteady figure of Pettigrew departing and looked back at her tenant.

"Your lease is up on March the twenty-fifth, Crockford," she reminded him. "I have come to tell you that I shall not be prepared to renew it."

The man simply blinked at her. His fuddled brain was not equal to grappling with such a catastrophe.

"Your farm is favourably situated," she continued, "and, although small, has great possibilities. I find you are dropping behind your neighbours and your crops are poorer each season. Have you saved any money, Crockford?"

"Saved any money," the man blustered, "with shepherd's wages alone at two pounds a week, and a week's rain starting in the day I began haymaking. Why, my barley—"

"You started your hay-making ten days too late," Segerson interrupted sternly. "You had plenty of warning. And as for your barley, you sold it in the King's Arms at Barnstaple, when you'd had too much to drink, at thirty per cent, below its value."

Jane turned towards the door.

"I need not stay any longer," she said. "I wanted to look at your farm for myself, Mr. Crockford, and I thought it only right that you should have early notice of my intention to ask you to vacate the place."

The cold truth was finding its way into the man's consciousness. It had a wonderfully sobering effect.

"Look here, ma'am," he demanded, "is it true that you lent Farmer Holroyd four hundred pounds to buy his own farm and the Crocombe brothers two hundred each?"

"Quite true," Jane replied coldly. "What of it?"

"What of it?" the man repeated. "You lend them youngsters money and then you come to me, a man who's been on this land for twenty-two years, and you've nothing to say but 'get out!' Where am I to find another farm at my time of life? Just answer me that, will you?"

"It is not my concern," Jane declared. "I only know that I decline to have any tenants on my property who do not do justice to the land. When I see that they do justice to it, then it is my wish that they should possess it. It is true that I have lent money to some of the farmers round here, but the greater part of what they have put down for the purchase of their holdings is savings,—money they had saved and earned by working early and late, by careful farming and husbandry, by putting money in the bank every quarter. You've had the same opportunity. You have preferred to waste your time and waste your money. You've had more than one warning you know, Crockford."

"Aye, more than a dozen," Segerson muttered.

The man looked at them both and there was a dull hate gathering in his eyes.

"It's easy to talk about saving money and working hard, you that have got everything you want in life and no work to do," he protested "It's enough to make a man turn Socialist to listen to un."

"Mr. Crockford," Jane said, "I am a Socialist and if you take the trouble to understand even the rudiments of socialism, you will learn that the drones have as small a part in that scheme of life as in any other. You have a right to what you produce. It is one of the pleasures of my life to help the deserving to enjoy what they produce. It is also one of the duties, when I find a non-productive person filling a position to which his daily life and character do not entitle him, to pull him up like a weed. That is my idea of socialism, Mr. Crockford. You will leave on March 25th."

They rode homeward into a gathering storm. A mass of black clouds was rolling up from the north, and an unexpected wind came bellowing down the coombs, bending the stunted oaks and dark pines and filling the air with sonorous but ominous music. The hills around soon became invisible, blotted out by fragments of the gathering mists. The cold sleet stung their faces. Out on the moors was no sound but time tinkling of distant sheep bells.

"There's snow coming," Segerson muttered, as he turned up his coat collar.

"It won't do any harm," she answered. "The earth lies warm under it."

The lights of Parracombe, precipitous and unexpected, were like flecks in the sky, wiped out by a sudden driving storm of sleet. A little while later they cantered up the avenue to Woolhanger and Jane slipped from her horse with a little sigh of relief.

"You'd better stay and have some tea, Mr. Segerson," she invited.

"John will take your horse and give him a rubdown."

She changed her habit and, forgetting her guest, indulged in the luxury of a hot bath. She descended some time later to find him sitting in front of the tea tray in the hall. A more than usually gracious smile soon drove the frown from his forehead.

"I really am frightfully sorry," she apologised, as she handed him his tea. "I had no idea I was so wet. You'll have rather a bad ride home."

"Oh, I'm used to it," he answered. "I'm afraid they'll lose a good many sheep on the higher farms, though, if the storm turns out as bad as it threatens. Hear that!"

A tornado of wind seemed to shake the ground beneath their feet. Jane shivered.

"I suppose," she reflected, "that man Crockford thought I was very cruel to-day."

"I will tell you Crockford's point of view," Segerson replied. "He doesn't exactly understand what your aims are, and wherever he goes he hears nothing but praise of the way you have treated your tenants and the way you have tried to turn them into small landowners. He isn't intelligent enough to realise that there is a principle behind all this. He has simply come to feel that he has a lenient landlord and that he has only to sit still and the plums will drop into his mouth, too. Crockford is one of the weak spots in your system, Lady Jane. There is no place for him or his kind in a self-supporting world."

She sighed.

"Then I am afraid he must go down," she said. "He simply stands in the way of better men."

"One reads a good deal of Mr. Tallente, nowadays," Segerson remarked, changing the conversation a little abruptly.

Jane leaned over and stroked the head of a dog which had come to lie at her feet.

"He seems to be making a good deal of stir," she observed.

The young man frowned.

"You know I am not unsympathetic with your views, Lady Jane," he said, a little awkwardly, "but I don't mind admitting that if I had a big stake in the country I should be afraid of Tallente. No one seems to be able to pin him down to a definite programme and yet day by day his influence grows. The Labour Party is disintegrated. The best of all its factions are joining the Democrats. He is practically leader of the Opposition Party to-day and I don't see how they are going to stop his being Prime Minister whenever he chooses."

"Don't you think he'll make a good Prime Minister?" Jane asked.

"No, I don't," was the curt answer. "He is too dark a horse for my fancy."

"I expect Mr. Tallente will be ready with his programme when the time comes," she observed. "He is a people's man, of course, and his proposals will sound pretty terrible to a good many of the old school. Still, something of the sort has to come."

The butler brought in the postbag while they talked. Segerson, as he rose to depart, glanced with curiosity at half a dozen orange-coloured wrappers which were among the rest of the letters.

"Fancy your subscribing to a press-cutting agency, Lady Jane!" he exclaimed. "You haven't been writing a novel under a pseudonym, have you?"

She laughed as she gathered up her correspondence in her hand.

"Don't pry into my secrets," she enjoined. "We may meet in Barnstaple to-morrow. If the weather clears, I want to go in and see those cattle for myself."

The young man took his reluctant departure. Jane crossed the hall, entered her own little sanctum, drew the lamp to the edge of the table and sank into her easy-chair with a little sigh of relief. All the rest of her correspondence she threw to one side. The orange-coloured wrappers she tore off, one by one. As she read, her face softened and her eyes grew very bright. The first cutting was a report of Tallente's last speech in the House, a clever and forceful attack upon the Government's policy of compromise in the matter of recent strikes. The next was a speech at the Holborn Town Hall, on workmen's dwellings, another a thoughtful appreciation of him from the pages of a great review. There was also a eulogy from an American journal and a gloomy attack upon him in the chief Whig organ. When she had finished the pile, she sat for some time gazing at the burning logs. The little epitome of his daily life—there were records there even of many of his social engagements-seemed to carry her into another atmosphere, an atmosphere far removed from this lonely spot upon the moors. She seemed to catch from those printed lines some faint, reflective thrill of the more vital world of strife in which he was living. For a moment the roar of London was in her ears. She saw the lighted thoroughfares, the crowded pavements, the faces of the men and women, all a little strained and eager, so different from the placid immobility of the world in which she lived. She rose to her feet and moved restlessly about the room. Presently she lifted the curtain and looked out. There was a pause in the storm and a great mass of black clouds had just been driven past the face of the watery moon. Even the wind seemed to be holding its breath, but so far as she could see, moors and hillsides were wrapped in one unending mantle of snow. There was no visible sign of any human habitation, no sound from any of the birds or animals who were cowering in their shelters, not even a sheep hell or the barking of a dog to break the profound silence. She dropped the curtain and turned back to her chair. Her feet were leaden and her heart was heavy. The struggle of the day was at an end. Memory was asserting itself. She felt the flush in her cheek, the quickening heat of her heart, the thrill of her pulses as she lived again through those few wild minutes. There was no longer any escape from the wild, confusing truth. The thing which she had dreaded had come.

CHAPTER V

The most popular hostess in London was a little thrilled at the arrival of the moment for which she had planned so carefully. She laid her hand on Tallente's arm and led him towards a comparatively secluded corner of the winter garden which made her own house famous. "I must apologise, Mrs. Van Fosdyke," he said, "for my late appearance. I travelled up from Devonshire this afternoon and found snow all the way. We were nearly two hours late."

"It is all the more kind of you to have turned out at all, then," she told him warmly. "I don't mind telling you that I should have been terribly disappointed if you had failed me. It has been my one desire for months to have you three—the Prime Minister, Lethbridge and you—under my roof at the same time."

"You find politics interesting over here?" Tallente asked, a little curiously.

She flashed a quick glance at him.

"Why, I find them absolutely fascinating," she declared. "The whole thing is so incomprehensible. Just look at to-night. Half of Debrett is represented here, practically the whole of the diplomats, and yet, except yourself, not a single member of the political party who we are told will be ruling this country within a few months. The very anomaly of it is so fascinating."

"There is no necessary kinship between Society and politics," Tallente reminded her. "Your own country, for instance."

Mrs. Van Fosdyke, who was an American, shrugged her shoulders.

"My own country scarcely counts," she protested. "After all, we came into being as a republic, and our aristocracy is only a spurious conglomeration of people who are too rich to need to work. But many of these people whom you see here to-night still possess feudal rights, vast estates, great names, and yet over their heads there is coming this Government, in which they will be wholly unrepresented. What are you going to do with the aristocracy, Mr. Tallente?"

"Encourage them to work," he answered, smiling.

"But they don't know how."

"They must learn. No man has a right to his place upon the earth unless he is a productive human being. There is no room in the world which we are trying to create for the parasite pure and simple."

"You are a very inflexible person, Mr. Tallente."

"There is no place in politics for the wobbler."

"Do you know," she went on, glancing away for a moment, "that my rooms are filled with people who fear you. The Labour Party, as it was understood here five or six years ago, never inspired that feeling. There was something of the tub-thumper about every one of them. I think it is your repression, Mr. Tallente, which terrifies them. You don't say what you are going to do. Your programme is still a secret and yet every day your majority grows. Only an hour ago the Prime Minister told me that he couldn't carry on if you threw down the gage in earnest."

Tallente remained bland, but became a little vague.

"I see Foulds amongst your guests," he observed. "Have you seen his statue of Perseus and Andromeda!'"

She laughed.

"I have, but I am not going to discuss it. Of course, I accept the hint, but as a matter of fact I am a person to be trusted. I ask for no secrets. I have no position in this country. Even my sympathies are at present wobbling. I am simply a little thrilled to have you here, because the Prime Minister is within a few yards of us and I know that before many weeks are past the great struggle will come between you and him as to who shall guide the destinies of this country."

"You forget, Mrs. Van Fosdyke," he objected, "that I am not even the leader of my party. Stephen Dartrey is our chief."

She shook her head.

"Dartrey is a brilliant person," she admitted, "but we all know that he is not a practical politician. The battle is between you and Horlock."

Tallente was watching a woman go by, a woman in black and silver, whose walk reminded him of Jane. His hostess followed his eyes.

"You are one of Alice Mountgarron's admirers?" she enquired.

"I don't even know her," he replied. "She reminded me of some one for a moment."

"She is one of the Duchess of Barminster's daughters," his companion told him. "She married Mountgarron last year. Her sister, Lady Jane, is rather inclined towards your political outlook. She lives in Devonshire and tries to do good."

His eyes followed the woman in black and silver until she had passed out of sight. The family likeness was there, appealing to him curiously, tugging at his heartstrings. His artificial surroundings slipped easily away. He was back on the moors, he felt a sniff of the strong wind, the wholesome exaltation of the empty places. A more wonderful memory still was seeping in upon him. His companion intervened chillingly.

"One never sees your wife, nowadays, Mr. Tallente."

"My wife is in America." he answered mechanically. "She has gone there to stay with some relatives."

"She is interested in politics?"

"Not in the least."

Mrs. Van Fosdyke welcomed a newcomer with a gracious little smile and Tallente rose to his feet. Horlock had left the group in the centre of the room and was making his way towards them.

"At least we can talk here," he said, shaking hands with Tallente, "without any suggestion of a conspiracy. The old gang, you know," he went on, addressing his hostess, "simply close around me when I try to have a word with Tallente. They are afraid of some marvellous combination which is going to shut them out."

"Lethbridge is the only one of them here to-night," She observed, "and he is probably in one of the rooms where they are serving things. Now I must go back to my guests. If I see him, I'll head him off."

She strolled away. The Prime Minister sank back upon a couch. His air of well-bred content with himself and life fell away from him the moment his hostess was out of sight.

"Tallente," he said, "I suppose you mean to break us?"

"I thought we'd been rather friendly," was the quiet reply. "We've been letting you have your own way for nearly a month."

"That is simply because we are on work which we are tackling practically in the fashion you dictated," Horlock pointed out. "When we have finished this Irish business, what are you going to do?"

"I am not the leader of the party," Tallente reminded him.

"From a parliamentary point of view you are," was the impatient protest. "Dartrey is a dreamer. He might even have dreamed away his opportunities if you hadn't come along. Miller would never have handled the House as you have. Miller was made to create factions. You were made to coalesce, to smooth over difficulties, to bring men of opposite points of view into the same camp. You are a genius at it, Tallente. Six months ago I was only afraid of the Democrats. Now I dread them. Shall I tell you what it is that worries me most?"

"If you think it wise."

"Your absence of programme. Why don't you say what you want to do—give us some idea of how far you are going to carry your tenets? Are we to have the anarchy of Bolshevists or the socialism of Marx,—a red flag republic or a classical dictatorship?"

"We are not out for anarchy, at all events," Tallente assured him, "nor for revolutions in the ordinary sense of the word."

"You mean to upset the Constitution?"

"Speaking officially, I do not know. Speaking to you as a fellow politician, I should say that sooner or later some changes are desirable."

"You'll never get away from party government."

"Perhaps not, but I dare say we can find machinery to prevent the house of Commons being used for a debating society."

Horlock, whose sense of humour had never been entirely crushed by the exigencies of political leadership, suddenly grinned.

"The old gang will commit suicide," he declared. "If they aren't allowed to spout, they'll either wither or die. Old man Lethbridge's monthly attacks of high-minded patriotism are the only things that keep him alive."

"I don't fancy," Tallente remarked, "that we shall abandon any of our principles for the sake of keeping Lethbridge alive."

"What the mischief are your principles?"

"No doubt Dartrey would enlighten you, if you chose to go to him," was the indifferent reply. "Within the course of the next few months we shall launch our thunderbolt. You will know then what we claim for the people."

"Hang the people!" Horlock exclaimed. "I've legislated for them myself until I'm sick of it. They're never grateful."

"Perhaps you confine yourself too much to one class," Tallente observed drily. "As a rule, the less intelligent the voter, the more easily he is caught by flashy legislation."

"The operative pure and simple," Horlock announced, "has no political outlook. He'll never see beyond his trades union. You'll never found a great national party with his aid."

His companion smiled.

"Then we shall fail and you will continue to be Prime Minister."

Mrs. Van Fosdyke came back to them, on the arm of a foreign diplomat.

She leaned over to Horlock and whispered:

"Lethbridge has heard that you two are here together and he is on your track. Better separate."

She passed on. The two men strolled away.

"Have you any personal feeling against me, Tallente?" Horlock asked.

"None whatever," his companion assured him. "You did me the best turn in your life when you left me stranded after Hellesfield."

Horlock sighed.

"Lethbridge almost insisted, he looked upon you as a firebrand. He said there would be no repose about a Cabinet with you in it."

"Well, it's turned out for the best," Tallente remarked drily. "Au revoir!"

On his way back to the reception rooms, an acquaintance tapped him on the shoulder.

"One moment, Tallente. Lady Alice Mountgarron has asked me to present you."

Tallente bowed before the woman who stood looking at him pleasantly, but a little curiously. She held out her hand.

"I seem to have heard so much of you from my sister Jane," she said.

"You are neighbours in Devonshire, aren't you?"

"Neighbours from a Devon man's point of view," he answered. "I live half-way down a precipice, and she five miles away, at the back of a Stygian moor, and incidentally a thousand feet above me."

"You seem to have surmounted such geographical obstacles."

"Your sister's friendship is worth greater efforts," Tallente replied.

Lady Alice smiled.

"I wish that some of you could persuade her to come to town occasionally," she said. "Jane is a perfect dear, of course, and I know she does a great deal of good down there, but I can't help thinking sometimes that she is a little wasted. Life must now and then be dreary for her." Tallente seemed for a moment to be looking through the walls of the room. "We are all made differently. Lady Jane is very self-reliant and Devonshire is one of those counties which have a curiously strong local hold."

"But when her moors and her farms are under snow, and Woolhanger is wreathed in mists, and one hears nothing except the moaning of animals in distress, what about the local attraction then?"

"You speak feelingly," Tallente observed, smiling. "I spent a fortnight with Jane last winter," she explains. "I had some idea of hunting. Never again! Only I miss Jane. She is such a dear and I don't see half enough of her."

"I saw her yesterday," Tallente said reminiscently. "This morning she told me she was going to ride out to inspect for herself the farm of the one black sheep amongst her tenants. I looked out towards Woolhanger as I came up in the train. It seemed like a miasma of driven snow and mists."

"Every one to his tastes," Lady Alice observed, as she turned away with a friendly little nod. "I have just an idea, however, that this morning's excursion was a little too much even for Jane."

"What do you mean?" Tallente asked eagerly. Lady Alice looked at him over the top of her fan. She was a woman of instinct. "I had a telegram from her just before I came out," she said. "There wasn't much in it, but it gave me an idea that after all perhaps she is thinking of a short visit to town. Come and see me, Mr. Tallente, won't you? I live in Mount Street—Number 17. My husband used to play cricket with you, I think."

She passed on and Tallente stood looking after her for a moment, a little dazed. A friend came up and took him by the arm.

"Unprotected and alone in the gilded halls of the enemy!" the newcomer exclaimed. "Come and have a drink. By the by, you look as though you'd had good news."

"I have," Tallente assented, smiling.

"Then we'll drink to it—Mum'll. Not bad stuff. This way."

CHAPTER VI

Tallente, for the first time in his life, was dining a few evenings later at Dartrey's house in Chelsea, and he looked forward with some curiosity to this opportunity of studying his chief under different auspices. Dartrey, notwithstanding the fact that he was a miracle of punctuality and devotion to duty, both at the offices in Parliament Street and at the House, seemed to have the gift of fading absolutely out of sight from the ken of even his closest friends when the task of the day was accomplished. He excused himself always, courteously but finally, from accepting anything whatever in the way of social entertainment, he belonged to no clubs, and, if pressed, he frankly confessed a predilection which amounted almost to passion for solitude during those hours not actually devoted to official duties. The invitation to dinner, therefore, was received by Tallente with some surprise. He had grown into the habit of looking upon Dartrey as a man who had no real existence outside the routine of their daily work. He welcomed with avidity, therefore, this opportunity of understanding a little more thoroughly Dartrey's pleasant but elusive personality.

The house itself, situated in a Chelsea square of some repute, was small and unostentatious, but was painted a spotless white and possessed, even from the outside, an air of quiet and unassuming elegance. A trim maid-servant opened the door and ushered him into a drawing-room of grey and silver, with a little faded blue in the silks of the French chairs. There were a few fine-point etchings upon the walls, a small grand piano in a corner, and very little furniture, although the little there was was French of the best period. There were no flowers and the atmosphere would have been chilly, but for the brightly burning fire. Tallente was scarcely surprised when Dartrey's entrance alone indicated the fact that, as was generally supposed, he was free from family ties.

"I am a little early, I am afraid," Tallente remarked, as they shook hands.

"Admirably punctual," the other replied. "I shall make no apologies to you for my small party. I have asked only Miss Miall and Miller to meet you—just the trio of us who came to lure you out of your Devonshire paradise."

"Miller?" Tallente repeated, with instant comprehension.

"Yes! I was thinking, only the other day, that you scarcely see enough of Miller."

"I see all that I want to," was Tallente's candid comment.

Dartrey laid his hand upon his guest's shoulder. In his sombre dinner garb, with low, turned-down collar and flowing black tie, his grey-black beard cut to a point, his high forehead, his straightly brushed-back hair, which still betrayed its tendency to natural curls, he looked a great deal more like an artist of the dreamy and aesthetic type than a man who had elaborated a new system of life and government.

"It is because of the feeling behind those words, Tallente," he said, "that I have asked you to meet him here to-night. Miller has his objectionable points, but he possesses still a great hold upon certain types of the working man. I feel that you should appreciate that a little more thoroughly. The politician, as you should know better than I, has no personal feelings."

"The politician is left with very few luxuries," Tallente replied, with a certain grimness.

Nora was announced, brilliant and gracious in a new dinner gown which she frankly confessed had ruined her, and close behind her Miller, a little ungainly in his overlong dress coat and badly arranged white tie. It struck Tallente that he was aware of the object of the meeting and his manner, obviously intended to be ingratiating, had still a touch of self-conscious truculence.

They went into dinner, a few minutes later, and their host's tact in including Nora in the party was at once apparent. She talked brightly of the small happenings of their day-by-day political life and bridged over the moments of awkwardness before general conversation assumed its normal swing. Dartrey encouraged Miller to talk and they all listened while he spoke of the mammoth trades unions of the north, where his hold upon the people was greatest. He spoke still bitterly of the war, from the moral effect of which, he argued, the working man had never wholly recovered. Tallente listened a little grimly.

"The fervour of self-sacrifice and so-called patriotism which some of the proletariat undoubtedly felt at the outbreak of the war," Miller argued, "was only an incidental, a purely passing sensation compared to the idle and greedy inertia which followed it. The war lost," he went on, "might have acted as a lash upon the torpor of many of these men. Won, it created a wave of immorality and extravagance from which they had never recovered. They spent more than they had and they earned more than they were worth. That is to say, they lived an unnatural life."

"It is fortunate, then," Tallente remarked, "that the new generation is almost here."

"They, too, carry the taint," Miller insisted. Tallente looked thoughtfully across towards his host.

"It seems to me that this is a little disheartening," he said. "It is exactly what one might have expected from Horlock or even Lethbridge. Miller, who is nearer to the proletariat than any of us, would have us believe that the people who should be the bulwark of the State are not fit for their position."

"I fancy," Dartrey said soothingly, "that Miller was talking more as a philosopher than a practical man."

"I speak according to my experience," the latter insisted, a little doggedly.

"Amongst your own constituents?" Tallente asked, with a faint smile, reminiscent of a recent unexpected defeat of one of Miller's partisans in a large constituency.

"Amongst them and others," was the somewhat acid reply. "Sands lost his seat at Tenchester through the apathy of the very class for whom we fight."

"Tenchester is a wonderful place," Nora intervened. "I went down there lately to study certain phases of women's labour. Their factories are models and I found all the people with whom I came in contact exceptionally keen and well-informed."

Miller gnawed his moustache for a moment.

"Then I was probably unpopular there," he said. "I have to tell the truth. Sometimes people do not like it."

The dinner was simply but daintily served. There were wines of well-known vintages and as the meal progressed Dartrey unbent. Eating scarcely anything and drinking less, the purely intellectual stimulus of conversation seemed to unloose his tongue and give to his pronouncements a more pungent tone. Naturally, politics remained the subject of discussion and Dartrey disclosed a little the reason for the meeting which he had arranged.

"The craft of politics," he pointed out, "makes but one inexorable demand upon her followers—the demand for unity. The amazing thing is that this is not generally realised. It seems the fashion, nowadays, to dissent from everything, to cultivate the ego in its narrowest sense rather than to try and reach out and grasp the hands of those around. The fault, I think, is in an over-developed theatrical sense, the desire which so many clever men have for individual notoriety. We Democrats have prospered because we have been free from it. We have been able to sink our individual prejudices in our cause. That is because our cause has been great enough. We aim so high, we see so clearly, that it is rare indeed to find amongst us those individual differences which have been the ruin of every political party up to to-day. We have no Brown who will not serve with Smith, no Robinson who declines to be associated with Jones. We forget the small things which are repugnant to us in a fellowman, because of the great things which bind us together."

"To a certain extent, yes," Tallente agreed, with some reserve in his tone, "yet we are all human. There are some prejudices which no man may conquer. If he pretends he does, he only lives in an atmosphere of falsehood. The strong man loves or hates."

They took their coffee in their host's very fascinating study. There was little room here for decoration. The walls were lined with books, there were a few choice bronzes here and there, a statue of wonderful beauty upon the writing table, and a figure of Justice leaning with outstretched arms over the world, presented to Dartrey by a great French artist. For the rest, there were comfortable chairs, an ample fire, and a round table on which were set out coffee and liqueurs of many sorts.

"You will find that I am not altogether an anchorite," Dartrey observed, as they settled into their places.

"I am a lover of old brandy. The '68 I recommend especially, Tallente, and bring your chair round to the fire. There are cigars and cigarettes at your elbow. Miller, I think I know your taste. Help yourself, won't you?"

Miller drank crème de menthe and smoked homemade Virginia cigarettes. Tallente watched him and sighed. Then, suddenly conscious of his host's critical scrutiny, he felt an impulse of shame, felt that his contempt for the man had in it something almost snobbish. He leaned forward and did his best. Miller had been a school-board teacher, an exhibitioner at college, and was possessed of a singular though limited intelligence. He could deal adequately with any one problem presented by itself and affected only by local conditions, yet the more Tallente talked with him, the more he realised his lack of breadth, his curious weakness of judgment when called upon to consider questions dependent upon varying considerations. As to the right or wrong wording of a clause in the Factory Amendment Act, he could be lucid, explanatory and convincing; as to the justice of the same clause when compared with other forms of legislation, he was vague and unconvincing, didactic and prejudiced. If Dartrey's object had been to bring these two men into closer understanding of each other, he was certainly succeeding. It is doubtful, however, whether the understanding progressed entirely in the fashion he had desired. Nora, curled up in an easy-chair, affecting to be sleepy, but still listening earnestly, felt at last that intervention was necessary. The self-revelation of Miller under Tallente's surgical questioning was beginning to disturb even their host.

"I am being neglected," she complained. "If no one talks to me, I shall go home."

Tallente rose at once and sat on the lounge by her side. Dartrey stood on the hearth rug and plunged into an ingenious effort to reconcile various points of difference which had arisen between his two guests. Tallente all the time was politely acquiescent, Miller a little sullen. Like all men with brains acute enough to deal logically with a procession of single problems, he resented because he failed altogether to understand that a wider field of circumstances could possibly alter human vision.

> Tallente walked home with Nora. They chose the longer way, by the Embankment.

"This is the Cockney's antithesis to the moonlight and hills of you country folk," Nora observed, as she pointed to the yellow lights gashing across the black water.

Tallente drew a long breath of content.

"It's good to be here, anyway. I am glad to be out of that house," he confessed.

"I'm afraid," she sighed, "that our dear host's party was a failure. You and Miller were born in different camps of life. It doesn't seem to me that anything will ever bring you together."

"For this reason," Tallente explained eagerly. "Miller's outlook is narrow and egotistical. He may be a shrewd politician, but there isn't a grain of statesmanship in him. He might make an excellent chairman of a parish council. As a Cabinet Minister he would be impossible."

"He will demand office, I am afraid," Nora remarked.

Tallente took off his hat. He was watching the lights from the two great hotels, the red fires from the funnel of a little tug, Mack and mysterious in the windy darkness.

"I am sick of politics," he declared suddenly. "We are a parcel of fools. Our feet move day and night to the solemn music."

"You, of all men," she protested, "to be talking like this!"

"I mean it," he insisted, a little doggedly. "I have spent too many of my years on the treadmill. A man was born to be either an egoist and parcel out the earth according to his tastes, or to develop like Dartrey into a dreamer.—Curse you!" he added, suddenly shaking his fist at the tall towers of the Houses of Parliament. "You're like an infernal boarding-school, with your detentions and impositions and castigations. There must be something beyond."

"A Cabinet Minister—" she began.

"The sixth form," he interrupted. "There's just one aspiration of life to be granted under that roof and to win it you are asked to stifle all the rest. It isn't worth it."

"It's the greatest game at which men can play," she declared.

"And also the narrowest because it is the most absorbing," he answered. "We have our triumphs there and they end in a chuckle. Don't you love sunshine in winter, strange cities, pictures, pictures of another age, pictures which take your thoughts back into another world, architecture that is not utilitarian, the faces of human beings on whom the strain of life has never fallen? And women—women whose eyes will laugh into yours, who haven't a single view in life, who don't care a fig about improving their race, who want just love, to give and to take?"

She gazed at him in astonishment, a little carried away, her eyes soft, her lips parted.

"But you have turned pagan!" she cried.

"An instant's revolt against the methodism of life," he replied, his feet once more upon the earth. "But the feeling's there, all the same," he went on doggedly. "I want to leave school. I have been there so long. It seems to me my holiday is overdue."

She passed her arm through his. She was a very clever and a very understanding woman.

"That comes of your having ignored us," she murmured.

"It isn't my fault if I have," he reminded her.

"In a sense it is," she insisted. "The woman in your life should be the most beautiful part of it. You chose to make her the stepping-stone to your ambition. Consequently you go through life hungry, you wait till you almost starve, and then suddenly the greatest things in the world which lie to your hand seem like baubles."

"You are hideously logical," he grumbled.

They were walking slower now, within a few yards of the entrance to her flat. Both of them were a little disturbed,—she, full as she was with all the generous impulses of sensuous humanity, intensely awakened, intensely sympathetic.

"Tell me, where is your wife?" she asked.

"In America."

"It is hopeless with her?"

"Utterly and irretrievably hopeless."

"It has been for long?"

"For years."

"And for the sake of your principles," she went on, almost angrily, "your stupid, canonical and dry-as-dust little principles, you've let your life shrivel up."

"I can't help it," he answered. "What would you have me do? Stand in the market place and shout my needs?"

She clung to his arm. "You dear thing!" she said. "You're a great baby!"

They were in the shadow of the entrance to the flats. He suddenly bent over her; his lips were almost on hers. There was a frightened gleam in her eyes, but she made no movement of retreat. Suddenly he drew himself upright.

"That wouldn't help, would it?" he said simply. "Thank you, all the same, Nora. Good-by!"

On his table, when he entered his rooms that night, lay the letter for which he had craved. He opened it almost fiercely. The few lines seemed like a message of hope:

"Don't laugh at me, dear friend, but I am coming to London for a week or two, to my little house in Charles Street. I don't know exactly when. You will find time to come and see me?"

Here the mists seem to have fallen upon us like a shroud, and we can't escape. I galloped many miles this morning, but it was like trying to find the edge of the world.

Please call on my sister at 17 Mount Street. She likes you and wants to see more of you.

JANE.

CHAPTER VII

For some weeks after his chief's dinner party, Tallente slackened a little in his grim devotion to work. A strangely quiescent period of day-by-day political history enabled him to be absent from his place in the House for several evenings during the week, and although he spent a good many hours with Dartrey at Demos House, carefully discussing and elaborating next season's programme, he still found himself with time to spare, and with Jane's note buttoned up in his pocket, he deliberately turned his face towards life in its more genial and human aspect.

He dined one night at the club to which he had belonged for many years, a club frequented chiefly by distinguished literary men, successful barristers, and a sprinkling of actors. His arrival created at first almost a sensation, a slight feeling of constraint even, amongst the little gathering of men drinking their apéritifs in the lounge under the stairs. Somehow or other, there was a feeling that many of the old ties had been broken. Tallente stood for new and menacing things in politics. He had to a certain extent cut himself adrift from the world which starts at Eton and Oxford and ends by making mild puns on the judicial bench, or uttering sonorous platitudes from a properly accredited seat in the House.

Tallente, fully appreciating the atmosphere, nevertheless made strenuous and not unsuccessful efforts to pick up the old threads. He abandoned even the moderation of his daily life. He drank cocktails, champagne and port, laughed heartily at the stories of the day and ransacked his brain to cap them. Of bridge, unfortunately, he knew nothing, but he played pool with some success, and left the club late, leaving behind him curiously mingled opinions as to the cause for this sudden return to his old haunts.

He himself walked through the streets, on his way homeward, conscious of at least partial success, feeling the pleasurable warmth of the wine he had drunk and the companionship for which he had so strenuously sought. He found himself thinking almost enviously of the men with whom he had associated,—Philipson, with whom he had been at college, with three plays running at different theatres, interested, even fascinated by his work, chaffing gaily with his principal actor as to the rendering of some of his lines. Then there was Fardell, also a schoolfellow, now a police magistrate, full of dry and pleasant humour, called by his intimates "The

Beak "; Amberson, poseur and dilettante thirty years ago, but always a good fellow, now an acknowledged master of English prose and a critic whose word was unquestioned. These men, one and all, seemed to be up to the neck in life, kept young and human by the taste of it upon their palate. The contemplation of their whole-sided existence, their sound combination of work and play, produced in him a sort of jealousy, for he knew that there was something behind it, which he lacked.

The night was bright and dry and there were still crowds about Leicester Square, Piccadilly Circle and Piccadilly itself. As he walked, he looked into the faces of the women who passed him by, struggling against his old abhorrence as against one of the sickly offshoots of an over-eclectic epicureanism. They typified not vice but weakness, the unhappy result of man's inevitable revolt against unnatural laws. Yet even then the mingled purity and priggishness encouraged by years of repression forbade any vital change in his sentiments. The toleration for which he sought, when it made its grudging appearance, was mingled with dislike and distrust. He breathed more freely as he turned into the quieter street in which his rooms were situated, passing them by, however, crossing Curzon Street and embarking upon a brief pilgrimage which had become almost a nightly one. Within a very few minutes he paused before a certain number in a street even more secluded than his own. At last the thing which he had so greatly anticipated had happened. There were lights in the house from top to bottom. Jane had arrived!

He walked slowly back and forth several times. The music in his blood, stirred already by the wine he had drunk and the revival of old memories, moved to a new and more wonderful tune. He knew now, without any possibility of self-deception, exactly what he had been waiting for, exactly where all his thoughts and hopes for the future were centered. Was she there now, he wondered, gazing at the windows like a moon-struck boy. He lingered about and fate was kind to him.

A limousine swung around the corner and pulled up in front of the door, a few minutes later. The footman on the box sprang down. He heard her voice as she said "Good-by" to some one. The car rolled smoothly away. She crossed the pavement with an involuntary glance at the tall, approaching figure.

"Jane!" he exclaimed.

She stood quite still, with the latch-key in her hand. The car was out of sight now and they seemed to be almost alone in the street. At first there was something almost unfamiliar in her rather startled face, her coiffured hair, her bare neck with its collar of diamonds. There was a moment of suspense. Then he saw something flash into her eyes and he was glad to be there.

"You?" she exclaimed, a little breathlessly. He plunged into explanations.

"My rooms are close by here in Charges Street," he told her. "I was walking home from the club and saw you step out of the car."

"How could you know that I was coming to-day?" she asked. "I only telephoned Alice after I arrived."

"To tell you the truth," he confessed, "I have got into the habit of walking this way home, in case—well, to-night I have my reward."

She turned the key in the latch and pushed the door open.

"You must come in," she invited.

"Isn't it too late?"

"What does that matter so long as I ask you?"

He followed her gladly into the hall, closing the door behind him.

"That wretched switch is somewhere near here," she said, feeling along the wall.

Her fingers suddenly met his and stayed passive in his grasp. She turned a little around as she realised the nearness of him.

"Jane," he whispered, "I have wanted you so much."

For a single moment she rested in his arms,—a wonderful moment, inexplicable, voluptuous, stirring him to the very depths. Then she slipped away. Her fingers sought the wall once more and the place was flooded with light.

"You must come in here for a moment," she said, opening the nearest door. "I shall not ask you to share my milk, and I am afraid I don't know where to get you a whisky and soda, but you can light a cigarette and just tell me how things are and when you are coming to see me."

He followed her into a comfortable little apartment, furnished in mid-Victorian fashion, but with an easy-chair drawn up to the brightly burning fire. On a table near was a glass of milk and some biscuits. The ermine cloak slipped from her shoulders. She stood with one foot upon the fender, half turned towards him. His eyes rested upon her, filled with a great hunger.

"Well?" she queried.

"You are wonderful," he murmured.

She laughed and for a moment her eyes fell.

"But, my dear man," she said, "I don't want compliments. I want to know the news."

"There is none," he answered. "We are marking time while Horlock digs his own grave."

"You have been amusing yourself?"

"Indifferently. I dined the other night with Dartrey, to-night at the Sheridan Club. The most exciting thing in the twenty-four hours has been my nightly pilgrimage round here."

"How idiotic!" she laughed. "Supposing you had not happened to meet me? You could scarcely have rung my bell at this hour of the night."

"I should have been content to have seen the lights and to have known that you had arrived."

"You dear man!" she exclaimed, with a sudden smile, a smile of entire and sweet friendliness. "I like the thought of your doing that. It is something to know that one is welcome, when one breaks away from the routine of one's life, as I have."

"Tell me why you have done it?" he asked.

She looked back into the fire.

"Everything was going a little wrong," she explained. "One of my farmers was troublesome, and the snow has stopped work and hunting. We lost thirty of our best ewes last week. I found I was getting out of temper with everybody and everything, so I suddenly remembered that I had an empty house here and came up."

"To the city of adventures," he murmured.

She shrugged her shoulders.

"London has never seemed like that to me. I find it generally a very ugly and a very sordid place, where I am hedged in with relatives, generally wanting me to do the thing I loathe.—You have really no news for me, then?"

"None, except that I am glad to see you."

"When will you come and have a long talk?"

"Will you dine with me to-morrow night?" he begged eagerly. "In the afternoon I have committee meetings. Thursday afternoon you could come down to the House, if you cared to."

"Of course I should, but hadn't you better dine here?" she suggested. "I can ask Alice and another man."

"I want to see you alone," he insisted, "for the first time, at any rate."

"Then will you take me to that little place you told me of in Soho?" she suggested. "I don't want a whole crowd to know that I am in town just yet. Don't think that it sounds vain, but people have such a habit of almost carrying one off one's feet. I want to prowl about London and do ordinary things. One or two theatres, perhaps, but no dinner parties. I shan't stay long, I don't suppose. As soon as I hear from Mr. Segerson that the snow has gone and that terrible north wind has died away, I know I shall be wanting to get back."

"You are very conscientious about your work there," he complained. "Don't you ever realise that you may have an even more important mission here?"

For a single moment she seemed troubled. Her manner, when she spoke, had lost something of its calm graciousness.

"Really?" she said. "Well, you must tell me all about it to-morrow night. I shall wear a hat and you must not order the dinner beforehand. I don't mind your ordering the table, because I like a corner, but we must sail into the place just like any other two wanderers. It is agreed?"

He bent over her fingers. His good angel and his instinct of sensibility, which was always appraising her attitude towards him, prompted his studied farewell.

"You will let yourself out?" she begged. "I have taken off my cloak and
I could not face that wind."

"Of course," he answered. "I shall call for you at a quarter to eight to-morrow night. I only wish I could make you understand what it means to have that to look forward to."

"If you can make me believe that," she answered gravely, "perhaps I shall be glad that I have come."

CHAPTER VIII

Whilst Tallente, rejuvenated, and with a wonderful sense of well-being at the back of his mind, was on his feet in the House of Commons on the following afternoon, leading an unexpected attack against the unfortunate Government, Dartrey sat at tea in Nora's study. Nora, who had had a very busy day, was leaning back in her chair, well content though a little fatigued. Dartrey, who had forgotten his lunch in the stress of work, was devoting himself to the muffins.

"While I think of it," he said, "let me thank you for playing hostess so charmingly the other night."

She made him a little bow.

"Your dinner party was a great success."

"Was it?" he murmured, a little doubtfully. "I am not quite so sure. I can't seem to get at Tallente, somehow."

"He is doing his work well, isn't he?"

"The mechanical side of it is most satisfactory," Dartrey confessed.
"He is the most perfect Parliamentary machine that was ever evolved."

"Surely that is exactly what you want? You were always complaining that there was no one to bring the stragglers into line."

"For the present," Dartrey admitted, "Tallente is doing excellently. I wish, though, that I could see a little farther into the future."

"Tell me exactly what fault you find with him?" Nora persisted.

"He lacks enthusiasm already. He makes none of the mistakes which are coincident with genius and he is a little intolerant. He takes no trouble to adapt himself to varying views, he has a fine, broad outlook, but no man can see into every corner of the earth, and what is outside his outlook does not exist."

"Anything else?"

"He is not happy in his work. There is something wanting in his scheme of life. I have built a ladder for him to climb. I have given him the chance of becoming the greatest statesman of to-day. One would think that he had some other ambition."

Nora sighed. She looked across at her visitor a little diffidently.

"I can help you to understand Andrew Tallente," she declared. "His condition is the greatest of all tributes to my sex. He has had an unhappy married life. From forty to fifty he has borne it philosophically as a man may. Now the reaction has come. With the first dim approach of age, he becomes suddenly terrified for the things he is missing."

Dartrey was thoughtful.

"I dare say you are right," he admitted, "but if he needs an Aspasia, surely she could be found?"

Nora rested her head upon her fingers. She seemed to be watching intently the dancing flames. Her broad, womanly forehead was troubled, her soft brown eyes pensive.

"He is fifty years old," she said. "It is rather an anomalous age. At fifty a man's taste is almost hypercritical and his attraction to my sex is on the wane. No, the problem isn't so easy."

Dartrey had finished tea and was feeling for his cigarette case.

"I rather fancied, Nora, that he was attracted by you."

"Well, he isn't, then," she replied, with a smile.

"He was rather by way of thinking that he was, the other night, but that was simply because he was in a curiously unsettled state and he felt that I was sympathetic."

"You are a very clever woman, Nora," he said, looking across at her.

"You could make him care for you if you chose."

"Is that to be my sacrifice to the cause?" she asked. "Am I to give my soul to its wrong keeper, that our party may flourish?"

"You don't like Tallente?"

"I like him immensely," she contradicted vigorously. "If I weren't hopelessly in love with some one else, I could find it perfectly easy to try and make life a different place for him."

He looked at her with trouble in his kind eyes. It was as though he had suddenly stumbled upon a tragedy.

"I have never guessed this about you, Nora," he murmured.

"You are not observant of small things," she answered, a little bitterly.

"Who is the man?"

"That I shall not tell you."

"Do I know him?"

"Less, I should say, than any one of your acquaintance."

He was silent for a moment or two. Then it chanced that the telephone rang for him, with a message from the House of Commons. He gave some instructions to his secretary.

"It is a queer thing," he remarked, as he replaced the receiver, "how far our daily work and our ambitions take us out of our immediate environment. I see you day by day, Nora, I have known you intimately since your school days—and I never guessed."

"You never guessed and I have no time to suffer," she answered. "So we go on until the breaking time comes, until one part of ourselves conquers and the other loses. It is rather like that just now with Andrew Tallente. A few more years and it will probably be like that with me."

He threw his cigarette away as though the flavour had suddenly become distasteful and sat drumming with his fingers upon the table, his eyes fixed upon Nora.

"Tallente's position," he said thoughtfully, "one can understand. He is married, isn't he, and with all the splendid breadth of his intellectual outlook he is still harassed by the social fetters of his birth and bringing up. I can conceive Tallente as a person too highminded to seek to evade the law and too scornful for intrigue. But you, Nora, how is it that your love brings you unhappiness? You are young and free, and surely," he concluded, with a little sigh, "when you choose you can make yourself irresistible."

She looked at him with a peculiar light in her eyes.

"I have proved myself very far from being irresistible," she declared. "The man for whose love my whole being is aching to-day is absolutely unawakened as to my desirability. I enjoy with him the most impersonal friendship in which two people of opposite sexes ever indulged."

"I thought that I was acquainted with all your intimates," Dartrey observed, in a puzzled tone. "Let me meet this man and judge for myself, Nora."

"Do you mean that?" she asked.

"Certainly."

"Very well, then," she acquiesced, "I'll ask him to dinner here. When are you free?"

He glanced through a thin memorandum book.

"On Sunday night?"

"At eight o'clock," she said. "You won't mind a simple dinner, I know. I can promise you that you will be interested. My friend is worth knowing."

Dartrey took his departure a little hurriedly. He had suddenly remembered an appointment at his committee rooms and went off with his mind full of the troubles of a northern constituency. On his way up Parliament Street he met Miller, who turned and walked by his side.

"Heard the news?" the latter asked curtly. "No. Is there any?" was the quick reply.

"Tallente's broken the truce," Miller announced. "There was rather an acid debate on the Compensation Clauses of Hensham's Allotment Bill. Tallente pulled them to pieces and then challenged a division. The Government Whips were fairly caught napping and were beaten by twelve votes." Dartrey's eyes flashed.

"Tallente is a most wonderful tactician," he said. "This is the second time he's forced the Government into a hole. Horlock will never last the session, at this rate."

"There are rumours of a resignation, of course," Miller went on, "but they aren't likely to go out on a snatched division like this."

"We don't want them to," Dartrey agreed. "All the time, though, this sort of thing is weakening their prestige. We shall be ready to give them their coup de grace in about four months."

The two men were silent for a moment. Then Miller spoke again a little abruptly.

"I can't seem to get on with Tallente," he confessed.

"I am sorry," Dartrey regretted. "You'll have to try, Miller. We can't do without him."

"Try? I have tried," was the impatient rejoinder. "Tallente may have his points but nature never meant him to be a people's man. He's too hidebound in convention and tradition. Upon my soul, Dartrey, he makes me feel like a republican of the bloodthirsty age, he's so blasted superior!"

"You're going back to the smaller outlook, Miller," his chief expostulated. "These personal prejudices should be entirely negligible. I am perfectly certain that Tallente himself would lay no stress upon them."

"Stress upon them? Damn it, I'm as good as he is!" Miller exclaimed irritably. "There's no harm in Tallente's ratting, quitting his order and coming amongst us Democrats, but what I do object to is his bringing the mannerisms and outlook of Eton and Oxford amongst us. When I am with him, he always makes me feel that I am doing the wrong thing and that he knows it."

Dartrey frowned a little impatiently.

"This is rubbish, Miller," he pronounced. "It is you who are to blame for attaching the slightest importance to these trifles."

"Trifles!" Miller growled. "Within a very short time, Dartrey, this question will have to be settled. Does Tallente know that I am promised a seat in his Cabinet?"

"I think that he must surmise it."

"The sooner he knows, the better," Miller declared acidly. "Tallente can unbend all right when he likes. He was dining at the Trocadero the other night with Brooks and Ainley and Parker and Saunderson—the most cheerful party in the place. Tallente seemed to have slipped out of himself, and yet there isn't one of those men who has ever had a day's schooling or has ever worn anything but ready-made clothes. He leaves his starch off when he's with them. What's the matter with me, I should like to know? I'm a college man, even though I did go as an exhibitioner. I was a school teacher when those fellows were wielding pick-axes."

Dartrey looked at his companion thoughtfully. For a single moment the words trembled upon his lips which would have brought things to an instant and profitless climax. Then he remembered the million or so of people of Miller's own class and way of thinking, to whom he was a leading light, and he choked back the words.

> "I find this sort of conversation a little peevish, Miller," he said. "As soon as any definite difference of opinion arises between you and Tallente, I will intervene. At present you are both doing good work. Our cause needs you both."

"You won't forget how I stand?" Miller persisted, as they reached their destination.

"No one has ever yet accused me of breaking my word," was the somewhat chilly rejoinder. "You shall have your pound of flesh."

CHAPTER IX

Jane leaned back in her chair, drew off her gloves and looked around her with an appreciative smile. She had somehow the subtle air of being even more pleased with herself and her surroundings than she was willing to admit. Every table in the restaurant was occupied. The waiters were busy: there was an air of gaiety. A faint smell of cookery hung about the place and its clients were undeniably a curious mixture of the bourgeois and theatrical. Nevertheless, she was perfectly content and smiled her greetings to the great Monsieur George, who himself brought their menu.

"We want the best of your ordinary dishes," Tallente told him, "and remember that we do not come here expecting Ritz specialities or a Savoy *chef d'oeuvre*. We want those special *hors d'oeuvres* which you know all about, a sole grilled *a la maison*, a plainly roasted chicken with an endive salad. The sweets are your affair. The savoury must be a cheese soufflé. And for wine—"

He broke off and looked across the table. Jane smiled apologetically.

"You will never bring me out again," she declared. "I want some champagne."

"I never felt more like it myself," he agreed. "The *Pommery*, George, slightly iced, an aperitif now, and the dinner can take its course. We will linger over the *hors d'oeuvres* and we are in no hurry."

George departed and Tallente smiled across at his companion. It was a wonderful moment, this. His steady success of the last few months, the triumph of the afternoon had never brought him one of the thrills which were in his pulses at that moment, not one iota of the pleasurable sense of well-being which was warming his veins. The new menace which had suddenly thrown its shadow across his path was forgotten. Governments might come or go, a career be made or broken upon the wheel. He was alone with Jane.

"Now tell me all the news at Woolhanger?" he asked.

"Woolhanger lies under a mantle of snow," she told him. "There is a wind blowing there which seems to have come straight from the ice of the North Pole and sounds like the devil playing bowls amongst the hills."

"The hunting?"

"All stopped, of course. A few nights ago, two stags came right up to the house and quite a troop of the really wild ponies from over Hawkbridge way. We've never had such a spell of cold in my memory. It reminded one of the snowstorm in 'Lorna Doone.'—But after all, I told you all about Woolhanger last night. I want your news."

"I seem to have settled down with the Democrats," he told her. "I do my best to keep the party in line. The great trades unions are, of course, our chief difficulty, but I think we are making progress even with them. Some of the miners' representatives dined with me at the Trocadero the other night. Good fellows they are, too. There is only one great difficulty," he went on, "in the consolidation of my party, and that is to get a little more breadth into the views of these men who represent the leading industries. They are obsessed with the duties that they owe to their own artificers and the labour connected with the particular industry they represent. It is hard to make them see the importance of any other subject. Yet we need these very men as lawmakers. I want them to study production and the laws of production from a universal point of view."

"I can quite understand," she acquiesced sympathetically, "that you have a difficult class of men to deal with. Tell me what the evening papers mean by their placards?"

"We had a small tactical success against the Government this afternoon," he explained. "It doesn't really amount to anything. We are not ready for their resignation at the moment, any more than they are ready to resign."

"You are an object of terror to all my people," she confided smilingly. "They say that Horlock dare not go to the country and that you could turn him out to-morrow if you cared to."

"So much for politics," he remarked drily.

"So much for politics," she assented. "And now about yourself?"

"A little finger of flame burning in an empty place," he sighed. "That is how life seems to me when I take my hand off the plough."

She answered him lightly, but her face softened and her eyes shone with sympathy.

"Aren't you by way of being just a little sentimental?"

"Perhaps," he admitted. "If I am, let me feel the luxury of it."

"One reads different things of you."

"For instance?"

"Town Topics says that you have become an interesting figure at many social functions. You must meet attractive people there."

"I only wish that I could find them so," he answered. "London has been almost feverishly gay lately and every one seems to have discovered a vogue for entertaining politicians. There seems to be a sort of idea that dangerous corners may be rubbed off us by a judicious application of turtle soup and champagne."

"Cynic!" she scoffed pleasantly.

"Well, I don't know," he went on. "From any other point of view, some of the entertainments to which I have been bidden appear utterly without meaning. However, it is part of my programme to prove to the world that we Democrats can open our arms wide enough to include every class in life. Therefore, I go to many places I should otherwise avoid. I have studied the attitude of the younger women whom I have approached, purely impersonally and without the slightest hypersensitiveness. They have all been perfectly pleasant, perfectly disposed for conversation or any of the usual social amenities. But they know that I have in the background a wife. To flirt with a married man of fifty isn't worth while."

"It appears to me," she said, with a slight note of severity in her tone, "that you have set your mind upon having a perfectly frivolous time."

"Not at all," he objected. "I have simply been experimenting."

The service of dinner had now commenced, and with George in the background, a haughty head waiter a few yards off, and a myrmidon handing them their dishes with a beatific smile, the conversation drifted naturally into generalities. When they resumed their more intimate talk, Tallente felt himself inspired by an ever-increasing admiration for his companion and her adaptability. During this brief interval he had seen many admiring and some wondering glances directed towards Jane and he realised that she was somehow a person entirely apart from any of the others, more beautiful, more distinguished, more desirable. Of the Lady Jane ruling at Woolhanger with a high hand, there was no trace. She looked out upon the gay room with its voluptuous air, its many couples and little parties carrées, with the friendly and sympathetic interest of one who finds herself in agreeable surroundings and whose only desire is to come into touch with them. Her plain black gown, her simple hat with its single quill, the pearls which were her sole adornment, all seemed part of her. She appeared wholly unconscious of the admiration she excited. She who was sometimes inclined, perhaps, to carry herself a little haughtily in her mother's drawing-room, was here only anxious to share in the genial atmosphere of friendliness which the general tone of her surroundings seemed to demand.

"Well, what was the final result of your efforts towards companionship?" she enquired, after they had praised the chicken enthusiastically and the wave of service had momentarily ebbed kitchenwards.

"They have led me to only one conclusion," he answered swiftly.

"Which is?"

"That if you remain on Exmoor and I in Westminster, the affairs of this country are not likely to prosper."

She laughed softly.

"As though I made any real' difference!"

Then she saw a transformed man. The firm mouth suddenly softened, the keen bright eyes glowed. A light shone out of his worn face which few had ever seen there.

"You make all the difference," he whispered. "You of your mercy can save me from the rocks. I have discovered very late in life, too late, many would say, that I cannot build the temples of life with hands and brain alone. Even though the time be short and I have so little to offer, I am your greedy suitor. I want help, I want sympathy, I want love."

There was nothing whatever left now of Lady Jane of Woolhanger. Segerson would probably not have recognised his autocratic mistress. The most timid of her tenant farmers would have adopted a bold front with her. She was simply a very beautiful woman, trembling a little, unsteady, nervous and unsure of herself.

"Oh, I wish you hadn't said that!" she faltered.

"But I must say it," he insisted, with that alien note of tenderness still throbbing in his tone. "You are not a dabbler in life. You have never been afraid to stand on your feet, to look at it whole. There is the solid, undeniable truth. It is a woman's glory to help men on to the great places, and the strangest thing in all the world is that there is only one woman for any one man, and for me—you are the only one woman."

Around them conversation had grown louder, the blue cloud of tobacco smoke more dense, the odour of cigarettes and coffee more pungent. Down in the street a wandering musician was singing a little Neapolitan love song. They heard snatches of it as the door downstairs was opened.

"You have known me for so short a time," she argued. "How can you possibly be sure that I could give you what you want? And in any case, how could I give anything except my eager wishes, my friendship—perhaps, if you will, my affection? But would that bring you content?"

"No!" he answered unhesitatingly. "I want your love, I want you yourself. You have played a woman's part in life. You haven't been content to sit down and wait for what fate might bring you. You have worked out your own destiny and you have shown that you have courage. Don't disprove it."

She looked him in the eyes, very sweetly, but with the shadow of a great disturbance in her face.

"I want to help you," she said. "Indeed, I feel more than you can believe—more than I could have believed possible—the desire, the longing to help. But what is there you can ask of me beyond my hand in yours, beyond all the comradeship which a woman who has more in her heart than she dare own, can give?"

Once more the door was opened below. The voice of the singer came floating up. Then it was closed again and the little passionate cry blotted out. His lips moved but he said nothing. It seemed suddenly, from the light in his face, that he might have been echoing those words which rang in her ears. She trembled and suddenly held her hand across the table.

"Hold my fingers," she begged. "These others will think that we have made a bet or a compact. What does it matter? I want to give you all that I can. Will you be patient? Will you remember that you have found your way along a very difficult path to a goal which no one yet has ever reached? I could tell you more but may not that be enough? I want you to have something to carry away with you, something not too cold, something that burns a little with the beginnings of life and love, and, if you will, perhaps hope. May that content you for a little while, for you see, although I am not a girl, these things, and thoughts of these things, are new to me?"

He drew a little breath. It seemed to him that there was no more beautiful place on earth than this little smoke-hung corner of the restaurant. The words which escaped from his lips were vibrant, tremulous.

"I am your slave. I will wait. There is no one like you in the world."

CHAPTER X

Tallente found a distant connection of his waiting for him in his rooms, on his return from the House at about half-past six,—Spencer Williams, a young man who, after a brilliant career at Oxford, had become one of the junior secretaries to the Prime Minister. The young man rose to his feet at Tallente's entrance and hastened to explain his visit.

"You'll forgive my waiting, sir," he begged. "Your servant told me that you were dining out and would be home before seven o'clock to change."

"Quite right, Spencer," Tallente replied. "Glad to see you. Whisky and soda or cocktail?"

The young man chose a whisky and soda, and Tallente followed suit, waving his visitor back into his chair and seating himself opposite.

"Get right into the middle of it, please," he enjoined.

"To begin with, then, can you break your engagement and come and dine with the Chief?"

"Out of the question, even if it were a royal command," was the firm reply. "My engagement is unbreakable."

"The Chief will be sorry," Williams said. "So am I. Will you go round to Downing Street and see him afterwards?"

"I could," Tallente admitted, "but why? I have nothing to say to him. I can't conceive what he could have to say to me. There are always pressmen loitering about Downing Street, who would place the wrong construction on my visit. You saw all the rubbish they wrote because he and I talked together for a quarter of an hour at Mrs. Van Fosdyke's?"

"I know all about that," Williams assented, "but this time, Tallente, there's something in it. The Chief quarrelled with you for the sake of the old gang. Well, he made a bloomer. The old gang aren't worth six-pence. They're rather a hindrance than help to legislation, and when they're wanted they're wobbly, as you saw this afternoon. Lethbridge went into the lobby with you."

Tallente smiled a little grimly.

"He took particularly good care that I should know that."

"Well, there you are," Williams went on. "The Chief's fed up. I can talk to you here freely because I'm not an official person. Can you discuss terms at all for a rapprochement?"

"Out of the question!"

"You mean that you are too much committed to Dartrey and the Democrats?"

> "'Committed' to them is scarcely the correct way of putting it," Tallente objected. "Their principles are in the main my principles. They stand for the cause I have championed all my life. Our alliance is a natural, almost an automatic one."

"It's all very well, sir," Williams argued, "but Dartrey stands for a Labour Party, pure and simple. You can't govern an Empire by parish council methods."

"That is where the Democrats come in," Tallente pointed out. "They have none of the narrower outlook of the Labour Party as you understand it—of any of the late factions of the Labour Party, perhaps I should say. The Democrats possess an international outlook. When they legislate, every class will receive its proper consideration. No class will be privileged. A man will be ranked according to his production."

Williams smiled with the faint cynicism of clairvoyant youth.

"Sounds a little Utopian, sir," he ventured. "What about Miller?"

"Well, what about him?"

"Are you going to serve with him?"

"Really," Tallente protested, "for a political opponent, or the representative of a political opponent, you're a trifle on the inquisitive side."

"It's a matter that you'll have to face sometime or other," the young man asserted. "I happen to know that Dartrey is committed to Miller."

"I don't see how you can happen to know anything of the sort," Tallente declared, a little bluntly. "In any case, Spencer, my political association or nonassociation with Miller is entirely my own affair, and you can hook it. Remember me to all your people, and give my love to Muriel."

"Nothing doing, eh?" Williams observed, rising reluctantly to his feet.

"You have perception," Tallente replied.

"The Chief was afraid you might be a little difficult about an interview. Those pressmen are an infernal nuisance, anyway. What about sneaking into Downing Street at about midnight, in a cloak and slouch hat, eh?"

"Too much of the cinema about you, young fellow,"
Tallente scoffed.
"Run along now. I have to dress."

Tallente held out his hand good-humouredly. His visitor made no immediate motion to take it.

"There was just one thing more I was asked to mention, sir," he said. "I will be quite frank if I may. My instructions were not to allude to it if your attitude were in the least conciliatory."

"Go on," Tallente bade him curtly.

"There has been a rumour going about that some years ago—while the war was on, in fact—you wrote a very wonderful attack upon the trades unions. This attack was so bitter in tone, so damning in some of its facts, and, in short, such a wonderful production, that at the last moment the late Prime Minister used his influence with you to suspend its publication. It was held over, and in the meantime the attitude of the trades unions towards certain phases of the war was modified, and the collapse of Germany followed soon afterwards. Consequently, that article was never published."

"You are exceedingly well informed," Tallente admitted. "Pray proceed."

"There is in existence," the young man continued, "a signed copy of that article. Its publication at the present moment would probably make your position with the Democratic Party untenable."

"Is this a matter of blackmail?" Tallente asked.

The young man stiffened.

"I am speaking on behalf of the Prime Minister, sir. He desired me to inform you that the signed copy of that article has been offered to him within the last few days."

Tallente was silent for several moments. The young man's subtle intimation was a shock in more ways than one.

"The manuscript to which you refer," he said at last, "was stolen from my study at Martinhoe under somewhat peculiar conditions."

"Perhaps you would like to explain those conditions to
Mr. Horlock,"
Williams suggested.

Tallente held open the door.

"I shall not seek out your Chief," he said, "but I will tell him the truth about that manuscript if at any time we should come together. In the meantime, I am perfectly in accord with the view which your Chief no doubt holds concerning it. The publication of that article at the present moment would inevitably end my connection with the Democratic Party and probably close my political career. This is a position which I should court rather than submit to blackmail direct or indirect."

"My Chief will resent your using such a word, sir," Williams declared.

"Your Chief could have avoided it by a judicious use of the waste-paper basket and an exercise of the gift of silence." Tallente retorted, as the young man took his departure.

Horlock came face to face with Tallente the following afternoon, in one of the corridors of the House and, scarcely troubling about an invitation, led him forcibly into his private room. He turned his secretary out and locked the door.

"A cigar?" he suggested.

Tallente shook his head.

"I want to see what's doing, in a few minutes," he said.

"I can tell you that," Horlock declared. "Nothing at all! I was just off when I happened to see you. You're looking very fit and pleased with yourself. Is it because of that rotten trick you played on us the other day?"

"Rotten? I thought it was rather clever of me," Tallente objected.

> "Perfectly legitimate, I suppose," the other assented grudgingly.
> "That's the worst of having a tactician in opposition."

"You shouldn't have let me get there," was the quick retort.

Horlock drew a paper knife slowly down between his fingers.

"I sent Williams to you yesterday."

"You did. A nice errand for a respectably brought-up young man!"

"Chuck that, Tallente."

"Why? I didn't misunderstand him, did I?"

"Apparently. He told me that you used the word 'blackmail.'"

"I don't think the dictionary supplies a milder equivalent."

"Tallente," said Horlock with a frown, "we'll finish with this once and for ever. I refused the offer of the manuscript in question."

"I am glad to hear it," was the laconic reply.

"Leaving that out of the question, then, I suppose there's no chance of your ratting?"

"Not the faintest. I rather fancy I've settled down for good."

Horlock lit a cigarette and leaned back in his chair.

"No good looking impatient, Tallente," he said. "The door's locked and you know it. You'll have to listen to what I want to say. A few minutes of your time aren't much to ask for."

"Go ahead," Tallente acquiesced.

"There is only one ambition," Horlock continued, "for an earnest politician. You know what that is as well as I do. Wouldn't you sooner be Prime Minister, supported by a recognised and reputable political party, than try to pull the chestnuts out of the fire for your friends Dartrey, Miller and company?"

"So this is the last bid, eh?" Tallente observed.

"It's the last bid of all," was the grave answer. "There is nothing more."

"And what becomes of you?"

"One section of the Press will say that I have shown self-denial and patriotism greater than any man of my generation and that my name will be handed down to history as one of the most single-minded statesmen of the day. Another section will say that I have been forced into a well-deserved retirement and that it will remain a monument to my everlasting disgrace that I brought my party to such straits that it was obliged to compromise with the representative of an untried and unproven conglomeration of fanatics. A third section—"

"Oh, chuck it!" Tallente interrupted. "Horlock, I appreciate your offer because I know that there is a large amount of self-denial in it, but I am glad of an opportunity to end all these discussions. My word is passed to Dartrey."

"And Miller?" the Prime Minister asked, with calm irony.

Tallente felt the sting and frowned irritably.

"I have had no discussions of any sort with Miller," he answered. "He has never been represented to me as holding an official position in the party."

"If you ever succeed in forming a Democratic Government," Horlock said, "mark my words, you will have to include him."

"If ever I accept any one's offer to form a Government," Tallente replied, "it will be on one condition and one condition only, which is that I choose my own Ministers."

"If you become the head of the Democratic Party," Horlock pointed out, "you will have to take over their pledges."

"I do not agree with you," was the firm reply, "and further, I suggest most respectfully that this discussion is not agreeable to me."

An expression of hopelessness crept into Horlock's face.

"You're a good fellow, Tallente," he sighed, "and I made a big mistake when I let you go. I did it to please the moderates and you know how they've turned out. There isn't one of them worth a row of pins. If any one ever writes my political biography, they will probably decide that the parting with you was the greatest of my blunders."

He rose to his feet, swinging the key upon his finger.

"One more word, Tallente," he added. "I want to warn you that so far as your further progress is concerned, there is a snake in the grass somewhere. The manuscript of which Williams spoke to you, and which would of course damn you forever with any party which depended for its existence even indirectly upon the trades unions, was offered to me, without any hint at financial return, on the sole condition that I guaranteed its public production. It is perfectly obvious, therefore, that there is some one stirring who means harm. I speak to you now only as a friend and as a well-wisher. Did I understand Williams to say that the document was stolen from your study at Martinhoe?"

"It was stolen," Tallente replied, "by my secretary, Anthony Palliser, who disappeared with it one night in August."

"'Disappeared' seems rather a vague term," Horlock remarked.

"A trifle melodramatic, I admit," Tallente assented. "So were the circumstances of his—disappearance. I can assure you that I have had the police inspector of fiction asking me curious questions and I am convinced that down in Devonshire I am still an object of suspicion to the local gossips."

"I remember reading about the affair at the time," Horlock remarked, as he unlocked the door. "It never occurred to me, though, to connect it with anything of this sort. Surely Palliser was a cut above the ordinary blackmailer?"

Tallente shrugged his shoulders. "A confusion of ethics," he said. "I dare say you remember that the young man conspired with my wife to boost me into a peerage behind my back However!—"

"One last word, Tallente," Horlock interrupted. "I am not at liberty to tell you from what source the offer as to your article came, but I can tell you this—Palliser was not or did not appear to be connected with it in any way."

"But I know who was," Tallente exclaimed, with a sudden lightning-like recollection of that meeting on the railway platform at Woody Bay.—"Miller!"

Horlock made no answer. To his visitor, however, the whole affair was now clear.

"Miller must have bought the manuscript from Palliser," he said, "when he knew what sort of an offer Dartrey was going to make to me and realised how it would affect him. Horlock, I am not sure, after all, that I don't rather envy you if you decide to drop out of politics. The main road is well enough, but the by-ways are pretty filthy."

Horlock remained gravely silent and Tallente passed out of the room, realising that he had finally severed his connection with orthodox English politics. The realisation, however, was rather more of a relief than otherwise. For fifteen years he had been cumbered with precedent in helping to govern by compromise. Now he was for the clean sweep or nothing. He strolled into the House and back into his own committee room, read through the orders of the day and spoke to the Government Whip. It was, as Horlock had assured him, a dead afternoon. There were a sheaf of questions being asked, none of which were of the slightest interest to any one. With a little smile of anticipation upon his lips, he hurried to the telephone. In a few moments he was speaking to Annie, Lady Jane's maid.

"Will you give her ladyship a message?" he asked. "Tell her that I am unexpectedly free for an hour or so, and ask if I may come around and see her?" The maid was absent from the telephone for less than a minute. When she returned, her message was brief but satisfactory. Her ladyship would be exceedingly pleased to see Mr. Tallente.

CHAPTER XI

Tallente found a taxi on the stand and drove at once to Charles Street. The butler took his hat and stick and conducted him into the spacious drawing-room upon the first floor. Here he received a shock. The most natural thing in the world had happened, but an event which he had never even taken into his calculation. There were half a dozen other callers, all, save one, women. Jane saw his momentary look of consternation, but was powerless to send him even an answering message of sympathy. She held out her hand and welcomed him with a smile.

"This is perfectly charming of you, Mr. Tallente," she said. "I know how busy you must be in the afternoons, but I am afraid I am old-fashioned enough to like my men friends to sometimes forget even the affairs of the nation. You know my sister, I think—Lady Alice Mountgarron? Aunt, may I present Mr. Tallente—the Countess of Somerham. Mrs. Ward Levitte—Lady English—oh! and Colonel Fosbrook."

Tallente made the best of a very disappointing situation. He exchanged bows with his new acquaintances, declined tea and was at once taken possession of by Lady Somerham, a formidable-looking person in tortoise-shell-rimmed spectacles, with a rasping voice and a judicial air.

"So you are the Mr. Tallente," she began, "who Somerham tells me has achieved the impossible!"

"Upon the face of it," Tallente rejoined, with a smile, "your husband is proved guilty of an exaggeration."

"Poor Henry!" his wife sighed. "He does get a little hysterical about politics nowadays. What he says is that you are in a fair way to form a coherent and united political party out of the various factions of Labour, a thing which a little time ago no one thought possible."

Tallente promptly disclaimed the achievement.

"Stephen Dartrey is the man who did that," he declared. "I only joined the Democrats a few months ago."

"But you are their leader," Lady Alice put in.

"Only in the House of Commons," Tallente replied.

"Dartrey is the leader of the party."

"Somerham says that Dartrey is a dreamer," the Countess went on, "that you are the man of affairs and the actual head of them all."

"Your husband magnifies my position," Tallente assured her.

Mrs. Ward Levitte, the wife of a millionaire and a woman of vogue, leaned forward and addressed him.

"Do set my mind at rest, Mr. Tallente," she begged. "Are you going to break up our homes and divide our estates amongst the poor?"

"Is there going to be a revolution?" Lady English asked eagerly. "And is it true that you are in league with all the Bolshevists on the continent?"

Tallente masked his irritation and answered with a smile.

"Civil war," he declared, "commences to-morrow. Every one with a title is to be interned in an asylum, all country houses are to be turned into sanatoriums and all estates will be confiscated."

"The tiresome man won't tell us anything," Lady Alice sighed.

"Of course, he won't," Mrs. Ward Levitte observed. "You can't announce a revolution beforehand truthfully."

"If there is a revolution within the next fifteen years," Tallente said, "I think it will probably be on behalf of the disenfranchised aristocracy, who want the vote back again."

Lady English and Mrs. Levitte found something else to talk about between themselves. Lady Somerham, however, had no intention of letting Tallente escape.

"You are a neighbour of my niece in Devonshire, I believe?" she asked.

He admitted the fact monosyllabically. He was supremely uncomfortable, and it seemed to him that Jane, who was conducting an apparently entertaining conversation with Colonel Fosbrook, might have done something to rescue him.

"My niece has very broad ideas," Lady Somerham went on. "Some of her fellow landowners in Devonshire are very much annoyed with the way she has been getting rid of her property."

"Lady Jane," he pronounced drily, "is in my opinion very wise. She is anticipating the legislation to come, which will inevitably restore the land to the people, from whom, in most cases, it was stolen."

"Well, my husband gave two hundred thousand pounds of good, hard-earned money for Stoughton, where we live," Mrs. Ward Levitte intervened. "So far as I know, the money wasn't stolen from anybody, and I should say that the robbery would begin if the Socialists, or whatever they call themselves, tried to take it away from us to distribute amongst their followers. What do you think, Mr. Tallente? My husband, as I dare say you know, is a banker and a very hard-working man."

"I agree with you," he replied. "One of the pleasing features of the axioms of Socialism adopted by the Democratic Party is that it respects the rights of the wealthy as well as the rights of the poor man. The Democrats may—in fact, they most certainly will—legislate to prevent the hoarding of wealth or to have it handed down to unborn generations, but I can assure you that it does not propose to interfere with the ethics of *meum* and *tuum*."

"I wish I could make out what it's all about," Lady Alice murmured.

"Couldn't you give a drawing-room lecture, Mr. Tallente, and tell us?" the banker's wife suggested.

"I am unfortunately a little short of time for such missionary enterprise," Tallente replied, with unappreciated sarcasm. "Dartrey's volume on 'Socialism in Our Daily Life' will tell you all about it." "Far too dry," she sighed. "I tried to read it but I never got past the first half-dozen pages."

"Some day," Tallente observed coolly, "it may be worth your while, all of you, to try and master the mental inertia which makes thought a labour; the application which makes a moderately good bridge player should be sufficient. Otherwise, you may find yourselves living in an altered state of Society, without any reasonable idea as to how you got there." Mrs. Ward Levitte turned to her hostess.

"Lady Jane," she begged, "come and rescue us, please. We are being scolded. Colonel Fosbrook, we need a man to protect us. Mr. Tallente is threatening us with terrible things."

"We're getting what we asked for," Lady Alice put in quickly.

Colonel Fosbrook caressed for a moment a somewhat scanty moustache. He was a man of early middle-age, with a high forehead, an aquiline nose and a somewhat vague expression.

"I'm afraid my protection wouldn't be much use to you," he said, regarding Tallente with mild interest. "I happen to be one of the few surviving Tories. I imagine that Mr. Tallente's opinions and mine are so far apart that even argument would be impossible."

Tallente acquiesced, smiling.

"Besides which, I never argue, outside the House," he added. "You should stand for Parliament, Colonel Fosbrook, and let us hear once more the Athanasian Creed of politics. All opposition is wholesome."

Colonel Fosbrook glared. The fact that he had three times stood for Parliament and three times been defeated was one of the mortifications of his life. He made his adieux to Jane and departed, and to Tallente's joy a break-up of the party seemed imminent. Mrs. Ward Levitte drifted out and Lady English followed suit. Lady Somerham also rose to her feet, but after a glance at Tallente sat down again.

"My dear Jane," she insisted, "you must dine with us to-night. You haven't been here long enough to have any engagements, and it always puts your uncle in such a good temper to hear that you are coming."

Jane shook her head.

"Sorry, aunt," she regretted, "but I am dining with the Temperleys. I met Diana in Bond Street this morning."

"Thursday, then."

"I am keeping Thursday for a friend. Saturday I am free."

"Saturday we are going into the country," her aunt said, a little ungraciously. "Heaven knows what for! Your uncle hates shooting and always catches cold if he gets his feet wet."

Tallente unwillingly held out his hand to his hostess. He seemed to have no alternative but to make his adieux. Jane walked with him towards the door.

"I am horribly disappointed," he confessed, under his breath.

She smiled a little deprecatingly.

"I couldn't help having people here, could I?"

"I suppose not," he answered, with masculine unreasonableness. "I only know that I wanted to see you alone."

"Men are such schoolboys," she murmured tolerantly. "Even you! I must see my friends, mustn't I, when they know that I am here and call?"

"About that friend on Thursday night?" he went on.

"I am waiting to hear from him," she answered, "whether he prefers to dine here or to take me out."

His ill-humour vanished, and with it some of his stiffness of bearing. His farewell bow from the door to Lady Somerham was distinguished with a new affability.

"If we may be alone," he said softly, "I should like to come here."

Nevertheless, his visit left him a little disturbed, perhaps a little irritable. With all the dominant selfishness which is part of a man's love, he had spent every waking leisure moment since their last meeting in a world peopled by Jane and himself alone, a world in which any other would have been an intruder. His eagerly anticipated visit to her had brought him sharply up against the commonplace facts of their day-by-day existence. He began to realise that she was without the liberty accorded to his sex, or to such women as Nora Miall, whose emancipation was complete. Jane's way through life was guarded by a hundred irritating conventions. He began to doubt even whether she realised the full import of what had happened between them. There was nothing gross about his love, not even a speculation in his mind as to its ultimate conclusion. He was immersed in a wave of sentimentality. He wanted her by his side, free from any restraint. He wanted the joy of her presence, more of those soft, almost reluctant kisses, the mute obedience of her nature to the sweet and natural impulse of her love. Of the inevitable end of these things he never thought. He was like a schoolboy in love for the first time. His desires led him no further than the mystic joy of her presence, the sweet, passionless content of propinquity. For the time the rest lay somewhere in a world of golden promise. The sole right that he burned to claim was the right to have her continually by his side in the moments when he was freed from his work, and even with the prospect of the following night before him, he chafed a little as he reflected that until then he must stand aside and let others claim her. In a fit of restlessness he abandoned his usual table in the House of Commons grillroom, and dined instead at the Sheridan Club, where he drank a great deal of champagne and absorbed with ready appreciation and amusement the philosophy of the man of pleasure. This was one of the impulses which kept his nature pliant even in the midst of these days of crisis.

CHAPTER XII

Whilst Tallente was trying to make up for the years of pleasant goodfellowship which his overstudious life had cost him and to recover touch with the friends of his earlier days, Stephen Dartrey, filled with a queer sense of impending disaster, was climbing the steps to Nora's flat. On the last landing he lingered for a moment and clenched his fingers.

"I am a coward," he reflected sadly. "I have asked for this and it has come."

He stood for a moment perfectly still, with half-closed eyes, seeking for self-control very much in the fashion of a man who says a prayer to himself. Then he climbed the last few stairs, rang the bell and held out both his hands to Nora, who answered it herself.

"Commend my punctuality," he began.

"Why call attention to the one and only masculine virtue?" she replied.
"Let me take your coat."

He straightened his tie in front of the looking-glass and turned to look at her with something like wonder in his eyes.

"Dear hostess," he exclaimed, "what has come to you?"

"An epoch of vanity," she declared, turning slowly around that he might appreciate better the clinging folds of her new black gown. "Don't dare to say that you don't like it, for heaven only knows what it cost me!"

"It isn't only your gown—it's your hair."

"Coiffured," she confided, "by an artist. Not an ordinary hairdresser at all. He only works for a few of our aristocracy and one or two leading ladies on the stage. I pulled it half down and built it up again, but it's an improvement, isn't it?"

"It suits you," he admitted. "But—but your colour!"

"Natural—absolutely natural," she insisted. "You can wet your finger and try if you like. It's excitement. If you look into the depths of my wonderful eyes—I have got wonderful eyes, haven't I?"

"Marvellous."

"You will see that I am suffering from suppressed excitement. To-night is quite an epoch. To tell you the truth, I am rather nervous about it."

"Is he here?"

"You shall see him presently," she promised. "Come along."

"Where is Susan?" he asked, as he followed her.

"Gone out. So has my maid. I had a fancy to turn every one else out of the flat. Your only hot course will be from a chafing-dish. You see, I am anxious to impress—him—with my culinary skill. I hope you will like your dinner, but it will be rather a picnic."

Dartrey glanced back at the hall stand. There was no hat or coat there except his own. He followed Nora into the little study, which was separated only by a curtain from the dining room.

"I think your idea is excellent," he pronounced. "And you will forgive me," he added, producing the parcel which he had been carrying under his arm. "See what I have brought to drink your health and his, even if he does not know yet the good fortune in store for him."

He set down a bottle of champagne upon the table. She laughed softly.

"You dear man!" she exclaimed. "Fancy your thinking of it! I thought you scarcely ever touched wine?"

"I am not a crank," he replied. "Sometimes my guests have told me that I have quite a reasonably good cellar for a man who takes so little himself. To-night I am going to drink a glass of champagne."

"Pommery!" she exclaimed. "I hope you'll be able to open it."

"That shall be my task," he promised. "You needn't worry about flippers. I have some in my pocket. And by the by," he added, glancing at the clock, "where is your other guest? It is ten minutes past eight, and I can hear your chafing-dish sizzling."

She threw back the curtain and took his arm. The table was laid for two. He looked at it in bewilderment and then back at her.

"He has disappointed you?"

She smiled up at him.

"He has disappointed me many, many times," she said, "but not to-night."

"I don't—understand," he faltered.

"I think you do," she answered.

He took the chair opposite to hers. The chafing-dish was between them. He was filled with a curious sense of unreality. It was a little scene, this, out of a story or a play. It didn't actually concern him. It wasn't Nora who sat within a few feet of him, bending down over the chafing-dish and stirring its contents vigorously.

"Of course," she said, "I am perfectly well aware that this is an anti-climax. I am perfectly well aware, too, that you will have a most uncomfortable dinner. You won't know what to say to me and you'll be dying all the time to look in your calendar and see if this is leap year. But even we working women sometimes," she went on, smiling bravely up at him, "have whims. I had a whim, Stephen, to let you know that I am very stupidly fond of you, and although it isn't your fault and I expect nothing from you except that you do not alter our friendship, you just stand in the way whenever I think of marrying any one."

Perhaps because speech seemed so inadequate, Dartrey said nothing. He sat looking at her with a queer emotion in his soft, studious eyes, drumming a little on the table with his finger tips, not quite sure what it meant that his heart was beating like a young man's and a queer sensation of happiness was stealing through his whole being.

"Nothing in the world," he murmured, "could alter our friendship."

"What you see before you," she went on, "is an oyster stew. The true hostess, you see, studying her guest's special tastes. It is very nearly cooked and if you do not pronounce it the most delicious thing you ever ate in your life, I shall be terribly disappointed."

Dartrey sat as still as a man upon whom some narcotic influence rested, and his words sounded almost unnatural.

"I am convinced," he assured her, "that I shall be able to gratify you."

"What you get afterwards you see upon the sideboard: cold partridges—both young birds though—ham, salad of my own mixing, and, behold! my one outburst of extravagance—strawberries. There is also a camembert cheese lying in ambush outside because of its strength. I would suggest that during the three minutes which will ensue before I serve you with the stew, you open the champagne. You are so dumbfounded at my audacity that perhaps a little exercise will be good for you."

Dartrey rose to his feet, produced the corkscrew and found the cork amenable. He filled Nora's glass and his own. Then he leaned over her and took her hand for a moment. His face was full of kindness and he was curiously disturbed.

"You are the dearest child on earth, Nora," he said. "I find myself wishing from the bottom of my heart that it were possible that you could be—something nearer and dearer to me."

She looked feverishly into his face and pushed him away.

"Go and sit down and don't be absurd," she enjoined. "Try and forget everything else except that you are going to eat an oyster stew. That is really the way to take life, isn't it—in cycles—and it doesn't matter then whether one's happy times are bounded by the coming night or the coming years. For five minutes, then, a paradise—of oyster stew."

"It is distinctly the best oyster stew I have ever tasted in my life," he pronounced a few minutes later.

"It is very good indeed," she assented. "Now your turn comes. Go to the sideboard and bring me something. Remember that I am hungry and don't forget the salad. And tell me, incidentally, whether you have heard anything of a rumour going around about Andrew Tallente?"

He served her and himself and resumed his seat.

"A rumour?" he repeated. "No, I have heard nothing. What sort of a rumour?"

"A vague but rather persistent one," she replied. "They say that it is in the power of certain people—to drive him out of political life at any moment."

Dartrey's smile was sufficiently contemptuous but there was a note of anxiety in his tone which he could not altogether conceal.

"These canards are very absurd, Nora," he declared. "The politician is the natural quarry of the blackmailer, but I should think no man of my acquaintance has lived a more blameless life than Andrew Tallente."

"I will tell you in what form the story came to me," she said. "It was from a journalist on the staff of one of our great London dailies. The rumour was that they had been indirectly approached to know if they would pay a large sum for a story, perfectly printable, but which would drive Tallente out of political life."

"Do you know the name of the newspaper?" he asked eagerly.

"I was told," Nora answered, "but under the most solemn abjuration of secrecy. You ought to be able to guess it, though. Then a woman whom I met in the Lyceum Chub this afternoon asked me outright if there was any truth in certain rumours about Tallente, so people must be talking about it."

The cloud lingered on Dartrey's face. He ate and drank in his usual sparing fashion, silently and apparently wrapped in thought. From the other side of the pink-shaded lamp which stood in the middle of the table, Nora watched him with a curious, almost a sardonic sadness in her clear eyes. An hour ago she had looked at herself in the mirror and had been startled at what she saw. The lines of her black gown, the most extravagant purchase of her life, had revealed the beauty of her soft and shapely figure. Her throat and bosom had seemed so dazzlingly white, her hair so rich and glossy, her eyes full of the hope, the softness, almost the anticipatory joy of the woman who has everything to offer to the one man in her life. She had felt as she had looked: almost a girl, with music on her lips and joyous things in her heart, nursing that wonderful gift to her sex,—the hopeless optimism begotten of love. And her little house of cards had tumbled so quickly to the ground, the little denouement on which she had counted had fallen so flat. They two were there alone. The little dinner which she had planned was as near perfection as possible. The champagne bubbled in their glasses. The soft light, the solitude, the stillness,—nothing had failed her, except the man. Stephen sat within a few feet of her, with furrowed brow and mind absorbed by a possible political problem.

Nora made coffee at the table, but they drank it seated in great easy chairs drawn up to the fire. She passed him silently a box of his favourite brand of cigarettes. Perhaps that evidence of her forethought, the mute resignation of her restrained conversation with its attempted note of cheerfulness forced its way through the chinks of his unnatural armour. His whole face suddenly softened. He leaned across and took her fingers into his.

"Dear Nora," he sighed, "what a brute I must seem to you and how difficult it is for me to try and tell you all that is in my heart!"

> "All tasks that are worth attempting are difficult,"
> she murmured.
> "Please go on."

"They are such simple things that I feel," he began, "simple and yet contradictory. I should miss you more out of my life than any other person. I shall resent from my very soul the man who takes you from me. And yet I know what life is, dear. I know how inexorable are its decrees. You have a fancy for me, born of kindness and sympathy, because you know that I am a little lonely. In our thoughts, too, we live so much in the same world. That is just one of the ironies of life, Nora. Our thoughts can move linked together through all the flowery and beautiful places of the world, but our bodies—alas, dear! Do you know how old I really am?"

"I know how young you are," she answered, with a little choke in her throat.

"I am fifty-four years old," he went on. "I am in the last lap of physical well-being, even though my mind should continue to flourish. And you are—how much younger! I dare not think."

"Idiot!" she exclaimed. "At fifty-four you are better and stronger than half the men of forty."

"I have good health," he admitted, "but no constitution or manner of living is of any account against the years. In six years' time I shall be sixty years old."

She leaned a little towards him. Now once more the light was coming back into her eyes. If that was the only thing with him!

"In twelve years' time from now," she said, "I, too, shall turn over a chapter, the chapter of my youth. What is time but a relative thing? Who shall measure your six years against my twelve? The years that count in the life of a man or a woman are the measure of their happiness."

She glided from her chair and sank on her knees beside him. Her lips pleaded. He took her gently, far too gently, into his arms.

"Dear Nora," he begged, "be kind to me. It is for your sake. I know what love should mean for you, what it must mean for every sweet woman. You see only the present. It is my hard task to look into the future for you."

"Can't you understand," she whispered feverishly, "that I would rather have that six years of your life, and its aftermath, than an eternity with any other man? Bend down your head, Stephen."

Her hands were clasped around his neck, her lips forced his. For a moment they remained so, while the room swam around her and her heart throbbed like a mad thing. Then she slowly unlocked her arms and drew away. As though unconscious of what she was doing, she found herself rubbing her lips softly with her handkerchief. She threw herself back in her chair a little recklessly.

"Very well, Stephen," she said, "you know your heart best. Drink your coffee and I'll be sensible again directly."

To his horror she was shaken with sobs. He would have consoled her, but she motioned him away.

"Dear Stephen," she pleaded, "I am sorry—to be such a fool—but this thing has lived with me a long time, and—would you go away? It would be kindest."

He rose to his feet, hesitated for one moment of agony, then crossed the room with a farewell glance at the sad little feast. He closed the door softly behind him, descended the stairs and stood for a moment in the entrance hall, looking out upon the street. A cheerless, drizzling rain was falling. The streets were wet and swept with a cold wind. He looked up and down, thought out the way to his club and shivered, thought out in misery the way back to Chelsea, the turning of his latch-key, the darkened rooms. The house opposite was brilliantly lit up. They seemed to be dancing there and the music of violins floated out into the darkness. Even as he stood there, he felt the bands of self-control weaken about him. A vision of the cold, grey days ahead terrified him. He was pitting his brain against his heart. Lives had been wrecked in that fashion. Philosophy, as the years creep on, is but a dour consolation. He saw himself with the jewel of life in his hand, prepared to cast it away. He turned around and ran up the stone steps, light-hearted and eager as a boy. Nora heard the door open and raised her head. On the threshold stood Stephen, transformed, rejuvenated, the lover shining out of his eyes, the look in his face for which she had prayed. He came towards her, speechless save for one little cry that ended like a sob in his throat, took her into his arms tenderly but fiercely, held her to him while the unsuspected passion of his lips brought paradise into the room.

"You care?" she faltered. "This is not pity?"

He held her to him till she almost swooned. The restraint of so many years was broken down.

"Must I, after all, be the teacher?" he asked passionately, as their lips met again. "Must I show you what love is?"

CHAPTER XIII

Tallente was seated at breakfast a few mornings later when his wife paid him an unexpected visit. She responded to his greeting with a cold nod, refused the coffee which he offered her and the easy-chair which he pushed forward to the fire.

"I got your letter, Andrew," she said, "in which you proposed to call upon me this afternoon. I am leaving town. I am on my way back to New York, as a matter of fact, and I shall have left the hotel by midday, so you see I have come to visit you instead."

"It is very kind," he answered.

She shrugged her shoulders and looked disparagingly around the plainly furnished man's sitting room.

"Not much altered here," she remarked. "It looks just as it did when I used to come to tea with you before we were married."

"The neighbourhood is a conservative one," he replied. "Still, I must confess that I am glad I never gave the rooms up. I don't think that nature intended me to dwell in palaces."

"Perhaps not," she agreed, a little insolently. "It is a habit of yours to think and live parochially. Now what did you want of me, please?"

"There is a scheme on foot," he began, "to bring about my political ruin."

"You don't mean to tell me," she exclaimed, with a sudden light in her eyes, "that you, my well-behaved Andrew, have been playing around? You are not going to be a corespondent or any-thing of that sort?"

"I used the word 'political,'" he reminded her coldly. "You would not understand the situation, but its interest and my danger centres round a certain document which was stolen from my study at Martinhoe on or just before the day of my arrival from London last August."

"How dull!" she murmured.

"That document," he went on, "was purloined by Anthony Palliser from the safe in my study. It was either upon him when he disappeared, or he disposed of it on the afternoon of my arrival to a political opponent of mine—James Miller."

"I had so hoped there was a lady in the case," she yawned.

"If you will give me your attention for one moment longer," he begged, "it will be all I ask. I want you to tell me, first of all, whether James Miller called at the Manor that afternoon and saw Palliser, whether any one called who might have been helping him, or—"

"Well?"

"Whether you have heard anything of Palliser since his disappearance?"

She looked at him hardly.

"You have brought me here to answer these questions?"

"Pardon me," he reminded her, "your coming was entirely your own idea."

"But why should you expect that I should give you information?" she demanded. "You refused to give me the thing I wanted more than anything in life and you have thrown me off like an old glove. If you are threatened with what you call political ruin, why on earth should I intervene to prevent it?"

He shrugged his shoulders.

"You take a severe and I venture to believe a prejudiced view of the situation between us," he replied. "I never promised you that I would make you a peeress. Such a thing never entered into my head. Every pledge I made to you when we were married, I kept. You cannot say the same."

"The man's point of view, I suppose," she scoffed. "Well, I'll tell you what I know, in exchange for a little piece of information from you, which is—what do you know about Anthony Palliser's disappearance?"

He was silent for several moments. The frown on his forehead deepened.

"Your very question," he observed, "answers one of the queries which have been troubling me."

"I have no objection to telling you," she said, "that since that night I have neither seen nor heard of Palliser."

"What happened that night was simple," Tallente explained calmly; "perhaps you would call it primitive. You left the room. I beckoned Palliser to follow me outside. The car was still in the avenue and the servants were taking my luggage in. The spot where we stood on the terrace, too, was exactly underneath your window. I took him by the arm and I led him along the little path towards the cliff. When we came to the open space by the wall, I let him go. I asked him if he had anything to say. He had nothing. I thrashed him."

"You bully!"

Tallente raised his eyebrows.

"Palliser was twenty years younger than I and of at least equal build and strength," he said. "It was not my fault that he seemed unable to defend himself."

"But his disappearance—tell me about that?"

"We were within a few feet of the edge of the cliff. I struck him harder, Perhaps, than I had intended, and he went over. I stood there and hooked down, but I could see nothing. I heard the crashing of some bushes, and after that—silence. I even called out to him, but there was no reply. Some time later, Robert and I searched the cliff and the bay below for his body. We discovered nothing."

"It was high tide that night!" she cried. "You know very well that he must have been drowned!"

"I have answered your question," Tallente replied quietly.

There was a cold fury in her eyes. The veins seemed to stand out on her clenched, worn hands. She looked at him with all the suppressed passion of a creature impotent yet fiercely anxious to strike.

"I shall give information," she cried. "You shall be charged with his murder!"

Tallente shook his head.

"You will waste your time, Stella," he said. "For one thing, a woman may not give evidence against her husband. Another thing, there cannot very well be a charge for murder unsupported by the production of the body. And for a third thing, I should deny the whole story."

Her fury abated, though the hate in her eyes remained.

"I think," she declared, "that you are the most coldblooded creature I ever knew."

The irony of the situation gripped at him. He rose suddenly to his feet, filled with an overwhelming desire to end it.

"Stella," he said, "to me you always seemed, especially during our last few years together, cold and utterly indifferent. I know now that I was mistaken. In your way you cared for Palliser. You starved me. My own fault, you would say? Perhaps. But listen. There is a way into every man's heart and a way into every woman's, but sometimes that way lies hidden except to the one right person, and you weren't the right person for me, and I wasn't the right person for you. Now answer the rest of my question and let us part."

"Tell me," she asked, with almost insolent irony, "do you believe that there could ever have been a right person for you?"

"My God, yes!" he answered, with a sudden fire. "I suffer the tortures of the damned sometimes because I missed my chance! There! I'm telling you this just so that you shall think a little differently, if you can. You and I between us have made an infernal mess of things. It was chiefly my fault. And as regards Palliser—well, I am sorry. Only the fellow—he may have been lovable to you, but he was a coward and a sneak to me—and he paid. I am sorry."

She seemed a little dazed.

"You mean to tell me, Andrew," she persisted, "that there is really some one you care for, care for in the big way—a woman who means as much to you as your place in Parliament—your ambition?"

"More," he declared vigorously. "There isn't a single thing I have or ever have had in life which I wouldn't give for the chance—just a chance—"

"And she cares for you?"

"I think that she would," he answered. "She has been brought up in a very old-fashioned school. She knows of you."

Stella smiled a little bitterly.

"Well," she said, "I suppose I am a brute, but I am glad to know that you can suffer. I hope you will suffer; it makes you seem more human anyhow. But in return for your confidence I will answer the other part of your question. The man Miller was at the Manor that afternoon. Palliser confessed to me that he had given him some important document."

"Given him!"

"Well, sold him, then. Tony hadn't got a shilling in the world and he would never take a halfpenny from me. He had to have money. He told me about it that night before you came. Miller gave him five thousand pounds for it—secret service money from one of the branches of his party. Now you know all about it."

"Yes, I know all about it," Tallente assented, a little bitterly. "You can take your trip to America without a single regret, Stella. I shall certainly never be a Cabinet Minister again, much less Prime Minister of England. Miller can use those papers to my undoing."

She shrugged her shoulders as she turned towards the door.

"You are like the fool," she said, "who tried to build the tower of his life without cement. All very well for experiments, Andrew, when one is young and one can rebuild, but you are a little old for that now, aren't you, and all your brain and all your efforts, and every thought you have been capable of since the day I met you have been given to that one thing. You'll find it a little difficult to start all over again.—Don't—trouble. I know the way down and I have a car waiting. You must take up golf and make a water garden at Martinhoe. I don't know whether you deserve that I should wish you good fortune. I can't make up my mind. But I will—and good-by!"

She left him in the end quite suddenly. He had not even time to open the door for her. Tallente looked out of the window and watched her drive away. His feelings were in a curiously numb state. For Stella he had no feeling whatever. Her confirmation of Palliser's perfidy had awakened in him no new resentment. Only in a vague way he began to realise that his forebodings of the last few days were founded upon a reality. Whether Palliser lived or was dead, it was too late for him to undo the mischief he had done.

Tallente took up the receiver and asked for Dartrey's number. In half an hour he was on his way to see him.

CHAPTER XIV

Tallente had the surprise of his life when he was shown into Dartrey's little dining room. A late breakfast was still upon the table and Nora was seated behind the coffee pot. She took prompt pity upon his embarrassment.

"You've surprised our secret," she exclaimed, "but anyhow, Stephen was going to tell you to-day. We were married the day before yesterday."

"That is why I played truant," Dartrey put in, "although we only went as far as Tunbridge Wells."

Tallente held out a hand to each. For a moment the tragedy in his own life was forgotten.

"I can't wish you happiness, because you have found it," he said. "Wise and wonderful people! Let me see if your coffee is what I should expect, Nora," he went on. "To tell you the truth, I have had rather a disturbed breakfast."

"So have we," Dartrey observed. "You mean the Leeds figures, of course?"

Tallente shook his head.

"I haven't even opened a newspaper."

"Horlock went down himself yesterday to speak for his candidate. Our man is in by five thousand, seven hundred votes."

"Amazing!" Tallente murmured.

"It is the greatest reversal of figures in political history," Dartrey declared. "Listen, Tallente. I was quite prepared to go the Session, as you know, but Horlock's had enough. He is asking for a vote of confidence on Tuesday. He'll lose by at least sixty votes."

"And then?"

"We can't put it off any longer. We shall have to take office. I shall be sent for as the nominal leader of the party and I shall pass the summons on to you. Here is a list of names. Some of them we ought to see unofficially at once."

Tallente looked down the slip of paper. He came to a dead stop with his finger upon Miller's name.

"I know," Dartrey said sympathetically, "but, Tallente, you must remember that men are not made all in the same mould, and Miller is the link between us and a great many of the most earnest disciples of our faith. In politics a man has sometimes to be accepted not so much for what he is as for the power which he represents."

"Has he agreed to serve under me?" Tallente inquired.

"We have never directly discussed the subject," Dartrey replied. "He posed rather as the ambassador when we came to you at Martinhoe, but as a matter of fact, if it interests you to know it, he was strongly opposed to my invitation to you. I am expecting him here every moment—in fact, he telephoned that he was on the way an hour ago."

Miller arrived, a few minutes later, with the air of one already cultivating an official gravity. He was dressed in his own conception of morning clothes, which fitted him nowhere, linen which confessed to a former day's service and a brown Homburg hat. It was noticeable that whilst he was almost fulsome in his congratulations to Nora and overcordial to Dartrey, he scarcely glanced at Tallente and confined himself to a nod by way of greeting.

"Couldn't believe it when you told me over the telephone," he said. "I congratulate you both heartily. What about Leeds, Dartrey?"

"Splendid!"

"It's the end, I suppose?"

"Absolutely! That is why I telephoned for you. Horlock is quite resigned. I understand that they will send for me, but I wish to tell you, Miller, as I have just told Tallente, that I have finally made up my mind that it would not be in the best interests of our party for me to attempt to form a Ministry myself. I am therefore passing the task on to Tallente. Here is a list of what we propose."

> Miller clenched the sheet of paper in his hand without glancing at it.
> His tone was bellicose.

"Do I understand that Tallente is to be Prime Minister?"

> "Certainly! You see I have put you down for the Home Office, Sargent as
> Chancellor of the Exchequer, Saunderson—"

"I don't want to hear any more," Miller interrupted. "It's time we had this out. I object to Tallente being placed at the head of the party."

"And why?" Dartrey asked coldly.

"Because he is a newcomer and has done nothing to earn such a position," Miller declared; "because he has come to us as an opportunist, because there are others who have served the cause of the people for all the years of their life, who have a better claim; and because at heart, mind you, Dartrey, he isn't a people's man."

"What do you mean by saying that I am not a people's man?" Tallente demanded.

"Just what the words indicate," was the almost fierce reply. "You're Eton and Oxford, not board-school and apprentice. Your brain brings you to the cause of the people, not your heart. You aren't one of us and never could be. You're an aristocrat, and before we knew where we were, you'd be legislating for aristocrats. You'd try and sneak them into your Cabinet. It's their atmosphere you've been brought up in. It's with them you want to live. That's what I mean when I say that you're not a people's man, Tallente, and I defy any one to say that you are."

"Miller," Dartrey intervened earnestly, "you are expounding a case from the narrowest point of view. You say that Tallente was born an aristocrat. That may or may not be true, but surely it makes his espousal of the people's cause all the more honest and convincing? For you to say that he is not a people's man, you who have heard his speeches in the house, who have read his pamphlets, who have followed, as you must have followed, his political career is sheer folly."

"Then I am content to remain a fool," Miller rejoined. "Once and for all, I decline to serve under Tallente, and I warn you that if you put him forward, if you go so far, even, as to give him a seat in the Cabinet of the Government it is your job to form, you will disunite the party and bring calamity upon us."

"Have you any further reason for your attitude," Tallente asked pointedly, "except those you have put forward?"

Miller met his questioner's earnest gaze defiantly.

"I have," he admitted.

"State it now, then, please."

Miller rose to his feet. He became a little oratorical, more than usually artificial.

"I make my appeal to you, Dartrey," he said. "You have put forward this man as your choice of a leader of the great Democratic Party, the party which is to combine all branches of Labour, the party which is to stand for the people. I charge him with having written in the last year of the war a scathing attack upon the greatest of British institutions, the trades unions, an article written from the extreme aristocratic standpoint, an article which, if published to-day and distributed broadcast amongst the miners and operatives of the north, would result in a revolution if his name were persisted in."

"I have read everything Tallente has ever written, and I have never come across any such article," Dartrey declared promptly.

"You have never come across it because it was never published," Miller continued, "and yet the fact remains that it was written and offered to the Universal Review. It was actually in type and was only held back at the earnest request of the Government, because on the very day that it should have appeared, an armistice was concluded between the railway men, the miners and the War Council, and the Government was terrified lest anything should happen to upset that armistice."

"Is this true, Tallente?" Dartrey asked anxiously.

"Perfectly. I admit the existence of the article and I admit that it was written with all the vigour I could command, on the lines quoted by Miller. Since, however, it was never published, it can surely be treated as nonexistent?"

"That is just what it cannot be," Miller declared. "The signed manuscript of that article is in the hands of those who would rather see it published than have Tallente Prime Minister."

"Blackmail," the latter remarked quietly.

"You can call it what you please," was the sneering reply. "The facts are as I have stated them."

"But what in the world could have induced you to write such an article, Tallente?" Dartrey demanded. "Your attitude towards Labour, even when you were in the Coalition Cabinet, was perfectly sound."

"It was more than sound, it was sympathetic," Tallente insisted. "That is why I worked myself into the state of indignation which induced me to write it. I will not defend it. It is sufficient to remind you both that when we were hard pressed, when England really had her back to the wall, when coal was the very blood of life to her, a strike was declared in South Wales and received the open sympathy of the faction with which this man Miller here is associated. Miller has spoken plainly about me. Let him hear what I have to say about him. He went down to South Wales to visit these miners and he encouraged them in a course of action which, if other industries had followed suit, would have brought this country into slavery and disgrace. And furthermore, let me remind you of this, Dartrey. It was Miller's branch of the Labour Party who sent him to Switzerland to confer with enemy Socialists and for the last eighteen months of the war he practically lived under the espionage of our secret service—a suspected traitor."

"It's a lie!" Miller fumed.

"It is the truth and easily proved," Tallente retorted. "When peace came, however, Miller's party altered their tactics and the hatchet was to have been buried. My article was directed against the trades unions as they were at that time, not as they are to-day, and I still claim that if public opinion had not driven them into an arrangement with the Government, my article would have been published and would have done good. To publish it now could answer no useful purpose. Its application is gone and the conditions which prompted its tone disappeared."

"I am beginning to understand," Dartrey admitted. "Tell me, how did the manuscript ever leave your possession, Tallente?"

"I will tell you," Tallente replied, pointing over at Miller. "Because that man paid Palliser, my secretary, five thousand pounds out of his secret service money to obtain possession of it."

Miller was plainly discomfited.

"Who told you that lie?" he faltered.

"It's no lie—it's the truth," Tallente rejoined. "You used five thousand pounds of secret service money to gratify a private spite."

"That's false, anyhow," Miller retorted. "I have no personal spite against you, Tallente. I look upon you as a dangerous man in our party, and if I have sought for means to remove you from it, it has been not from personal feeling, but for the good of the cause."

"There stands your leader," Tallente continued. "Did you consult him before you bribed my secretary and hawked about that article, first to Horlock and now to heaven knows whom?"

"It is the first I have heard of it," Dartrey said sternly.

"Just so. It goes to prove what I have declared before—that Miller's attack upon me is a personal one."

"And I deny it," Miller exclaimed fiercely. "I don't like you, Tallente, I hate your class and I distrust your presence in the ranks of the Democratic Party. Against your leadership I shall fight tooth and nail. Dartrey," he went on, "you cannot give Tallente supreme control over us. You will only court disaster, because that article will surely appear and the whole position will be made ridiculous. I am strong enough—that is to say, those who are behind me will take my word on trust—to wreck the position on Thursday. I can keep ninety Labour men out of the Lobby and the Government will carry their vote of confidence. In that case, our coming into power may be delayed for years. We shall lose the great opportunity of this century. Tallente is your friend, Dartrey, but the cause comes first. I shall leave the decision with you."

Miller took his departure with a smile of evil triumph upon his thin lips. He had his moment of discomfiture, however, when Dartrey coldly ignored his extended hand. The two men left behind heard the door slam.

"This is the devil of a business, Tallente!" Dartrey said grimly.

CHAPTER XV

Nora returned to the room as Miller left.

"I don't know whether you wanted me to go," she said to Dartrey, "but I cannot sit and listen to that man talk. I try to keep myself free from prejudices, but there are exceptions. Miller is my pet one. Tell me exactly what he came about? Something disagreeable, I am sure?"

They told her, but she declined to take the matter seriously.

"A position like this is necessarily disagreeable," she argued, "but I have confidence in Mr. Tallente. Remember, this article was written nine years ago, Stephen, and though for twenty-four hours it may make things unpleasant, I feel sure that it won't do nearly the harm you imagine. And think what a confession to make! That man, who aims at being a Cabinet Minister, sits here in this room and admits that he bribed Mr. Tallente's secretary with five thousand pounds to steal the manuscript out of his safe. How do you think that will go down with the public?"

"A certain portion of the public, I am afraid," Tallente said gravely, "will say that I discovered the theft—and killed Palliser."

"Killed Palliser!" Nora repeated incredulously. "I never heard such rubbish!"

"Palliser certainly disappeared on the evening of the day when he parted with the manuscript to Miller," Tallente went on, "and has never been seen or heard of since."

"But there must be some explanation of that," Dartrey observed.

There was a short silence, significant of a curious change in the atmosphere. Tallente's silence grew to possess a queer significance. The ghost of rumours to which neither had ever listened suddenly forced its way back into the minds of the other two. Dartrey was the first to collect himself.

"Tallente," he said, "as a private person I have no desire to ask you a single question concerned with your private life, but we have come to something of a crisis. It is necessary that I should know the worst. Is there anything else Miller could bring up against you?"

"To the best of my belief, nothing," Tallente replied calmly

"That is not sufficient," Dartrey persisted. "Have you any knowledge, Tallente, which the world does not share, of the disappearance of this man Palliser? It is inevitable that if you discovered his treachery there should have been hard words. Did you have any scene with him? Do you know more of his disappearance than the world knows?"

"I do," Tallente replied. "You shall share that knowledge with me to a certain extent. I had another cause for quarrel with Palliser to which I do not choose to refer, but on my arrival home that night I summoned him from the house and led him to an open space. I admit that I chose a primitive method of inflicting punishment upon a traitor. I intended to thrash Palliser, a course of action in which I ask you, Dartrey, to believe, as a man of honour, I was justified. I struck too hard and Palliser went over the cliff."

Neither Nora nor Dartrey seemed capable of speech. Tallente's cool, precise manner of telling his story seemed to have an almost paralysing effect upon them.

"Afterwards," Tallente continued, "I discovered the theft of that document. A faithful servant of mine, and I, searched for Palliser's body, risking our lives in vain, as it turns out, in the hope of recovering the manuscript. The body was neither in the bay below nor hung up anywhere on the cliff. One of two things, then, must have happened. Either Palliser's body must have been taken out by the tide, which flows down the Bristol Channel in a curious way, and will never now be recovered, or he made a remarkable escape and decided, under all the circumstances, to make a fresh start in life."

Nora came suddenly over to Tallente's side. She took his arm and somehow or other the strained look seemed to pass from his face.

"Dear friend," she said, "this is very painful for you, I know, but your other cause of quarrel with Palliser—you will forgive me if I ask—was it about your wife?"

"It was," Tallente replied. "You are just the one person in the world, Nora, in whom I am glad to confide to that extent."

She turned to Dartrey.

"Stephen," she said, "either Palliser is dead and his death can be brought to no one's door, or he is lying hidden and there is no one to blame. You can wipe that out of your mind, can you not? All that we shall have to consider now is the real effect upon the members of our party as a whole, if this article is published."

"Have you a copy of it?" Dartrey asked.

Tallente shook his head.

"I haven't, but if a certain suspicion I have formed is true, I might be able to get you one. In any case, Dartrey, don't come to any decision for a day or two. If it is for the good of the party for you to throw me overboard, you must do it, and I can assure you I'll take the plunge willingly. On the other hand, if you want me to fight, I'll fight."

Dartrey smiled.

"It is extraordinary," he said, "how one realises more and more, as time goes on, how inhuman politics really are. The greatest principle in life, the principle of sticking to one's friends, has to be discarded. I shall take you at your word, Tallente. I am going to consider only what I think would be best for the welfare of the Democratic Party and in the meantime we'll just go on as though nothing had happened."

"If Horlock approaches me," Tallente began—

"He can go out either on a vote of confidence or on an adverse vote on any of the three Bills next week," Dartrey said. "We don't want to drive them out like a flock of sheep. They can go out waving banners and blowing tin horns, if they like, but they're going. It's time the country was governed, and the country, after all, is the only thing that counts.—I am sorry to send you back to work, Tallente, in such a state of uncertainty, but I know it will make no difference to you. Strike where you can and strike hard. Our day is coming and I tell you honestly I can't believe—nothing would make me believe—that you won't be in at the death."

"Don't forget that we meet to-night in Charles Street," Tallente reminded them, as he shook hands.

"Trust Nora," Dartrey replied. "She has been looking forward to it every day."

"I now," Tallente said, as he took up his hat and stick, "am going to confront an editor."

"You are going to try and get me a copy of the article?"

Tallente nodded.

"I am going to try. If my suspicions are correct, you shall have it in twenty-four hours."

Tallente, however, spent a somewhat profitless morning, and it was only by chance in the end that he succeeded in his quest. He strolled into the lounge at the Sheridan Club to find the man he sought the centre of a little group. Greetings were exchanged, cocktails drunk, and as soon as an opportunity occurred Tallente drew his quarry on one side.

"Greening," he said, "if you are not in a hurry, could I have a word with you before lunch?"

"By all means," the other replied. "We'll go into the smoking room."

They strolled off together, followed by more than one pair of curious eyes. An interview between the editor of the daily journal having the largest circulation in Great Britain and Tallente, possible dictator of a new party in politics, was not without its dramatic interest. Tallente wasted no words as soon as they had entered the smoking room and found it empty.

"Do you mind talking shop, Greening?" he asked. "I've been down to your place twice this morning, but couldn't find you."

"Go ahead," the other invited. "I had to go round to Downing Street and then on to see the chief. Sorry you had a fruitless journey."

"I will be quite frank with you," Tallente went on. "What I am going to suggest to you is pure guesswork. A political opponent, if I can dignify the fellow with such a term, has in his possession an article of mine which I wrote some years ago, during the war. I have been given to understand that he means to obtain publication of it for the purpose of undermining my position with the Labour Party. Has he brought it to you?"

"He has," Greening answered briefly.

"Are you going to use it?"

"We are. The article is in type now. It won't be out for a day or two. When it does, we look upon it as the biggest political scoop of this decade."

"I protest to you formally," Tallente said, "against the publication by a respectable journal of a stolen document."

Greening shook his head.

"Won't do, Tallente," he replied. "We have had a meeting and decided to publish. The best I can do for you is to promise that we will publish unabridged any comments you may have to make upon the matter, on the following day."

"I have always understood that there is such a thing as a journalistic conscience," Tallente persisted. "Can you tell me what possible justification you can find for making use of stolen material?"

"The journalistic conscience is permitted some latitude in these matters," Greening answered drily. "We are not publishing for the sake of any pecuniary benefit or even for the kudos of a scoop. We are publishing because we want to do our best to drive you out from amongst the Democrats."

"Did Horlock send Miller to you?" Tallente enquired.

Greening shook his head once more.

"I cannot answer that sort of question. I will say as much as this in our justification. We stand for sane politics and your defection from the ranks of sane politicians has been very seriously felt. We look upon this opportunity of weakening your present position with the Democratic Party as a matter of political necessity. Personally, I am very sorry, Tallente, to do an unfriendly action, but I can only say, like the school-master before he canes a refractory pupil, that it is for your own good."

"I should prefer to remain the arbiter of my own destiny," Tallente observed drily. "I suppose you fully understand that that noxious person, Miller, paid my defaulting secretary five thousand pounds for that manuscript?"

"My dear fellow, if your pocket had been picked in the street of that manuscript and it had been brought to us, we should still have used it," was the frank reply.

Tallente stared gloomily out of the window.

"Then I suppose there is nothing more to be said," he wound up.

"Nothing! Sorry, Tallente, but the chief is absolutely firm. He looks upon you as the monkey pulling the chestnuts out of the fire for the Labour Party and he has made up his mind to singe your paws."

"The Democrats will rule this country before many years have passed," Tallente said earnestly, "whether your chief likes it or not. Isn't it better to have a reasonable and moderate man like myself of influence in their councils than to have to deal with Miller and his lot?"

Greening shrugged his shoulders and glanced at the clock.

"Orders are orders," he declared, "and even if I disbelieved in the policy of the paper, I couldn't afford to disobey. Come and lunch, Tallente."

"Can I have a proof of the article?"

"By all means," was the prompt reply. "Shall I send it to your rooms or here?"

"Send it direct to Stephen Dartrey at the House of Commons."

"I see," Greening murmured thoughtfully, "and then a council of war, eh? Don't forget our promise, Tallente. We'll publish your counterblast, whatever the consequences."

Tallente sighed.

"It isn't decided yet," he said, as they made their way towards the luncheon room, "whether there is to be a counterblast."

CHAPTER XVI

"We have achieved a triumph," Jane declared, when the last of the servants had disappeared and the little party of four were left to their own devices. "We have sat through the whole of dinner and not once mentioned politics."

"You made us forget them," Tallente murmured.

"A left-handed compliment," Jane laughed. "You should pay your tribute to my cook. Mr. Dartrey, I have told you all about my farms and your wife has explained all that I could not understand of her last article in the National. Now I am going to seek for further enlightenment. Tell my why the publication of an article written years ago is likely to affect Mr. Tallente's present position so much?"

"Because," Dartrey explained, "it is an attack upon the most sensitive, the most difficult, and the section of our party furthest removed from us—the great trades unions. Some years ago, Lady Jane, since the war, one of our shrewdest thinkers declared that the greatest danger overshadowing this country was the power wielded by the representatives of these various unions, a power which amounted almost to a dictatorship. We have drawn them into our party through detaching the units. We have never been able to capture them as a whole. Even to-day their leaders are in a curiously anomalous position. They see their power going in the dawn of a more socialistic age. They cannot refuse to accept our principles but in their hearts they know that our triumph sounds the death knell to their power. This article of Tallente's would give them a wonderful chance. Out of very desperation they will seize upon it."

"Have you read the article?" Jane enquired.

"This evening, just before I came," Dartrey replied gravely.

"I can understand," Tallente intervened, "that you feel bound to take this seriously, Dartrey, but after all there is nothing traitorous to our cause in what I wrote. I attacked the trades unions for their colossal and fiendish selfishness when the Empire was tottering. I would do it again under the same circumstances. Remember I was fresh from Ypres. I had seen Englishmen, not soldiers but just hastily trained citizens—bakers, commercial travellers, clerks, small tradesmen—butchered like rabbits but fighting for their country, dying for it—and all the time those blackguardly stump orators at home turned their backs to France and thought the time opportune to wrangle for a rise in wages and bring the country to the very verge of a universal strike. It didn't come off, I know, but there were very few people who really understood how near we were to it. Dartrey, we sacrifice too much of our real feelings to political necessity. I won't apologize for my article; I'll defend it."

Dartrey sighed.

"It will be a difficult task, Tallente. The spirit has gone. People have forgotten already the danger which we so narrowly escaped—forgotten before the grass has grown on the graves of our saviours."

"Still, you wouldn't have Mr. Tallente give in without a struggle?" Jane asked.

"I hope that Tallente will fight," Dartrey replied, "but I must warn you, Lady Jane, that I am the guardian of a cause, and for that reason I am an opportunist. If the division of our party which consists of the trades unionists refuses to listen to any explanation and threatens severance if Tallente remains, then he will have to go."

"So far as your personal view is concerned," Tallente asked, "you could do without Miller, couldn't you?"

"I could thrive without him," Dartrey declared heartily.

"Then you shall," Tallente asserted. "We'll show the world what his local trades unionism stands for. He has belittled the whole principle of cooperation. He twangs all the time one brazen chord instead of seeking to give expression to the clear voices of the millions. Miller would impoverish the country with his accursed limited production, his threatened strikes, his parochial outlook. Englishmen are brimful of common sense, Dartrey, if you know where to dig for it. We'll materialise your own dream. We'll bring the principles of socialism into our human and daily life and those octopus trades unions shall feel the knife."

Jane laid her hand for a moment upon his arm.

"Why aren't you oftener enthusiastic?"

He glanced at her swiftly. Their eyes met. Fearlessly she held his fingers for a moment,—a long, wonderful moment.

"I was getting past enthusiasms," he said; "I was dropping into the dry-as-dust school—the argumentative, logical, cold, ineffectual school. The last few months have changed that. I feel young again. If Dartrey will give me a free hand, I'll deliver up to him Miller's bones."

Dartrey had come to the dinner in an uncertain frame of mind. No one knew better than he the sinister power behind Miller. Yet before Tallente had finished speaking he had made up his mind.

"I'll stand by you, Tallente," he declared, "even if it puts us back a year or so. Miller carries with him always an atmosphere of unwholesome things. He has got the Bolshevist filth in his blood and I don't trust him. No one trusts him. He shall take his following where he will, and if we are not strong enough to rule without them, we'll wait."

It was a compact of curious importance which the two men sealed impulsively with a grip of the hands across the table, and down at Woolhanger, through some dreary months, it was Jane's greatest pleasure to remember that it was at her table it had been made.

Tallente, seeking about for some excuse to remain for a few moments after the departure of the Dartreys, was relieved of all anxiety by Jane's calm and dignified remark.

"I can't part with you just yet, Mr. Tallente," she said. "You are not in a hurry, I hope, and you are so close to your rooms that the matter of taxies need not worry you. And, Mr. Dartrey, next time you come down to my county you must bring your wife over to see me. Woolhanger is so typically Devonshire, I really think you would be interested."

"I shall make Stephen bring me in the spring," Nora promised. "I shall never forget how fascinated we were with the whole place this last summer. Don't forget that you are coming to the House with me tomorrow afternoon."

Jane smiled.

"I am looking forward to it," she declared. "The only annoying part is that that stupid man won't promise to speak."

"I shall have so much to say within the next week or so," Tallente observed, a little grimly, "that I think I had better keep quiet as long as I can."

The moment for which Tallente had been longing came then. The front door closed behind the departing guests. Jane motioned to him to come and sit by her side on the couch.

"I love your friends," she said. "I think Mrs. Dartrey is perfectly sweet and Dartrey is just as wonderful as I had pictured him. They are so strangely unusual," she went on. "I can scarcely believe, even now, that our dinner actually took place in my little room here—Stephen Dartrey, the man I have read about all my life, and this brilliant young wife of his. Thank you so much, dear friend, for bringing them."

"And thank you, dear perfect hostess," he answered. "Do you know what you did? You created an atmosphere in which it was possible to think and talk and see things clearly. Do you realise what has happened? Dartrey has done a great thing. He has thrown over the one menacing power in the advancing cause of the people. He is going to back me against Miller."

"What exactly is Miller's position?" she asked.

"Let me tell you another time," he begged. "I have looked forward so to these few minutes with you. Tell me how much time you are going to spare me this next week?"

She looked at him with the slight, indulgent smile of a woman realising and glad to realise her power. To Tallente she had never seemed more utterly and entirely desirable. It was not for him to know that a French modiste had woven all the cunning and diablerie of the sex lure into the elegant shape, the apparent simplicity of the black velvet which draped her limbs. In some mysterious way, the same spirit seemed to have entered into Jane herself. The evening had been one of unalloyed pleasure. She felt the charm of her companion more than ever before. The pleasant light in her eyes, the courteous, half-mocking phrases with which, as a rule, she fenced herself about in those moments when he sought to draw her closer to him, were gone. Her eyes were as bright as ever, but softer. Her mouth was firm, yet somehow with a faint, womanly voluptuousness in its sweet curves. The fingers which lay unresistingly in his hand were soft and warm.

"As much time as you can spare," she promised him. "I thought, though, that you would be busy tearing Miller bone from bone."

"The game of politics is played slowly," he answered, "sometimes so slowly that one chafes. Dear Jane, I want to see you all the time. So much of what is best in me, best and most effective, comes from you."

"If I can help, I am proud," she whispered.

"You help more than you will ever know, more than my lips can tell you. It is you who have lit the lamp again in my life, you from whom come the fire and strength which make me feel that I shall triumph, that I shall achieve the one thing I have set my heart upon."

"The one thing?" she murmured rashly.

"The one thing outside," he answered, "the desire of my brain. The desire of my heart is here."

She lay in his arms, her lips moved to his and the moments passed uncounted. Then, with a queer little cry, she stood up, covered her face for a moment with her hands and then held them both out to him.

"Dear man," she begged, "dearest of all men—will you go now? To-morrow—whenever you have time—let your servant ring up. I will free myself from any engagement—but please!"

He kissed her fingers and passed out with a murmured word. He knew so little of women and yet some wonderful instinct kept him always in the right path. Perhaps, too, he feared speech himself, lest the ecstasy of those few moments might be broken.

CHAPTER XVII

This is how a weekly paper of indifferent reputation but immense circulation brought Tallente's love affair to a crisis. In a column purporting to set out the editor's curiosity upon certain subjects, the following paragraphs appeared:

Whether a distinguished member of the Democratic Party is not considered just now the luckiest man in the world of politics and love.

Whether the young lady really enjoys playing the prodigal daughter at home and in the country, and what her noble relatives have to say about it.

Whether there are not some sinister rumours going about concerning the politician in question.

Jane's mother, who had arrived in London only the day before, was in Charles Street before her prodigal daughter had finished breakfast. She brandished a copy of the paper in her hand. Jane read the three paragraphs and let the paper slip from her fingers as though she had been handling an unclean thing. She rang the bell and pointed to where it lay upon the floor.

"Take that into the servants' hall and let it be destroyed, Parkins," she ordered.

The Duchess held her peace until the man had left the room. Then she turned resolutely to Jane.

"My dear," she said, "that's posing. Besides, it's indiscreet. Parkins will read it, of course, and it's what that sort of person reads, nowadays, that counts. We can't afford it. The aristocracy has had its fling. To-day we are on our good behaviour."

"I should have thought," Jane declared, "that in these democratic days the best thing we could do would be to prove ourselves human like other people."

"And people call you clever!" her mother scoffed. "Why, my dear child, any slight respect which we still receive from the lower orders is based upon their conviction that somehow or other we are, after all, made differently from them. Sometimes they hate us for it and sometimes they love us for it.

The great thing, nowadays, however, is to cultivate and try and strengthen that belief of theirs."

"How did you come to see this rag?" Jane enquired mildly.

"Your Aunt Somerham brought it round this morning while I was in bed," her mother replied. "It was a great shock to me. Also to your father. He was anxious to come with me but is threatened with an attack of gout."

"And what do you want to say to me about it? Just why did you bring me that rag and show me those paragraphs?"

"My dear, I must know how much truth there is in them. Have you been going about with this man Tallente?"

"To a certain extent, yes," Jane admitted, after a moment's hesitation.

"Chaperoned?"

"Pooh! You know I finished with all that sort of rubbish years ago, mother."

"I am informed that Mr. Tallente is a married man."

Jane flinched a little for the first time.

"All the world knows that," she answered. "He married an American, one of William Hunter's daughters."

"Who has now, I understand, left him?" Lady Jane shrugged her shoulders.

"I do not discuss Mr. Tallente's matrimonial affairs with him."

"Surely," her mother remarked acidly, "in view of your growing intimacy they are of some interest to you both?"

Jane was silent for a moment.

"Just what have you come to say, mother?" she asked, looking up at her, clear-eyed and composed. "Better let's get it over."

The Duchess cleared her throat.

"Jane," she said, "we have become reconciled, your father and I, against our wills, to your strange political views and the isolation in which you choose to live, but when your eccentricities lead you to a course of action which makes you the target for scandal, your family protests. I have come to beg that this intimacy of yours with Mr. Tallente should cease."

"Mother," Jane replied, "for years after I left the schoolroom I subjected myself to your guidance in these matters. I went through three London seasons and made myself as agreeable as possible to whatever you brought along and called a man. At the end of that time I revolted. I am still in revolt. Mr. Tallente interests me more than any man I know and I shall not give up my friendship with him."

"Your aunt tells me that Colonel Fosbrook wants to marry you."

"He has mentioned the fact continually," Jane assented. "Colonel Fosbrook is a very pleasant person who does not appeal to me in the slightest as a husband."

"The Fosbrooks are one of our oldest families," the Duchess said severely. "Arnold Fosbrook is very wealthy and the connection would be most desirable. You are twenty-nine years old, Jane, and you ought to marry. You ought to have children and bring them up to defend the order in which you were born."

"Mother dear," Jane declared, smiling, "this conversation had better cease. Thanks to dear Aunt Jane, I have an independent fortune, Woolhanger, and my little house here. I have adopted an independent manner of life and I have not the least idea of changing it. You have three other daughters and they have all married to your complete satisfaction. I don't think that I shall ever be a very black sheep but you must look upon me as outside the fold.—I hope you will stay to lunch. Colonel Fosbrook is bringing his sister and the Princess is coming."

The Duchess rose to her feet. The family dignity justified itself in her cold withdrawal.

"Thank you, Jane," she said, "I am engaged. I am glad to know, however, that you still have one or two respectable friends."

The setting was the same only the atmosphere seemed somehow changed when Jane received her second visitor that day. She was waiting for him in the small sitting room into which no other visitor save members of the family were ever invited. There was a comfortable fire burning, the roses which had come from him a few hours before were everywhere displayed, and Jane herself, in a soft brown velvet gown, rose to her feet, comely and graceful, to welcome him.

"So we are immortalised!" she exclaimed, smiling.

"That wretched rag!" he replied. "I was hoping you wouldn't see it."

"Mother was here with a copy before eleven o'clock."

Tallente made a grimace.

"Have you sworn to abjure me and all my works?"

"So much so," she told him, "that I have been here waiting for you for at least half an hour and I have put on the gown you said you liked best. Some one said in a book I was reading last week that affection was proved only by trifles. I have certainly never before in my life altered my scheme of clothes to please any man."

He raised her fingers to his lips.

> "You are exercising," he said, "the most wonderful gift of your sex. You are providing an oasis—more than that, a paradise—for a disheartened toiler. It seems that I have enemies whose very existence I never guessed at."

"Well, does that matter very much?" she asked cheerfully. "It was one of your late party, wasn't it, who said that the making of enemies was the only reward of political success?"

"A cheap enough saying," Tallente sighed, "yet with the germs of truth in it. I don't mind the allusion to a sinister rumour. The air will be thick with them before long. The other—well, it's beneath criticism but it hurts."

She laughed whole-heartedly.

"Andrew," she said, "for the first time in my life I am ashamed of you. Here am I, hidebound in conventions, and I could just summon indignation enough to send the paper down to the kitchen to be burnt. Since then I have not even thought of it. I was far more angry that any one should anticipate the troubles which you have to face. Come and sit down."

She led him to the couch and held his fingers in hers as she leaned back in a corner.

"I honestly believe," she went on gently, "that the world is not sufficiently grateful to those who toil for her. Criticism has become a habit of life. Nobody believes or wants to believe in the altruist any longer. I believe that if to-day a rich man stripped himself of all his possessions and obeyed the doctrines of the Bible by giving them to the poor, the Daily something or other would worry around until they found some interested motive, and the Daily something or other else would succeed in proving the man a hypocrite."

He smiled and in the lightening of his face she appreciated for the first time a certain strained look about his eyes and the drawn look about the mouth.

"You are worrying about all this!" she exclaimed.

"Yes, in a way I am worrying," he confessed simply. "Not about the storm itself. I am ready to face that and I think I shall be a stronger and a saner man when the battle has started. In the meantime, I think that what has happened to me is this. I have arrived just at that time of life when a man takes stock of himself and his doings, criticises his own past and wonders whether the things he has proposed doing in the future are worth while."

"You of all men in the world need never ask yourself that," she declared warmly. "Think of your lifelong devotion to your work. Think of the idlers by whom you are surrounded."

"I work," he admitted, "but I sometimes ask myself whether I work with the same motives as I did when I was young. I started life as an altruist. I am not sure now whether I am not working in self-defence, from habit, because I am afraid of falling behind."

"You mean that you have lost your ideals?"

"I wonder," he speculated, "whether any man can carry them through to my age and not be afflicted with doubts as to whether, after all, he has been on the right path, whether he may not have been worshipping false gods."

"Tell me exactly how you started life," she begged.

"Like any other third or fourth son of a bankrupt baronet," he replied. "I went to Eaton and Oxford with the knowledge that I had to carve out my own career and my ambitions when I left the University were entirely personal. I chose diplomacy. I did moderately well, I believe. I remember my first really confidential mission," he went on, with a faint smile, "brought me to Paris, where we met.—Then came Parliament—afterwards the war and a revolution in all my ideas. I suddenly saw the strength and power of England and realised whence it came. I realised that it was our democracy which was the backbone of the country. I realised the injustice of those centuries of class government. I plunged into my old socialistic studies, which I had taken up at Oxford more out of caprice than anything, and I began to have a vision of what I have always since looked upon as the truth. I began to realise that there was some super-divine truth in the equality of all humans, notwithstanding the cheap arguments against it; that by steady and broad-minded government for a generation or so, human beings would be born into the world under more level conditions; and with the fading away of class would be born or rather generated the real and wonderful spirit of freedom. My parliamentary career progressed by leaps and bounds, but when in '15 the war began to go against us, I turned soldier."

"You don't need to tell me anything about that part of your career," she interrupted, with a little smile almost of proprietory pride. "I never forget it."

"When I came back," he continued, "I was almost a fanatic. I worked not from the ranks of the Labour Party itself, because I flatter myself that I was clear-sighted enough to see that the Labour Party as it existed after the war, split up by factions, devoted to the selfish interests of the great trades unions and with the taint of Miller retarding all progress, had nothing in it of the real spirit of freedom. It was every man for his own betterment and the world in which he lived might go hang. I stayed with the Coalitionists, though I was often a thorn in their side, but because I was also useful to them I bent them often towards the light. Then they began to fear me, or rather my principles. It was out of my principles, although I was not nominally one of them, that Dartrey admits freely to-day he built up the Democratic Party. He had been working on the same lines for years, a little too much from the idealistic point of view. He needed the formula. I gave it to him. Horlock came into office again and I worked with him for a time. Gradually, however, my position became more and more difficult. In the end he offered me a post in the Cabinet, induced me to resign my own seat, which I admit was a doubtful one, and sent me to fight Hellesfield, which it was never intended that I should win. Then Miller dug his own grave. He opposed me there and I lost the seat. Horlock was politely regretful, scarcely saw what could be done for me at the moment, was disposed to join in a paltry little domestic plot to send me to the Lords. This was at the time I came down to Martinhoe, the time, except for those brief moments in Paris, when I first met you."

"Pruning roses in a shockingly bad suit of clothes," she murmured.

"And taken for my own gardener! Well, then came Dartrey's visit. He laid his programme before me, offered me a seat and I agreed to lead the Democrats in the House. There I think I have been useful. I knew the game, which Dartrey didn't. Whilst he has achieved almost the impossible, has, except so far as regards Miller's influence amongst the trades unions, brought the great army of the people into line, I accomplished the smaller task of giving them their due weight in the House."

"Very well, then," Jane declared, looking at him with glowing eyes, "there is your stocktaking, taken from your own, the most modest point of view. With your own lips you confess to what you have achieved, to where you stand. What doubts should any sane man have? How can you say that the lamp of your life has burned dull?"

"Insight," he answered promptly. "Don't think that I fear the big fight. I don't. With Dartrey on my side we shall wipe Miller into oblivion. It isn't true to-day to say that he represents the trades unions, for the very reason that the trades unions as solid bodies don't exist any longer. The men have learnt to think for themselves. Many of them are earnest members of the Democratic Party. They have learnt to look outside the interests of the little trade in which they earn their weekly wage. No, it isn't Miller that I am afraid of."

"Then what is it?" she demanded.

"How can I put it?" he went on thoughtfully. "Well, first of all, then, I feel that the Democrats, when they come into power, are going to develop as swiftly as may be all the fevers, the sore places, the jealousies and the pettiness of every other political party which has ever tried to rule the State. I see the symptoms already and that is what I think makes my heart grow faint. I have given the best years of my life to toiling for others. Who believes it? Who is grateful? Who would not say that because I lead a great party in the House of Commons, I have all that I have worked for, that my reward is at hand? And it isn't. If I am Prime Minister in three months' time, there will still be something left of the feeling of weariness I carry with me to-day."

It was a new phase of the man who unconsciously had grown so dominant in her life. She felt the pull at her heartstrings. Her eyes were soft with unshed tears as her arm stole through his.

"Please go on," she whispered.

"There is the ego," he confessed, his voice shaking. "Why it has come to me just at this period of life—but there it is. I have neglected human society, human intercourse, sport, pleasures, the joys of a man who was born to be a man. I am philosopher enough not to ask myself whether it has been worth while, but I do ask myself—what of the next ten years?"

"Who am I to give you counsel?" she asked, trembling.

"The only person who can."

"Then I advise you to go on. This is just a mood. There are muddy places through which one must pass, even in the paths that lead to the mountain tops, muddy and ugly and depressing places. As one climbs, one loses the memory of them."

"But I climb always alone," he answered, with a sudden fierceness. "I walk alone in life. I have been strong enough to do it and I am strong enough no longer.—Jane," he went on, his voice a little unsteady, his hands almost clutching hers, "it is only since I have known you that I have realised from what source upon this earth a man may draw his inspiration, his courage, the strength to face the moving of mountains, day by day. My heart has been as dry as a seed plot. You have brought new things to me, the soft, humanising stimulus of a new hope, a new joy. If I am to fight on to the end, I must have you and your love."

She was trembling and half afraid, but her hands yielded their pressure to his. Her lips and her eyes, the little quivering of her body, all spoke of yielding.

"I have done foolish things in my life," he went on, drawing her nearer to him. "When I was young, I felt that I had the strength of a superman, and that all I needed in life was food for the brain. I placed woman in her wrong place. I sold myself and my chance of happiness that I might gain more power, a wider influence. It was a sin against life. It was a greater crime against myself. Now that the thunder is muttering and the time is coming for the last test, I see the truth as I have never seen it before. Nature has taken me by the hand—shows it me.—Tell me it isn't too late, Jane? Tell me you care? Help me. I have never pleaded for help before. I plead to you."

Her eyes were wet and beautiful with the shine of tears. It seemed to him in that moment of intense emotion that he could read there everything he desired in life. Her lips met his almost eagerly, met his and gave of their own free will.

"Andrew," she murmured, "you see, you are the only man except those of my family whom I have ever kissed, and I kiss you now—again—and again—because I love you."

CHAPTER XVIII

Tallente, notwithstanding the glow of happiness which had taken him down to Westminster with the bearing of a young man, felt occasional little shivers of doubt as he leaned back in his seat during the intervals of a brief but portentous debate and let his mind wander back to that short hour when he seemed to have emptied out all the hidden yearnings which had been lurking in the dark corners of his heart and soul. His love for Jane had no longer the boyish characteristics of a vague worship. He made no further pretences to himself. It was Jane herself, and not the spirit of her sex dwelling in her body, which he desired. A tardy heritage of passion at times rejuvenated him and at others stretched him upon the rack.

He walked home later with Dartrey, clinging to the man with a new sympathy and drinking in with queer content some measure of his happiness. Dartrey himself seemed a little ashamed of its exuberance.

"If it weren't that Nora is so entirely a disciple of our cause, Tallente," he said, "I think I should feel a little like the man in the 'Pilgrim's Progress,' who stopped to pick flowers by the way. She is such a help, though. It was she who pointed out the flaw in that second amendment of Saunderson's, which I had very nearly passed. Did you read her article in the National, too?"

"Wonderful!" Tallente murmured. "There is no living woman who writes such vivid and convincing prose."

"And the amazing part of it all is," Dartrey went on, "that she seeks no reward except just to see the cause prosper. She hasn't the faintest ambition to fill any post in life which could be filled by a man. She would write anonymously if it were possible. She has insight which amounts to inspiration, yet whenever I am with her she makes me feel that her greatest gift is her femininity."

"It must be the most wonderful thing in life to have the help of any one like Nora," Tallente said dreamily.

"My friend," the other rejoined, "I wish I could make you believe this. There is room in the life of the busiest man in the world for an understanding woman. I'll go further. No man can do his best work without her."

"I believe you are right," Tallente assented.

His friend pressed his arm kindly.

"You've ploughed a lonely furrow for a good many years, Tallente," he said. "Nora talks of you so often and so wistfully. She is such an understanding creature.—No, don't go. Just one whisky and soda. It used to be chocolate, but Nora insists upon making a man of me."

Tallente was a little in the shadow of the hall and he witnessed the greeting between Nora and her husband: saw her come out of the study,—a soft, entrancing figure in the little circle of firelight gleaming through the open door. She threw her arms around Dartrey's neck and kissed him.

"Dear," she exclaimed, "how early you are! Come and have an easy-chair by the fire and tell me how every one's been behaving."

Dartrey, with his arm around her waist, turned to Tallente.

"An entirely unrehearsed exhibition, I can assure you, Tallente," he declared.

Nora pouted and passed her other arm through Tallente's.

"That's just like Stephen," she complained, "advertising his domestic bliss. Never mind, there is room for an easy-chair for you."

Tallente took a whisky and soda but declined to sit down.

"I walked home with Stephen," he said, "and then I felt I couldn't go away without seeing you just for a moment, Nora."

"Dear man," she answered, "I should have been terribly hurt if you had. Do make yourself comfortable by the fire. You will be able to check all that Stephen tells me about the debate to-night. He is so inexact."

Tallente shook his head. "I am restless to-night, Nora," he said simply. "I shall walk up to the club."

She let him out herself, holding his hand almost tenderly. "Oh, you poor dear thing!" she said. "I do wish I knew—"

"What?"

"What to wish you—what to hope for you."

He walked away in silence. They both understood so well.—He found his way to the club and ate sandwiches with one or two other men, also just released from the House, but the more he tried to compose himself, the more he was conscious of a sort of fierce restlessness that drove the blood through his veins at feverish pace. He wandered from room to room, played a game of billiards, chafing all the time at the necessity of finishing the game. He hurried away, pleading an appointment. In the hall he met Greening, who led him at once to a secluded corner.

"Prepared with your apologia, Tallente?" he enquired.

"It's in your office at the present moment," Tallente replied, "finished this morning."

Greening stroked his beard. He was a lank, rather cadaverous man, with a face like granite and eyes like polished steel. Few men had anything to say against him. No one liked him.

"How are you regarding the appearance of these outpourings of yours, Tallente?" he asked.

"With equanimity," was the calm rejoinder. "I think I told you what I thought of you and your journalism for having any dealings with a thief and for making yourself a receiver of stolen property. I have nothing to add to that. I am ready to face the worst now and you may find the thunders recoil on your own head."

"No one will ever be able to blame us," Greening replied, "for publishing material of such deep interest to every one, even though it should incidentally be your political death warrant. As a matter of fact, Tallente, I was rather hoping that I might meet you here to-night. The chief and Horlock appear to have had a breeze."

"How does that concern me?" Tallente asked bluntly.

"It may concern you very much indeed. A few days ago I should have told you, as I did, that nothing in the world could stop the publication of that article. To-day I am not so sure. At any rate, I believe there is a chance. Would you care to see the chief?"

"I haven't the slightest desire to," Tallente replied. "I have made my protest. Nothing in the world can affect the morality of your action. At the same time, I have got over my first dread of it. I am prepared with my defence, and perhaps a little in the way of a counterattack. No, I am not going hat in hand to your chief, Greening. He must do as he thinks well."

"If that is your attitude," Greening observed, "things will probably take their course. On the other hand, if you were inclined to have a heart-to-heart talk with the chief and our other editors, I believe that something might come of it."

"In other words," Tallente said coldly, "your chief, who is one of the most magnificent opportunists I ever knew, has suddenly begun to wonder whether he is backing the right horse."

"Something like it, perhaps," Greening admitted. "Look here, Tallente," he went on, "you're a big man in your way and I know perfectly well that you wouldn't throw away a real advantage out of pique. Consider this matter. I can't pledge the paper or the chief. I simply say—see him and talk it over."

Tallente shook his head.

"I am much obliged, Greening," he said, "but I don't want to go through life with this thing hanging over me. Miller has a copy of the article, without a doubt. If you turn him down, he'll find some one else to publish it. I should never know when the thunderbolt was going to fail. I am prepared now and I would rather get it over."

"Is Dartrey going to back you?" Greening asked.

Tallente smiled.

"I can't give away secrets."

Greening turned slowly away.

"I am off for a rubber of bridge," he said. "I am sorry, Tallente. Better dismiss this interview from your mind altogether. It very likely wouldn't have led to anything. All the same, I envy you your confidence. If I could only guess at its source, I'd have a leader for to-morrow morning."

Tallente walked down the stairs with a smile upon his lips. He put on his hat and coat and hesitated for a moment on the broad steps. Then a sudden wonderful thought came to him, an impulse entirely irresistible. He started off westward, walking with feverish haste.

The spirit of adventure sat in his heart as he passed through the crowded streets. The night was wonderfully clear, the stars were brilliant overhead and from behind the Colliseum dome a corner of the yellow moon was showing. He was conscious of a sudden new feeling of kinship with these pleasure-seeking crowds who jostled him here and there upon the pavement. He was glad to find himself amongst them and of them. He felt that he had come down from the chilly heights to walk the lighted highways of the world. The keen air with its touch of frost invigorated him. There was a new suppleness in his pulses, a queer excitement in his whole being, which he scarcely understood until his long walk came to an end and he found himself at a standstill in front of the house in Charles Street, his unadmitted destination.

He glanced at his watch and found that it was half an hour after midnight. There was a light in the lower room into which Jane had taken him on the night of her arrival in town. Above, the whole of the house seemed in darkness. He walked a little way down the street and back again. Jane was dining, he knew, with the Princess de Fénaples, her godmother, and had spoken of going on to a ball with her afterwards. In that case she could scarcely be home for hours. Yet somehow he had a joyful conviction that history would repeat itself, that he would find her, as he had once before, entering the house. His fortune was in the ascendant. Not even the emptiness of the street discouraged him. He strolled a little way along and back again. As he passed the door once more, something bright lying underneath the scraper attracted his notice. He paused and stooped down. Almost before he had realised what he was doing, he had picked up a small key, her latch-key, and was holding it in his hand.

He passed down the street again and there seemed something unreal in the broad pavement, the frowning houses, the glow of the gas lamps. The harmless little key burned his flesh. All the passionate acuteness of life seemed throbbing again in his veins. He retraced his steps, making no plans, obeying only an ungovernable instinct. The street was empty. He thrust the key into the lock, opened the door, replaced the key under the scraper, entered the house and made his way into the room on the right.

Tallente stood there for a few minutes with fast-beating heart. He had the feeling that he had burned his boats. He was face to face now with realities. There was no sound from anywhere. A bright fire was burning in the grate. An easy-chair was drawn up to the side of a small table, on which was placed a tumbler, some biscuits, a box of cigarettes and some matches. A copper saucepan full of milk stood in the hearth, side by side with some slippers,—dainty, fur-topped slippers. Even these slight evidences of her coming presence seemed to thrill him. Time dissolved away into a dream of anticipation. Minutes or hours might have passed before he heard the motor stop outside, her voice bidding some friend a cheerful good night, the turning of the key in the door, the drawing of a bolt, a light step in the hall, and then—Jane.

She was wrapped from head to foot in white furs, a small tiara of emeralds and diamonds on her head. She entered, humming a tune to herself, serene, desirable.

"Andrew!"

Her exclamation, the light in her eyes, the pleasure which swiftly took the place of her first amazement, intoxicated him. He drew her into his arms and his voice shook.

"Jane," he confessed, "I tried to keep away and I couldn't. I stole in here to wait for you. And you're glad—thank heavens you're glad!"

"But how long have you been here?" she asked wonderingly.

He shook his head.

"I don't know. I walked down the street, hoping for a miracle. Then I saw your key under the scraper. I let myself in and waited.—Jane, how wonderful you are!"

Unconsciously she had unfastened and thrown aside her furs. Her arms and neck shone like alabaster in the shaded light. She looked into his face and began to tremble a little.

"You ought not to have done this," she said.

"Why not?" he pleaded.

"If any one had seen you—if the servants knew!"

He laughed and stopped her mouth with a kiss.

"Dear, these things are trifles. The things that count lie between us two only. Do you know that you have been in my blood like a fever all day? You were there in the House this afternoon, you walked the streets with me, you drew me here.—Jane, I haven't felt like this since I was a boy. You have brought me back my youth. I adore you!"

Again she rested willingly enough in his arms, smiling at him, as he drew near to her, with wonderful kindness. The fire of his lips, however, seemed to disturb her. She felt the enveloping turmoil of his passion, now become almost ungovernable, and extricated herself gently from his arms.

"Put my saucepan on the fire, please," she begged. "You will find some whisky and soda on the sideboard there. Parkins evidently thinks that I ought to have a male escort when I come home late."

"I don't want whisky and soda, Jane," he cried passionately. "I want you!"

She rested her hand upon his shoulder.

"And am I not yours, dear," she asked,—"foolishly, unwisely perhaps, but certainly yours?—They were all talking about you to-night at dinner and I was so proud," she went on, a little feverishly. "Our host was almost eloquent. He said that Democracy led by you, instead of proving a curse, might be the salvation of the country, because you have political insight and imperialistic ideas. It is those terrible people who would make a parish council of Parliament from whom one has most to fear."

Tallente made no reply. He was standing on the hearth rug, a few feet away from her, watching as she stirred her milk, watching the curve of her body, the grace of her long, smoothly shining arms. And beyond these things he strove to read what was at the back of her mind.

"We must talk almost in whispers," she went on. "And do have your whisky and soda, Andrew, because you must go very soon."

"It would disturb you very much if your servants were to know of my presence here?" he asked, in a queer, even tone.

"Of course it would," she answered, without looking at him. "As you know, I have lived, from my standpoints, an extraordinarily unconventional life, but that was because I knew myself and was safe. But—I have never done anything like this before in my life."

"You have never been in the same position," he reminded her. "There has never been any one else to consider except yourself."

"True enough," she admitted, "but oughtn't that to make one all the more careful? I loved seeing you when I came in, and I have loved our few minutes together, but I am getting a little nervous. Do you see that it is past two o'clock?"

"There is no one to whom you are accountable for anything in life except to me," he told her passionately.

She laughed softly but a little uneasily.

"Dear Andrew," she said, "there is my own sense of what is seemly and—must I use the horrid word?—my reputation to be considered. As it is, you may be seen leaving the house in the small hours of the morning."

A little shiver passed through him. All the splendid warmth of living seemed to be fading away from his heart and thoughts. He was back again in that empty world of unreal persons. Jane had been a dream. This kindly faced, beautiful but anxious girl was not the Jane to whose arms he had come hotfoot through the streets.

"I ought not to have come," he muttered.

"Dear, I don't blame you in the least," she answered, "only be very careful as you go out. If there is any one passing in the street, wait for a moment."

"I understand," he promised. "I will take the greatest care."

He took up his hat and coat mechanically. She thrust her arm through his and led him to the door, looking furtively into his face as though afraid of what she might find there. Her own heart was beginning to beat faster. She was filled with a queer sense of failure.

"You are not angry with me, Andrew? You know that I have been happy to see you?"

"I am not angry," he answered.

There was a little choking in her throat. She felt the rush of strange things. Her eyes sought his, filled with almost terrified anticipation. It chanced that he was looking away. She clenched her hands. His moment had passed.

"There is something else on your mind, Andrew, I know, but to-night we cannot talk any longer," she said, in something resembling her old tone. "Be very careful, dear. To-morrow—you will come to-morrow."

He walked down the hall with the footsteps of a cat, let himself out silently into the empty street and walked with leaden footsteps to his rooms. It was not until he had reached the seclusion of his study that the change came. A sudden dull fury burned in his heart. He poured himself out whisky and drank it neat. Then he seated himself before his desk and wrote. He did not once hesitate. He did not reread a single sentence. He dug up the anger and the bitterness from his heart and set them out in flaming phrases. A sort of lunacy drove him into the bitterest of extremes. His brain seemed fed with the inspiration of his suffering, fed with cruel epigrams and biting words. He dragged his idol down into the dust, scoffed at the piecemeal passion which measures its gifts, the complacency of an analysed virtue, the sense of well-living and self-contentment achieved in the rubric of a dry-as-dust morality. She had failed him, offered him stones instead of bread.—He signed the letter, blotted it with firm fingers, addressed the envelope, stamped it and dropped it himself into the pillar box at the corner of the street. Then he turned wearily homeward, filled with the strange, almost maniacal satisfaction of the man who has killed the thing he loves.

CHAPTER XIX

There followed days of sullen battle for Tallente, a battle with luck against him, with his back to the wall, with despair more than once yawning at his feet. The house in Charles Street was closed. There had come no word to him from Jane, no news even of her departure except the somewhat surprised reply of Parkins, when he had called on the following afternoon.

"Her ladyship left for Devonshire, sir, by the ten-fifty train."

Tallente went back to the fight with those words ringing in his ears. He had deliberately torn to pieces his house of refuge. Success or failure, what did it matter now? Yet with the dogged courage of one loathing failure for failure's own sake, he flung himself into the struggle.

On the fifth day after Jane's departure, the thunderbolt fell. Tallente's article was printed in full and the weaker members of the Democratic Party shouted at once for his resignation. At a question cunningly framed by Dartrey, Tallente rose in the House to defend his position, and acting on the soundest axiom of military tactics, that the best defence is attack, he turned upon Miller, and with caustic deliberation exposed the plot framed for his undoing. He threw caution to the winds, and though repeatedly and gravely called to order, he poured out his scorn upon his enemy till the latter, white as a sheet, rose to demand the protection of the Speaker. There were very few in the House that day who ever forgot the almost terrifying spectacle of Miller's collapse under his adversary's hurricane assault, or the proud and dignified manner in which Tallente concluded his own defence. But this was only the first step. The Labour Press throughout the country took serious alarm at an attack which, though out of date and influenced by conditions no longer predominant, yet struck a very lusty blow at the very existence of their great nervous centres. Miller, as Chairman of the Associated Trades Unions, issued a manifesto which, notwithstanding his declining influence, exercised considerable effect. It seemed clear that he could rely still upon a good ninety votes in the House of Commons. Horlock became more cheerful. He met Tallente leaving the House one windy March evening and the two men shared a taxi together, westwards.

"Looks to me like another year of office, thanks to you," the Prime Minister observed. "Lenton tells me that we shall have a majority of forty on Thursday week. It is Thursday week you're going for us again, isn't it?"

"Many things may happen before then," Tallente replied, with a little affirmative nod. "Dartrey may decide that I am too expensive a luxury and make friends with Miller."

"I don't think that's likely," Horlock pronounced. "Dartrey is a fine fellow, although he is not a great politician. He is out to make a radical and solid change in the government of this country and he knows very well that Miller's gang will only be a dead weight around his neck. He'd rather wait until he has weaned away a few more votes—even get rid of Miller if he can—and stick to you."

"I think you are right," Tallente said. "I am keeping the Democrats from a present triumph, but if through me they shake themselves free from what I call the little Labourites, I think things will pan out better for them in the long run."

"And in the meantime," Horlock went on, lighting a cigar and passing his case to Tallente, "I must give you the credit of playing a magnificent lone hand. I expected to see Miller fall down in a fit when you went for him in the House. If only his army of adherents could have heard that little duel, I think you'd have won straight through!"

"Unfortunately they couldn't," Tallente sighed, "and it's so hard to capture the attention, to reach the inner understanding, of a great mixed community."

"It's a curious thing about Englishmen," Horlock reflected, "especially the Englishman who has to vote. The most eloquent appeals on paper often leave him unmoved. A perfectly convincing pamphlet he lays down with the feeling that no doubt it's all right but there must be another side. It's the spoken words that tell, every time. What about Miller's election next week?"

"A great deal depends upon that," Tallente replied. "Miller himself says that it is a certainty. On the other hand, Saunderson is going to be proposed, and, with Dartrey's influence, should have a pretty good backing."

They travelled on in silence for a short time. Tallente looked idly through the rain-streaming window at the block of traffic, the hurrying passers-by, the cheerful warmth of the shops and restaurants.

"You take life too seriously, Tallente," his companion said, a little abruptly.

"Do I?" Tallente answered, with a thin smile.

"You do indeed. Look at me. I haven't a line on my face as compared with yours and I've held together a patchwork Government for five years. I don't know when I may be kicked out and I know perfectly well that the Government which succeeds mine is going to undo all I have done and is going to establish a state of things in this country which I consider nothing short of revolutionary. I am not worrying about it, Tallente. The fog of Downing Street stinks sometimes in my nostrils, but I have a little country house—you must come and see me there some day—down in Buckinghamshire, one of these long, low bungalow types, you know, with big gardens, two tennis courts, and a golf course just across the river. My wife spends most of her time there now and every week-end, when I go down, I think what a fool I am to waste my time trying to hold a reluctant nation to principles they are thoroughly sick of. Tallente, you can turn me out whenever you like. The day I settle down for two or three months' rest is going to be one of the happiest of my life."

"You have a wonderful temperament," Tallente remarked, a little sadly.

"Temperament be damned!" was the forcible reply. "I have done my best. When you've said those four words, Tallente, any man ought to have philosophy enough to add, 'Whatever the result may be, it isn't going to be my funeral.' Look at you—haggard, losing weight every day, poring over papers, scheming, planning, writing articles, pouring out the great gift of your life twice as fast as you need. No one will thank you for it. It's quite enough to give half your soul and the joy of living to work for others. Keep something up your sleeve for yourself, Tallente. Mark you, that's the soundest thing in twentieth century philosophy you'll ever hear of.—Corner of Clarges Street right for you, eh?"

Tallente held out his hand.

"Horlock," he said, "thank you. I know you're right but unfortunately I am not like you. I haven't an idyllic retreat, a charming companion waiting for me there, a life outside that's so wonderful. I am driven on because there's nothing else."

Horlock laid his hand upon his companion's shoulder. His tone was suddenly grave—amply sympathetic.

"My friend—and enemy," he said. "If that is so—I'm sorry for you."

CHAPTER XX

There was a tense air of expectation amongst the little company of men who filed into one of the smaller lecture rooms attached to Demos House a few afternoons later. Two long tables were arranged with sixty or seventy chairs and a great ballot box was placed in front of the chairman. A little round of subdued cheers greeted the latter as he entered the room and took his place,—the Right Honourable John Weavel, a Privy Councillor, Member for Sheffield and Chairman of the Ironmaster's Union. Dartrey and Tallente appeared together at the tail end of the procession. Miller sprang at once to his feet and addressed the chairman.

"Mr. Chairman," he said, "I call attention to the fact that two honorary members of this company are present. I submit that as these honorary members have no vote and the present meeting is called with the sole object of voting a chairman for the year, honorary members be not admitted."

Mr. Weavel shook his head.

"Honorary members have the right to attend all meetings of our society," he pronounced. "They can even speak, if invited to do so by the chairman for the day. I am sure that we are all of us very pleased indeed to welcome Mr. Dartrey and Mr. Tallente."

> There was a murmur of approval, in one or two cases a
> little dubious.
> Dartrey smiled a greeting at Weavel.

"I have asked Mr. Tallente to accompany me," he explained, "because, in face of the great issues by which the party to which we all belong is confronted, some question might arise on to-day's proceedings which would render his presence advisable. He does not wish to address you. I, however, with the chairman's permission, before you go to the vote would like to say a few words."

Miller again arose to his feet.

"I submit, Mr. Chairman," he said arrogantly, "that when I had the privilege of being elected last April, no honorary member was present or allowed to speak."

Mr. Weavel rose to his feet.

"Gentlemen," he said, "you know what this meeting is. It is a meeting of fifty-seven representatives of the various trades unions of the country, to elect a single representative to take the chair whenever meetings of this company shall be necessary. This gathering does not exist as a society in any shape or form and we have therefore neither rules nor usages. Mr. Dartrey and Mr. Tallente, although they are honorary members, are, I am sure, welcome guests, and whatever either of them wishes to say to us will, I am sure, be listened to. There is no business. All that we have to do is to vote, to choose our leader for the next twelve months. There are two names put forward—Saunderson and Miller. It is my business only to count the votes you may record. Presuming that no one else wishes to speak, I shall ask Mr. Dartrey to say those few words."

Miller sat frowning and biting his nails. Dartrey moved to the farther end of the room and looked down the long line of attentive faces.

"Weavel," he said, "and you, my friends, I am not here to say a word in favour of either of the two candidates between whom you have to choose to-day. I am here just because you are valued members of the great party which before very long will be carrying upon its shoulders the burden of this country's government, to tell you of one measure which some of you know of already, which may help you to realise how important your to-day's choice will be. You know quite as much about politics as I do. You know very well that the present Government is doomed. But for an unfortunate difference of opinion between two of our supporters who are present to-day, there is not the slightest doubt that the Government would lose their vote of confidence to-morrow, and that in that case, if I still remained your chief, I should be asked to form a Democratic Government, a task which, when the time comes, it is my intention to pass on to one more skilled in Parliamentary routine. I want to explain to you that we consider the representative you elect to-day to be one of the most important personages in that Government. We have not issued our programme yet. When we do, we are going to make the country a wonderful promise. We are going to promise that there shall be no more strikes. That sounds a large order, perhaps, but we shall keep our word and we are going to end for ever this bitter struggle between capital and labour by welding the two into one and by making the interests of one the interests of the other. Our scheme is that the person whom you elect to-day will be chairman of an inner conference of twelve. We shall ask you to elect a further three from amongst yourselves, which will give the trades unions four representatives upon this inner council. Four representative Cabinet Ministers will be chosen by ballot to add to their number. Four employers of labour, elected by the Employers' Association, will also join the council and the whole will be presided over by the person whom you elect to-day. There will be a select committee, or rather fifty-seven select committees, of each industry always at hand, and we consider that we shall frame in that manner a body of men competent to deal with the inner workings of every industry. They will decide what proportion of the earnings of each industry shall be allocated to labour and what to capital. In other words, they will fix or approve of or revise the wages of the country. They will settle every dispute and their decision will be final. The funds held by the various trades unions will form charitable funds or be returned as bonuses to the contributors. I have given you the barest outline of the scheme which has been drawn up to form a part of our programme when the time comes for us to present one. To-day you are only concerned to elect the one representative. I am here to beg, gentlemen, that you elect one whose theories, whose principles, whose antecedents and whose general attitude towards labour problems will fit him to take a very important place in the future government of the country."

There was a little murmur of applause. Miller was once more on his feet.

"I claim," he said, "that this is neither the time nor the place to spring upon us an utterly new method of dealing with Labour questions. What you propose seems to me a subtle attack upon the trades unions themselves. They have been the guardians of the people for the last fifteen years, and even though some strikes have been necessary and although all strikes may not have been successful, yet on the whole the trades unions have done their work well. I shall not accept, in the event of my election, the programme which Mr. Dartrey has laid down, unless I am elected with a special mandate to do so."

Saunderson rose to his feet, a man of different type, blunt of speech, rugged, the typical working-man's champion except for his voice, which was of unexpected tone and quality.

"Mr. Weavel and the rest of you," he said, "I differ from Miller. That's lucky, because you can vote now not only for the man but the principle. I have loathed strikes all my life, just because I am political economist enough to loathe waste and to hate to see production fettered,—that is, where the fruits of the production are shared fairly with Labour. I like Dartrey's scheme and I am prepared to stand by it."

Saunderson sat down. Dartrey and Tallente left the room while the business of voting went on. Dartrey had a private room of his own in the rear of the building and he and Tallente made their way there.

"Those men have a good deal to decide," Tallente reflected. "It's queer how the balance of things has changed. I don't suppose any Cabinet Council for years has had to tackle a more important problem."

"I wonder how they'll vote," Dartrey speculated. "Weavel's our man."

"You can't tell," Tallente replied. "You've given them something fresh to think about. They may even decide not to vote to-day at all. Miller has some strong supporters. He appeals tremendously to a certain class of labour—and that class exists, you know, Dartrey—which loves the excitement and the loafing of a strike, which feels somehow or other that benefits got in any other way than by force are less than they ought to have been."

There was a knock at the door. Northern put in his head.
He was the Boot and Shoe representative.

"Thought I'd let you know how the thing's gone," he said. "There's an unholy row there. They've chucked Miller. Saunderson's in by five votes. I'm off back again. Miller's up speaking, tearing mad."

He nodded and disappeared. Dartrey held out his hand.

"Thank God!" he exclaimed. "Let's clear cut, Tallente. Nora must know about this at once. We'll call at the House and enter your amendment against the vote of confidence. And then—Nora. I am not sure, Tallente—the man's a subtle fellow—but I rather think we've driven the final nail into Miller's coffin."

CHAPTER XXI

The great night came and passed with fewer thrills than any one had imagined possible. Horlock himself undertook the defence of his once more bitterly assailed Government and from the first it was obvious what the end must be. He spoke with the resigned cynicism of one who knows that words are fruitless, that the die is already cast and that his little froth of words, valedictory in their tone from the first, was only a tribute to exacting convention. Tallente had never been more restrained, although his merciless logic reduced the issues upon which the vote was to be taken to the plainest and clearest elements. He remained studiously unemotional and nothing which he said indicated in any way his personal interest in the sweeping away of the Horlock regime. He was the impersonal but scathing critic, paving the way for his chief. It was Dartrey himself who overshadowed every one that night. He spoke so seldom in the House that many of the members had forgotten that he was an orator of rare quality. That night he lifted the debate from the level of ordinary politics to the idyllic realms where alone the lasting good of the world is fashioned. He pointed out what government might and should be, taking almost a Roman view of the care of the citizen, his early and late education, his shouldering of the responsibilities which belong to one of a great community. From the individual he passed to the nation, sketching in a few nervous but brilliant phrases the exact possibilities of socialistic legislation; and he wound up with a parodied epigram: Government, he declared, was philosophy teaching by failures. In the end, Miller led fourteen of his once numerous followers into the Government lobby to find himself by forty votes upon the losing side.

Horlock found Tallente once more slipping quietly away from the House and bundled him into his car. They drove off rapidly. "So it's Buckinghamshire for me," the former observed, not without jubilation. "After all, it has been rather a tame finale. We were beaten before we opened our mouths."

"Even your new adherent," Tallente said, smiling, "could not save you."

Horlock made a grimace.

"You can have Miller and his faithful fourteen," he declared.
"We don't want him. The man was a Little Englander, he has

become a Little Labourite. Heaven knows where he'll end! Are you going to be Prime Minister, Tallente?"

"I don't know," was the quiet reply. "Just for the moment I am weary of it all. Day after day, fighting and scheming, speaking and writing, just to get you fellows out. And now we've got you out, well, I don't know that we are going to do any better. We've got the principles, we've got some of the men, but is the country ready for our programme!"

"If you ask me, I think the country's ready for anything in the way of a change," Horlock replied. "I am sure I am. I have been Prime Minister before, but I've never in my life had such an army of incompetents at the back of me. Take my tip, Tallente. Don't you have a Chancellor of the Exchequer who refuses to take a bit off the income tax every year."

"We shall abolish the income tax before long," Tallente declared.

"I shall invest my money in America," Horlock observed, "my savings, that is. Where shall I put you down?"

"In Chelsea, if you would," Tallente begged. "We are only just turning off the Embankment. I want to see Mrs. Dartrey."

Horlock gave an order through the tube.

"I am going down to Belgrave Square," he said, "then I am going back to Downing Street for to-night. To-morrow a dutiful journey to Buckingham Palace, Saturday a long week-end. I shall take out a season ticket to Buckinghamshire now. You're not going to nationalise the railways—or are you, Tallente; what about season tickets then?"

"Nationalisation is badly defined," Tallente replied. "The Government will certainly aim at regulating the profits of all public companies and applying a portion of them to the reduction of taxation."

"Well, good luck to you!" Horlock said heartily, as the car pulled up outside Dartrey's little house. "Here's just a word of advice from an old campaigner. You're going to tap the people's pockets, that's what you are going to do, Tallente, and I tell you this, and you'll find it's the truth— principles or no principles, your own party or any one else's—the moment you touch the pockets of any class of the community, from the aristocrat to the stone-breaker, they'll be up against you like a hurricane. Every one in the world hugs their principles, but there isn't any one who'd hold on to them if they found it was costing them money.—So long, and the best of luck to you, Tallente. We may meet in high circles before long."

Horlock drove away, a discomfited man, jubilant in his thoughts of freedom. Tallente was met by Nora in the little hall—Nora, who had kept away from the house at Stephen's earnest request.

"Stephen has done it," Tallente announced triumphantly. "He made the only speech worth listening to. Horlock crumbled to pieces. Miller only got fourteen of the ragtail end of his lot to vote with him. We won by forty votes. Horlock brought me here. He is to have a formal meeting of the party. He'll offer his resignation on Thursday."

"It's wonderful!" Nora exclaimed.

"Stephen will be sent for," Tallente went on. "That, of course, is a foregone conclusion. Nora, I wish you'd make him see that it's his duty to form a Government. There isn't any reason why he should pass it on to me. I can lead in the Commons if he wants me to, so far as the debates are concerned. We are altering the procedure, as I dare say you know. Half the government of the country will be done by committees."

"It's no use," Nora replied. "Stephen simply wouldn't do it. You must remember what you yourself said—procedure will be altered. So much of the government of the country will be done outside the House. Stephen has everything mapped out. You are going to be Prime Minister."

Tallente left early and walked homeward by the least frequented ways. A soft rain was falling, but the night was warm and a misty moon made fitful appearances. The rain fell like little drops of silver around the lampposts. There was scarcely a breath of wind and in Curzon Street the air was almost faint with the odour of spring bulbs from the window boxes. Tallente yielded to an uncontrollable impulse. He walked rather abruptly up Clarges Street, past his rooms, and paid a curious little visit, almost a pilgrimage, to the closed house in Charles Street. It seemed to him that those drawn blinds, the dead-looking windows, the smokeless chimneys typified in melancholy fashion the empty chambers in his own heart. Weeks had passed now and no word had come from Jane. He pictured her still smarting under the sting of his brutal words. Some of his phrases came back to his mind and he shivered with remorse. If only—He started. It seemed for a moment as though history were about to repeat itself. A great limousine had stolen up to the kerbstone and a woman in evening dress was leaning out.

"Mr. Tallente," she called out, "do come and speak to me, please."

Tallente approached at once. In the dim light his heart gave a little throb. He peered forward. The woman laughed musically. "I do believe that you have forgotten me," she said, "I am Alice Mountgarron—Jane's sister.

I saw you there and I couldn't help stopping for a moment. Can I drop you anywhere?"

"Thank you so much," he answered. "My rooms are quite close by here in Clarges Street."

"Get in, please, and I will take you there," she ordered. "Tell the man the number. I want just one word with you."

The car started off. Lady Alice looked at her companion and shook her head.

"Mr. Tallente," she said, "I am very much a woman of the world and Jane is a very much stronger person than I am, in some things, and a great baby in others. You and she were such friends and I have an idea that there was a misunderstanding."

"There was," he groaned. "It was my fault."

"Never mind whose fault it was," she went on. "You two were made for each other. You have so much in common. Don't drift apart altogether, just because one has expected too much, or the other been content to give too little. Jane has a great soul and a great heart. She wants to give but she doesn't quite know how. And perhaps there isn't any way. But two people whose lives seem to radiate towards each other, as yours and hers, shouldn't remain wholly apart. Take a day or two's holiday soon, even from this great work of yours, and go down to Devonshire. It would be very dangerous advice," she went on, smiling, "to a different sort of man, but I have a fancy that to you it may mean something, and I happen to know—that Jane is miserable."

The car stopped. Tallente held Lady Alice's hand as he had seldom held the hand of a woman in his life. A curious incapacity for speech checked the words even upon his lips.

"Thank you," he faltered.

CHAPTER XXII

Upon the moor above Martinhoe and the farm lands adjoining, spring had fallen that year as gently as the warm rain of April. Tallente, conscious of an unexpected lassitude, paused as he reached the top of the zigzag climb from the Manor and rested for a moment upon a block of stone. Below him, the forests of dwarf oaks which stretched down to the sea were tipped with delicate green. The meadows were like deep soft patches of emerald verdure; the fruit trees in his small walled garden were pink and white with blossoms. The sea was peaceful as an azure lake into which the hulls of the passing steamers cut like knives, leaving behind a long line of lazy foam. Little fleecy balls of cloud were dotted across the sky, puffs of soft wind cooled his cheeks when he rose to his feet and faced inland.

Soon he left the stony road and walked upon the springy turf bordering the moorland. Little curled-up shoots of light green were springing from the bracken. Here and there, a flame of gorse filled the air with its faint, almond-like blossom. And the birds! Farmlands stretched away on his left-hand side, and above the tender growth of corn, larks invisible but multifarious filled the air with little quiverings of melody. Bleatng lambs, ridiculously young, tottered around on this new-found, wonderful earth. A pair of partridges scurried away from his feet; the end of a drooping cloud splashed his face with a few warm raindrops.

Tallente, as he swung onwards, carrying his cap in his hand, felt a great glow of thankfulness for the impulse which had brought him here. Already he was finding himself. The tangled emotions of the last week were loosening their grip upon his brain and consciousness. Behind him London was in an uproar, his name and future the theme of every journal. Journalists were besieging his rooms. Embryo statesmen were telephoning for appointments. Great men sent their secretaries to suggest a meeting. And in the midst of it all he had disappeared. The truth as to his sudden absence from town was unknown even to Dartrey. At the very moment when his figure loomed large and triumphant upon one of the great canvasses in history, he had simply slipped away, a disappearance as dramatic as it was opportue. And all because he had a fancy to see how spring sat upon the moors,—and because he had walked back to his rooms by way of Charles Street and because he had met Lady Alice.

The last ascent was finished and below him lay the house and climbing woods,—woods that crept into the bosom of the hills, the closely growing trees tipped with tender greens melting into the softest of indeterminate greys as the breeze rippled through their tops like fingers across a harp. The darker line of moorland in the background, scant as ever of herbage, had yet lost its menacing bareness and seemed touched with the faint colour of the earth beneath, almost pink in the generous sunshine. The avenue into which he presently turned was starred on either side with a riot of primroses, running wild into the brambles, with here and there a belt of bluebells. The atmosphere beneath the closely growing trees—limes, with great waxy buds—became enervating with spring odours and a momentary breathlessness came to Tallente, fresh from his crowded days and nights of battle. The sun-warmed wave of perfume from the trim beds of hyacinths in the suddenly disclosed garden was almost overpowering and he passed like a man in a dream through their sweetness to the front door. The butler who admitted him conducted him at once to Jane's sanctum. Without any warning he was ushered in.

"Mr. Tallente, your ladyship."

He had a strange impression of her as she rose from a very sea of newspapers. She was thinner—he was sure of that—dressed in indoor clothes although it was the middle of the morning, a suggestion of the invalid about her easy-chair and her tired eyes. It seemed to him that for a moment they were lit with a gleam of fear which passed almost instantaneously. She had recovered herself even before the door was closed behind the departing servant.

"Mr. Tallente!" she repeated. "You! But how is this possible?"

"Everything is possible," he answered. "I have come to see you, Jane."

She was glad but amazed. Even when he had obeyed her involuntary gesture and seated himself by her side, there was something incredulous about her expression.

> "But what does it mean that you are here just now?" she persisted.

"According to the newspapers you should be at Buckingham Palace to-day."

"To-morrow," he corrected her. "I hired a very powerful car and motored down yesterday afternoon. I am starting back when the moon rises to-night. For these few hours I am better out of London."

"But why—" she faltered.

He was slowly finding himself.

"I came for you, Jane," he said, "on any terms—anyhow. I came to beg for your sympathy, for some measure of your affection, to beg you to come back to Charles Street. Is it too late for me to abase myself?"

Her eyes glowed across at him. She suddenly rose, came over and knelt by the side of his chair. Her arms went around his neck.

"Andrew," she whispered, "I have been ashamed. I was wrong. That night—the thought of my pettiness—my foolish, selfish fears.—Oh, I was wrong! I have prayed that the time might come when I could tell you. And if you hadn't come, I never could have told you. I couldn't have written. I couldn't have come to London. But I wanted you to know."

She drew his head down and kissed him upon the lips. Tallente knew then why he had come. The whole orchestra of life was playing again. He was strong enough to overcome mountains.

"Andrew," she faltered, "you really—"

He stopped her.

"Jane," he said, "I have some stupid news. It seems to me incredibly stupid. Let me pass it on to you quickly. You knew, didn't you, that I was married in America? Well, my wife has divorced me there. We married in a State where such things are possible."

"Divorced you?" she exclaimed.

"Quite legally," he went on. "I saw a lawyer before I started yesterday morning. But listen to the rest of it. Stella is married—married to the man I thought I had thrown over the cliff. She is married to Anthony Palliser."

"Then you are free?" Jane murmured, drawing a little away. "Not in the least," he replied. "I am engaged to marry you."

At luncheon, with Parkins in attendance, it became possible for them to converse coherently.

"When I found you at home in the middle of the morning," he said, "I was afraid that you were ill."

"I haven't been well," she admitted. "I rode some distance yesterday and it fatigued me. Somehow or other, I think I have had the feeling, the last few weeks, that my work here is over. All my farms are sold. I have really now no means of occupying my time."

"It is fortunate," he told her, with a smile, "that I am able to point out to you a new sphere of usefulness."

She made a little grimace at him behind Parkins' august back.

"Tell me," she asked, "how did you ever make your peace with the trades unions after that terrible article of yours?"

"Because," he replied, "except for Miller, their late chief, there are a great many highly intelligent men connected with the administration of the trades unions. They realised the spirit in which I wrote that article and the condition of the country at the time I wrote it. My apologia was accepted by every one who counted. The publication of that article," he went on, "was Miller's scheme to drive me out of politics. It has turned out to be the greatest godsend ever vouchsafed to our cause, for it is going to put Mr. Miller out of the power of doing mischief for a—many years to come."

"How I hated him when he called here that day! Jane murmured reminiscently."

"Miller is the type of man," Tallente declared, "who was always putting the Labour Party in a false position. He was born and he has lived and he has thought parochially. He is all the time lashing himself into a fury over imagined wrongs and wanting to play the little tin god on Olympus with his threatened strikes. Now there will be no more strikes."

"I was reading about that," she reflected. "How wonderful it sounds!"

"The greatest power in the country," Tallente explained, "is that wielded by these trades unions. There will be no more fights between the Government and them, because they are coaling into the Government. I am afraid you will think our programme revolutionary. On the other hand, it is going to be a Government of justice. We want to give the people their due, each man according to his worth. By that means we wipe out all fear forever of the scourge of eastern and mid-Europe, the bolshevism and anarchy which have laid great empires bare. We are not going to make the poor add to the riches of the rich, but on the other hand we are not going to take from the rich to give to the poor. The sociological scheme upon which our plan of government will be based is to open every avenue to success equally to rich and poor. The human being must sink or swim, according to his capacity. Ours will never be a State-aided socialism."

Parkins had left the room. She held out her hand.

"How horrid of you!" she murmured. "You are gibing at me because I lent my farmers a little money." He laughed softly.

"You dear!" he exclaimed. "On my honour, it never entered into my head. Only I want to bring you gradually into the new way of thinking, because I want so much from you so much help and sympathy."

"And?" she pleaded.

He looked around to be sure that Parkins was gone and, leaning from his place, kissed her.

"If you care for moonlight motoring," he whispered, "I think I can give you quite a clear outline of all that I expect from you."

She drew a little sigh of relief.

"If you had left me behind," she murmured, "I should have sat here and imagined that it was all a dream. And I am just a little weary of dreams."